Lightning Disciple

Heirloom Earth Book 1

Elliot Hendry

CONTENTS

PROLOGUE

An explosion rumbled somewhere deep below Dr Linette Cooper, throwing her against the wall of the corridor. The central AI - or what was left of it - made its inscrutable calculations and decided enough was enough; lights dropped from the ceiling and began to pulse orange in a slow, steady heartbeat. A warning tone blared into life for three piercing seconds before that too spluttered and died. Linette could hear the robotic evacuation message echoing from down the corridor but here, at least, the speakers were shot to hell. She could feel the ship's death throes in her bones, though, the usual steady humming vibration given over to a choking, irregular spasm. She didn't need to see a damage report to know how little time she had.

The doors to the Terraforming Control Laboratory were gone, a victim of the war, blown open and leaving only a jagged wound in their wake. Bodies lay in various states of decay, crumpled in corners and behind makeshift barricades and Linette could not tell loyalist from rebel. The labs hadn't been the first area to be targeted but they had been one of the most desperately contested, taken and re-taken over and over as the balance of power had swung to and fro. Here she passed one of the security crew, rifle still in hand; there she passed the chief engineer, dead in their sleep. The fight to recapture the life support systems had taken a week.

The control panels still lived, if only just. Bullet holes pierced all but a few, black holes from which dead pixels fragmented outward, and those that remained flickered in and out of life. Linette picked the one that seemed the least damaged and swiped her palm across the security panel at its side. A message flickered across the screen.

**** Access Denied ****

The words took a moment to sink in and when they did Linette's heart seized - until she looked down at her palm. The entirety of it was covered in dirt and grime and blood, dry and brown, to the point that it was unrecognisable even to Linette. It cost her two whole bottles of water, taken from the galley after the final battle, to wash her palm clean enough for the security panel to recognise her.

**** Access Granted ****

**** Welcome: Acting Captain Doctor Linette Cooper ****

Somehow Linette found it in herself to laugh. Acting Captain! Just look at her go - all it took was a mutiny and dumb luck. No gilded birthright for her! Not that the central AI cared; it just tallied up the remaining life-signs, worked its way down the order of succession and called it a day. Or at least, that's what she assumed. Who knew what really went on in those supercooled plasma matrices that it called a brain? Artificial Intelligences didn't think like humans thought, didn't see the world the same way. It just knew data and data said she was, at long last, calling the shots.

The computer took an age to spin up through its start-up procedure; checks and re-checks and verification of both. Another rumble shook the room, thunder in the walls, and Linette heard the echoing message cut off mid-sentence. There was a distinct tang of ozone and burnt wiring in the air and now and then the lights would flicker. The war had not been gentle and the damage done had been extensive. Linette knew that she had precious little time left.

Finally, the control panel flashed into readiness, neat rows of information plastered across its surface. Linette knew them in her soul, now, after so many years of preparation. All of the lines shone a healthy green, all the numbers falling into place - all except one.

**** Geographical Dataset not found ****

All the noise around Linette faded away and her skin flashed cold, despite the warm and stuffy air. With a trembling finger, she reached out and double-tapped the warning message. The control panel thought for a second or two and the message was replaced with a spinning circle. Then it came to a decision and the words appeared again.

**** Geographical Dataset not found ****

Somehow, out of all of the possibilities that had been running through her mind on the way to the lab, this was the one error that Linette hadn't considered. The data storage had five layers of redundancies built-in and was backed up in three different locations. For the data to just disappear would take a level of physical damage that would have ripped the ship apart hours ago. Either that or -

Or one final "Fuck You" from the captain, one last petty, small-minded act of evil before they had taken the bridge.

The thought filled her mind and she knew, with a grim certainty born of bloodshed and weariness, that the old man had done it. It was the whole bloody conflict summed up in a single act; a pathological inability to share taken to its ultimate conclusion. What good was a rising tide if everyone else had a boat too? Power seldom let itself be diluted.

Well, she was captain now. She had access to all that remained. A flurry of taps across the screen and the central AI began to reach out its tendrils, caressing every corner of the network, anywhere that the data might have been squirrelled away, either accidentally or as insurance. The control panel screen faded into a single looping animation as it worked, while the floor shook and the walls groaned.

**** Searching ... ****

An explosion rocked the corridor outside and before Linette could respond it was answered by a second, then a third. Flames licked around the corner of the doors as the fire suppression systems struggled to bring the sudden inferno under control, a spray of white foam disappearing into the blaze. Linette covered her mouth with her sleeve, choking back tears as the acrid smell of burning plastic hit her. Klaxons began to ring out - mechanical, dependable and final. It had been a long time since flight training but Linette knew the sound the way miners knew the tell-tale crack of a rockfall: abandon ship.

But she couldn't leave. It had cost her - and so many more - everything to reach this point. The AI was still searching. The payload below the floor was still locked into position. There was nothing left of the war except her and the rapidly decaying structure around her but if she left now it was all for nothing. Every drop of blood shed would burn up and be forgotten, every sacrifice rendered meaningless. Linette just needed time; time to think, to figure this out, to search -

**** Search complete. Non-standard geographical dataset located ****

Non-standard? Coughing into her sleeve and waving the gathering smoke from in front of her eyes, Linette pulled herself to the control panel. Sure enough, the central AI had found geographical data that matched the terrain - in the cultural media servers, of all places. Hidden by the captain? Someone's personal project? She neither knew nor cared. Whatever "non-standard" meant, data was data. If the AI could work with it that was all that mattered.

**** Extrapolate data? ****

Despite the fire now spilling into the room, the smoke burning her lungs more and more with every breath, Linette paused. This was something new, something that she had never seen before despite years of staring at this very control panel, alongside the men and women who had built it. Extrapolate? From what? The panel offered no clues but she suspected the central AI's invisible hand. The scientist in her wanted more time to study it, to figure out what it all meant, but the realist in her knew there was no time.

A pipe burst free from the ceiling and fell towards the doorway; in an instant, the gas inside ignited and turned a strong fire into a furnace. The heat hit Linette in one great wall, sending her tumbling behind the cover of the control panel with a scream as her skin blistered. There was no time.

Pulling her jacket over her head for protection, Linette peeked over the rim of the control panel just long enough to hit ** Yes ** and ** Execute Launch ** then fell backwards again. She felt the floor tremble and groan as the payload launch mechanisms below her ground into life, heard the dull thud as each one slammed into the launch tube and the whine of the servos, straining in the heat.

The exit back into the corridor was blocked by fire but the labs had their own bank of escape pods. Smoke poured down from the ceiling; crawling on her hands and knees, Linette raced the flames to the row of hatches along the far wall. Smoke clawed at her eyes until she had to close them; fire licked at her heels until she was sure her shoes would melt from her feet. When her arm hit the wall and her blind grasping found the escape pod hatch she cried out in joy, instantly regretting it. The space inside the pod was small and spartan but - when she pulled the hatch closed behind her - blessedly cool and free of smoke.

Years of drills coerced her limbs into motion and she strapped herself into a seat within seconds. When she slapped the launch button - satisfyingly blocky and physical - there was a dreadful moment where nothing happened. The terrifying certainty that it had jammed reached her throat just as the pod lurched sideways and she surrendered her scream to the acceleration. For a few seconds, the view back through the hatch window was of darkness, the fire rushing away into an ever-shrinking point. Then the pod broke free of the launch tube and the world outside became a chaotic patchwork of light and the deepest dark.

As gravity lost its artificial hold on her, Linette watched the bulk of the *SF Eden* fall away. Its swooping, superficial curves were shattered by countless explosions, whole panels floating away in dozens of extravagant pieces. Underneath, the blocky superstructure was cracked and bleeding; fire and oxygen escaped from a constellation of holes. Even as she pulled the first aid kit from its spot on the wall, dry-swallowing the two pain tablets she found, large chunks of the ship began to drift free from one another. Escaping debris propelled it in a slow tumble, revealing a broken spine and bow. The running lights flickered out and even the fires couldn't last long, choked out by the vacuum of space. Within minutes the *Eden* was dead; three generations of humanity's finest, most misguided work extinguished.

But as Linette watched, a bright point of light shot away from the underbelly of the ship. It was followed a second later by another; then another. Soon a long line of the lights stretched out from the corpse of the *Eden* and beyond the edge of the hatch view-port. Linette unbuckled herself and floated across the pod to press her face against the view-port, her heart rate - and, despite everything that had happened, her hopes - rising.

If the payloads had launched then the central AI must have found and extrapolated - whatever that entailed - the data. If the payloads made landfall and the data was intact, if they had a full template and the terraforming process began -

It had worked. Her life's work, the work of two-dozen different men and women united as one, was complete. Winning that stupid, stupid war had been worth it after all.

She felt a great bubble of grief and relief and a thousand other emotions burst up from her chest. For the first time in forever, she let herself relax and she let herself cry, great fat tears that floated through the escape pod. Through her own private constellation, she watched the lights speed away from the wreck of the crippled ship, settling into their gentle, spiralling path to the planet below.

The Earth was saved.

CHAPTER ONE

The earth was doomed.

That's what Alan's dad said. It was a slow doom but not slow enough for them. The men and women of the Old World had caged nature and let it starve, poisoned the water and let it boil away. A quiet extinction without even the spark of nuclear war, just an apathetic retreat as the land and the people on it grew ever-less fertile. Nobody liked it when he said it and Alan's mum had often scolded him for it - but now she was gone, lost to one of the thousand diseases whose names had been forgotten. Alan couldn't stand to tell his dad to stop worrying people in her place. So Alan's dad said it, while he and Alan worked the dry, unyielding soil behind their house and prayed for one more mild, seasonless year. Another year survived but not lived, scraping by on roots and gritty grain.

And, if Alan's nerve held, rabbits.

The riverbank below the village was dotted with warrens. Most of them were empty and half-collapsed. A generation or two ago they had been teeming with rabbits so fat that one would feed a family for a week if stretched out with grain and vegetables. A generation or two before that, of course, nobody had paid much attention to how fat or numerous they were - why would you, when food came in tins from all over the world? Alan didn't know if he believed it but his dad swore it was true, in that special tone he used to show that this time he definitely wasn't pulling Alan's leg, honest.

But that was then and this was now. Alan crept along the riverbank in the fading light of dusk, sling in his hand and nothing in his stomach. Harvest was a week away and the dry skeleton of the nearby forest had been picked clean. His dad had told him to sleep off the hunger pangs until the handful of oats rationed for breakfast but Alan couldn't wait until morning. Wouldn't.

Something flickered in the corner of Alan's vision and he paused, crouching in the rough, dry grass. Slowly, silently, he slipped one hand into a pocket and pulled out a river-polished stone. Not moving his eyes from the spot where he was sure he had seen movement, he wrapped the stone in the sling and held it loose behind him. Eighteen years of practice crouched with him, ready to strike. A single stone was all he needed to knock a rabbit dead. Hunger was, if nothing else, a powerful motivator.

He crouched there as the sun sank, the only movement the lengthening of the shadows. The river was little more than a silent, sickly trickle this deep into summer. Even the wind had died. For a long time, there was no sign that his prey existed anywhere other than in his mind; no tell-tale twitching of grass, no scratch of claw on stone. Then, suddenly -

A pair of ears twitched into view. They were a little off to the left of where he was looking, the tips just visible over the top of a rock buried in the bank. The bulk of the rabbit was shielded from view - and, more importantly, a clear shot. Alan felt his grip on the sling tighten involuntarily as frustration joined hunger in gripping his chest.

He hadn't eaten meat in a month. It had been an oily scrap of fish, traded for a day's back-breaking toil in old Cariss's field and stretched out over three meals. He was sick of flour and scavenged roots; sick of grain not fit for pigs (but who had seen a pig recently?) and working a field that grew more rocks than plants. He didn't care if the meat was tough and gamey and boiled into mush - he wanted it. He wanted that rabbit *now*.

The ears twitched; Alan's eyes strained to follow them as the setting sun smudged them deeper into the shadows with every passing second. The rabbit moved forward, just a little. Then a little more. Then a little more. Alan's pulse quickened; a few more tentative hops and the rabbit's head would be visible. Not by much - but enough. He was sure of it.

Alan raised the sling behind him and began to whirl it round, the stone orbiting a point behind his head. It whistled softly in the still air and Alan hoped it sounded enough like wind to go unnoticed. The ears did twitch a little in his direction - but the rabbit hopped forward again, either unaware or - like him - hungry enough to risk it. It was close now. Alan stayed like that for minute after agonising minute, a growing ache in his wrist as the sling kept on whirling round. The rabbit didn't move. Whatever patch of grass it had found seemed to have grabbed its attention entirely; it lingered just out of sight behind the rock as the sun sank lower and the light got worse and his wrist began to throb. Frustration built in Alan's chest; if the rabbit took just one more hop he would have it, just one more inch. He could see the tip of its nose, snuffling in the dirt. If only he were a couple of feet to the side of where he had frozen …

Screw it. He wanted the rabbit. He could take the rabbit.

Sling still whirling behind him, eyes still locked on his prey, Alan took a broad step to his right. His foot found a rock in the ground and he shifted his weight to it - but the mud beneath gave way without warning. The rock shot out from under his foot, his foot shot out from under him and Alan fell backwards, letting out a startled cry as the sling wrapped around his arm and the stone smacked into his wrist. Crashing onto his back, Alan heard the rabbit leap away into the denser grass, the rapid patter of its paws quickly fading into the distance.

Damn it!

Alan smacked the earth with both palms, crying out in desperation. Every time! Every damn time! If the rabbit had just hopped one hop further - But it hadn't. And with the commotion he had raised there wouldn't be an animal for miles around that wasn't now on guard. Choking down the bitter taste of failure, Alan pushed himself from the ground, gathered the sling and begrudgingly headed for home.

It wasn't a long journey. Hungry as he was, Alan wasn't one to roam far from the village walls by himself. Especially not once it got dark. Once or twice a year they lost precious livestock to wild dogs. There hadn't been an attack on humans in Alan's lifetime but everyone and everything was getting more desperate. Even if the wildlife wasn't quite ready to make a move, other people were. His dad spoke about law and order but they were relics of his dad's dad's time. As the world wound down so did certain peoples' empathy. When they found each other - and once one of them had beaten their way to the top of the pile - they bent the world around them, drawing in food and Old World tech and fear with their power. There was still safety in numbers to a point but nobody with a brain went travelling down certain paths or after dark.

A dark part of Alan, a part that fed on his hunger and frustration, envied that power. His dad always said that he couldn't understand what drove men and women to become bandits. The dirty little secret that shamed Alan whenever he thought about it was that he could understand only too well.

As he reached the old road and its relatively root-free surface, Alan could afford to turn his eyes upwards. It was a clear night, although thick black clouds had been gathering on the horizon all day. Something about the air in what remained of summer made lightning storms a common occurrence. They usually spat themselves out before they could gather much size but this was looking to be a monster of a storm - the sort that stripped and drowned fields, rather than replenishing them. Another reason for the rabbit hunt. The heat and humidity made working the fields even more miserable than usual - Alan was at least looking forward to the coming storm clearing the air. He just hoped that there was a harvest left at the end of it. The Old World had spent centuries trying to bottle nature but he had only ever known it to have the upper hand.

For now, though, the clouds kept their distance and the stars and the moon were the only things in the sky. Alan's dad had tried in vain to teach him the constellations but it had never stuck. It was bad enough that he had forced Alan to learn to read, one painfully dry page of the dictionary at a time. Alan had never seen the point - not like Carl, who had by now begged and bartered nearly twenty books from passing travellers. It was just one of those Old World traditions that hadn't died just yet.

Movement. Movement in a place where movement was impossible.

It took Alan a moment to recognise what he was seeing. Something about the stars was wrong. Then it hit him - they were moving! Some of them, anyway. A thin band reaching across the sky from the west. They were faint at first and only noticeable because the rest of the sky was so still. Then, as he stopped there in the middle of the old road, a couple at the front of the band flared brighter, developed a tail. Soon more and more of them did the same, not all of them but most, cutting the sky in sharp lines of fire. Alan turned his head to watch them go, arcing over him and into the horizon - all except for one. One star burned brighter than the others but didn't seem to move. It simply grew; larger and larger and -

Oh.

Alan's eyes widened and he threw himself flat against the ground, covering the back of his head with his hands. As it turned out his fear was unwarranted; the star screamed its way over him, still far above. Alan raised his head only when the false noon it brought with it faded back to dusk, the light dragged away across the landscape. He had been sure it would hit him but the depths of the sky had disguised how far away it really was. The star briefly illuminated the village ahead as it passed over, before crashing silently through the canopy of the forest beyond. Nothing for a second - then a brief pulse of light and sound suddenly seemed to catch up, a distant bang echoing back to where Alan lay on the old road and stared up in awe.

He had once seen lightning strike the big oak tree on the hill above the village. It had been the greatest moment of his life, a single instant of raw, blinding power. He wasn't sure that a star falling from the sky quite beat that but it came closer than anything else he had ever known.

He jogged the rest of the way to the village, keeping one eye on the road and one on the thin band of moving stars that continued to drift from west to east. There was nobody on guard at the gate but that was hardly new; it was Michael Arton's shift tonight and Alan knew he'd be three cups deep back in his house by now. It wasn't an exciting or even very important duty; even the closest bandits wouldn't travel this far at night. And if they did? What chance would one person with a long pole and a whistle stand? It was - as Samuel, one of the older and self-proclaimed-wiser villagers, often said - about sending a message.

The village was quiet on the other side of the crumbling stone wall, quiet and dark - nobody wasted candles or firewood on lighting in the short nights. Alan's footsteps echoed off of the stone houses as he passed - several generations old even before the Old World had ended - and he traced his way back to the house he shared with his dad. It was squat and crumbling but then they all were - built to last, yes, but in kinder times.

He paused at the front door, one hand on the latch, his eyes turned in the direction where the star had fallen. He had never seen a star up close and the thought thrilled him. Carl had told him once that they were massive things, larger than anything had a right to be, and so very far away. This one had been close, though, and small enough to disappear into the forest. A sudden urge to see it gripped him, to jog straight on through the village and out into the night, to see something, anything, he hadn't seen yesterday and every day before that.

He was halfway back down the garden path when he came back to reality. The forest was dark and full of danger - both beast and man, as there was said to be a bandit camp on the other side, full of Old World weapons and Old World power. The star would still be there in the morning, he assumed - maybe it had fallen close enough to the border that he could tempt Carl into going along with him. His friend was built from skin, bones and curiosity and what was more curious than what a star looked like during the day? But for now … For now, Alan let his baser instincts guide him into and through the silent house to a threadbare bed and hungry dreams. There was always tomorrow, the same as today.

While he slept the clouds grew closer and the stars continued to fall.

CHAPTER TWO

Alan woke the next morning to a distant scream carrying across the quiet village.

The instant he opened his eyes, he realised why. The curtains still hung across the window from the night before, leaving his bedroom a dark picture painted in shades of black. Only years of habit let him know where everything was - not that it was a long list. Half of it was stuffed into a rough canvas day pack by the door while the rest cluttered the old chest at the foot of his bed. He could navigate the darkness with his eyes closed, so little did it change. And yet -

And yet a pale blue and silver vision hung in front of his eyes, turning with his head. The shock of it propelled him back across the mattress and the vision moved with him, chasing him to the wall. It was utterly silent.

**** Welcome to Heirloom Online ****

The letters were thick and ornately drawn and reminded Alan of the few remaining windows in the village church. It took him a second to decipher them. They were surrounded by a ring of symbols that he didn't recognise, some angular and harsh, others soft and flowing in long, looping curves. The text beneath was plain by comparison, which made it far easier to read, and each word shimmered slightly as he focused on it.

**** <u>Please choose an option:</u> ****
**** Load Existing Character ****
**** Create New Character ****
**** Log Off ****

Alan had never seen anything quite like it. The closest sight he could recall was a large painting that a merchant caravan had shown off once long ago when he was much younger, what they had called a 'poster' for a 'film'. This, though, was partly see-through and when he reached out to touch it his fingers went straight through. The image didn't even ripple, the way a reflection in water would.

Alan briefly wondered if he was still dreaming - right up until his wrist, still tender from his mishap with the sling, knocked against the wall behind him. He winced at the sudden stab of pain. Alan held his wrist up to the glowing panel to get a better look at it but the panel shed no light outside of itself. It wasn't until he got up and drew back the curtains that he could make out the shape of the bruise gripping his lower arm, as dark and ugly and purple as the clouds gathering in the sky outside. He tried to push aside thoughts of a sprain - or worse, a break - and turned back to the panel floating in front of him.

"What are you?" he wondered.

When he didn't get a response he traced a finger across the first line of plain text, sounding out each word as he went in halting, uncertain syllables.

"Low-duh eks-is-ting ca- car-act-er."

A soft, dull thud sounded in his ear and a new line of text flashed briefly across his vision.

**** No Character Data Found. ****

Stranger and stranger. This was clearly magic and magic meant the Old World and the Old World meant trouble. But what kind of trouble? There were Old World machines all over the village, built into the buildings and roads. Tall metal trees with glass fruit could still be seen here and there on the street - lanterns of some sort, apparently. Even the ceiling of his bedroom - he looked up and saw the faint glimmer of dusty glass there too. It was all dead - dead for as long as he could remember and just as well. This, though - this was new and alive. The thought sent a shiver down his spine.

Alan's thoughts were interrupted, however, by the approaching thud of footsteps in the hall, terminating a second before the door was flung open. His dad stood on the other side, only a little taller than Alan and twice as gaunt, with as deep a frown as Alan had ever seen carved across his face.

"You too?" His dad's voice was soft, no energy to waste on volume, but with an undercurrent of concern running through it.

Alan didn't bother asking what he meant. Even if he hadn't known his dad so well, he could still put two and two together.

"Yeah. What's it mean?"

His dad shrugged.

"No idea. It was there when I woke up so I told it to sod off."

"Did it?"

"Course. Old World crap's clever like that. You do it too."

So it was Old World magic! Alan clenched his bruise-free fist in silent triumph, being careful to keep the other from his dad's sight. No need for both of them to be worrying.

"Sure, in a bit." Alan's mind was already racing and he almost didn't see his dad tense through the silver and blue panel.

"Now, Alan". There was an edge to his dad's voice now. Even as curious as Alan was, he wasn't going to miss that - there was never anything sharp about his dad.

"Come on," he said, "you aren't even interested in what it means? I mean, look at -"

"No!"

For the first time in Alan's life, his dad roared, the cry echoing around the little room and stunning them both into temporary silence. His dad's face was - even through the blue and silver - shaded in red. As Alan watched the colour faded away and his dad seemed to sag with it, as though the energy of it had been the only thing propping him up.

"... It kills people Al," his dad said, voice soft again and full of shame. "The Old World died when my dad was a boy and it still keeps killing people. I won't have it taking any more of my family."

Alan winced and looked away, the panel still tracking with his sight. There was no name for what had killed his mum, not any more, but everyone thought - everyone knew - that there was a stain in the world now. An old poison. It was the go-to culprit to blame whenever the crops failed and animals - or people - took sick and died. Nobody could say whether it was intentional or accidental, an act of spite by generations gone or just the slow decay of hubris. Nobody cared either way, now.

"With the storm brewing, I need you paying attention to the fields, not this rubbish." His dad's voice took on a pleading tone. "For chrissake, Arthur Gumley's running around telling everyone that he's a fighter now - man never threw a punch in his life! It's a daydream, Alan. You can't eat daydreams."

Alan's stomach rumbled at the mere mention of food and he knew his dad noticed. Both of them were skinny, even for the village, and his dad's face had grown gaunter and gaunter over the past few weeks.

"Get rid of it, get your head back down here and get on out to the fields; daylight's wasting. I'm heading to the forest - there's bound to be some mushrooms somewhere."

Alan opened his mouth to argue, then closed it again when he saw his dad raise an eyebrow. He couldn't argue with him. Nobody could - or at least, nobody would - since Alan's mum had died. Hunger and grief kept the man's eyes facing forward and down, always looking to the soil and the shrubs for his next meal. Everyone was the same in the village and Alan wished with all his strength that he could learn to do the same.

He nodded instead, not trusting himself to speak. His dad nodded too and a little tension seeped from his shoulders as he stepped away, drawing the bedroom door closed behind him. Footsteps faded away and Alan waited until they had withdrawn to the ground floor before beginning to gather his things. He waited until the footsteps disappeared down the garden path entirely before making his move.

There was no way Alan was letting this - whatever this was - go. There was a long day of sun ahead of him and plenty of time to tend the fields. It was still early enough that most of the village would still be asleep, content to let the fields wait for them. At least, those villagers with slightly more fertile soil, anyway. Alan's fields had been there every day of his life and would be there an hour from now. This, though, this was new and fleeting - who knew if it would leave as unexpectedly as it had arrived?

He studied the lines of text again. The first option hadn't gotten him anywhere but it had at least responded to him - what about the second?

"Cree-ate new car-act-er."

The vision instantly flashed white in front of him, although the light didn't spread to the rest of the room. When it faded the ornate text and the list of options were replaced with a new list, a list of names that Alan barely recognised. As he looked to the bottom of it the text scrolled, revealing more and more choices.

**** <u>Choose Your Class:</u> ****
**** Knight ****
**** Fighter ****
**** Ranger ****
**** Druid ****
**** ... ****

Alan recognised knights from the stories his mum had told him when he was young. It was pretty obvious what a fighter was. A ranger, though? Or a dru-id?

**** ... ****
**** Cleric ****
**** Apostate ****
**** Titan ****
**** Shaper ****
**** ... ****

The words were gibberish, like something a drunk would say. What did they mean? As he wondered, a small box popped up in front of the larger list.

**** <u>Shaper (Mag/Phys Hybrid)</u> ****

**** A shaper is a mage that has learnt to mould their flesh like clay, taking inspiration from the deadliest predators that the world has to offer. They have a focus on close combat and stealth. ****

**** Starting Abilities: *Mould Face, Bone Claws* ****

That made barely any more sense to Alan, although what he did understand sounded terrifying. Was this vision asking him what kind of person he was? The kind of person he wanted to be? Either way, he didn't want to read any more about whatever a "Shaper" was - and as he thought that, the box disappeared. He kept scrolling down.

** ... **

** **Dragon Knight** **

** **Crow Sage** **

** **Lightning Disciple** **

** ... **

Alan's eyes snapped to the latest entry on the list. Now the strange system of "classes" was starting to get interesting! Without him having to say anything, the small box returned.

** <u>Lightning Disciple (Magic)</u> **

** **The lightning disciple draws inspiration from the awesome natural power of thunderstorms to strike down their foes. They focus on high DPS against solo targets.** **

** **Starting Abilities:** *Lightning Strike, Thunderclap* **

The words in front of him made more sense than before - not a lot, but more. He thought back to the struck tree above the village and the sound of thunder on stormy nights; the power and freedom of the storms that swept across the village each summer, appearing and disappearing over the horizon. This was him, he told himself, this was who he wanted to be. This described him perfectly. He had no idea what the last couple of lines meant but who cared?

As he thought that, a new box popped up.

** **Confirm Class Selection?** **

** **Warning: class re-selection is not currently available on this server. Are you happy with your choice?** **

Why wouldn't he be happy? The vision seemed to know what he was thinking - was this a trick question?

"Yes," he said, the words loud in the quiet room.

For a second nothing happened. Then the vision flickered and disappeared, leaving only his room before him. The same view greeted him as on thousands of mornings before and the damning ordinariness of it made him flinch.

"Hello?" Alan wondered where the vision had gone - or where it had come from for that matter. "Vision?"

Nothing. Just a faint tingle in his limbs that felt like nothing more than excitement rapidly fading away. Alan's heart sank. It was like his dad had said - just some Old World hocus pocus, a dream he'd already woken up from. There were always rumours of Old World tech running with the caravans, always a village or two away, and the rumours always ended the same: with the last of the Old World fading away for good. Nice and neat and as comfortable as endings got any more. He had just hoped that this time, when it came to him ...

He had just hoped.

Alan stretched and reached down to pull his boots on, letting rote practicality guide his body as his mind wallowed in disappointment. He could ponder the momentary flash of excitement while he worked. Let the lightning strike over the horizon, as always.

The instant that he stepped out of the house, though, a soft chime rang in his head.

**** Location Discovered: Riverford Village (+100 XP) ****
**** Spawn Point Set: #N/A ****
**** Quest Gained: Be Vewy, Vewy Quiet! ****

The text this time was small and clustered in the bottom-left corner of Alan's vision and faded away when he focused elsewhere. He couldn't help himself - a grin stretched across his face. Whatever Old World magic this was, it wasn't dead yet! He had no idea how it knew the name of the village or what a spawn point or XP were but he knew what a quest was. Or, rather, he knew someone who would know what a quest was.

The streets of the village were quiet; it was still early and the few people up were those with too much work to dream or daydream. Like most mornings, he heard Carl before he saw him, the sound of an argument drifting through the air. As he reached Carl's house and rounded the last corner he found his friend staring daggers at his twin sister Ella, both perched on the garden wall. The similarities between the two were obvious - both were tall and dark-eyed and favoured close-cropped air. The differences ran deeper; where Carl was quick and daring - so long as his nose wasn't buried in a book - his sister was cautious and rather heavy-handed with her words.

They trailed off their argument as Alan approached, for which he breathed a sigh of relief. Their arguments were fierce and free-flowing, founded in that deep frustration that only family could bring about, and all-too-happy to drag in anyone unlucky enough to wander past.

"Tell her she's being an idiot," Carl said, dropping down from the walls.

"Yeah, no," Alan said, clasping Carl's hand as they met. "I'm not making that mistake again. Ella."

"Alan." Ella dropped down from the wall, her movements mirroring her brother's, although she stopped short of reaching out to Alan. "What class did you pick?"

"Class? I don't know what you're talking about." Alan maintained a puzzled face for all of three seconds before the disbelieving stares from the two siblings forced him to smile. "Who said I chose anything? Dad said it was a load of rubbish and to get out to the fields."

"Yeah, and here you are," Carl said. "Come on mate, what did you go for? Warchief? Mistwalker?"

Behind him, Ella snorted and rolled her eyes.

"Check it out: Lightning Disciple!" Alan spread his hands out in what he hoped was a dramatic manner and waggled his fingers - only for Carl to groan and kick at the ground while Ella burst into laughter.

"What?"

"Told you," Ella said, as Carl cursed under his breath. "Idiot."

"Makes a change," he snapped back. Ella just kept on laughing.

"She bet me you'd go for that one just based on the name," Carl said. "Thanks a lot - I owe her my crusts next time there's bread."

"What, I'm that predictable?" Alan wasn't sure how offended he actually was but put on an air of hurt anyway. It didn't fool either of the two for a second.

"You and lightning, man." Carl shook his head. "I'll never get it. It's just weather."

"Whatever," Alan said, "I bet you don't even know what's going on." His friend bristled at the affront to his knowledge - but his sister answered first.

"Not a clue," she said, grinning at her brother's annoyed scowl. "We made characters, though. Like in one of Carl's books."

"It's more like a play, actually," Carl muttered. "We're all characters and the class is like the type of person we have to pretend to be. A noble wandering knight, a - well, whatever a lightning disciple is supposed to act like. You get the idea."

Alan grinned. "Knew you wouldn't be able to resist. What'd you pick?"

"Scholar," Carl said. "Apparently it means that I derive abilities from rare texts, which I thought was rather appropriate."

Behind him, his sister rolled her eyes so hard Alan was worried she'd burst a vein and muttered something that was probably "dork" under her breath. Carl shot her a glare, to no effect.

"I kept it nice and simple." Ella thumped one fist against her chest. "Fighter."

Alan waited a moment but that was apparently all that Ella felt like sharing.

"So," he said, once it was clear no more was forthcoming, "you have any idea what it all actually is?" Alan looked to both Carl and Ella for politeness' sake - but really, he was looking to Carl, who unfortunately shook his head.

"No clue," Carl said, "it's Old World stuff - got to be - and who knows what that means? An heirloom is like an old-fashioned ... thing, that you hand down to your kids. Don't know what 'online' means. Guess that doesn't really help."

It really didn't.

"You see a message about a quest?"

"Yeah." Ella nodded and jerked her head at Carl. "He says it's like a job."

"A quest is far more than a job," Carl said, his voice taking on a clipped tone that everyone in the village knew far too well. "A quest is a mythical undertaking, a journey so monumental and epic that it -"

"It's rabbits." Ella shook her head. "It's just hunting damn rabbits."

Alan's grind faded. Really? Seemed like a lot of drama all for the sake of hunting rabbits. Hell, he'd done that the night before without needing some fancy new magic vision telling him what to do. The fact that he'd failed was neither here nor there.

"How do you know?"

"Because - oh, just think about it real hard. The quest, I mean. You'll see."

As soon as Alan concentrated on the idea that he had a quest - even if he still wasn't sure what it meant - a new window appeared over his vision, crowding out Carl's and Ella's faces.

**** <u>Quest: Be Vewy, Vewy Quiet!</u> ****
**** Difficulty: Tutorial ****
**** Reward: 100 XP ****
**** Description: Proceed to the marked area and kill five rabbits. ****
**** Quest Progress: 0 / 5 rabbits killed ****

A tugging sensation pulled at Alan's mind and when he turned his head he could see a golden fleck of light slide across the top of his vision, hovering to the south-west. Sure enough, it was the direction of the riverbank that he had been hunting on the night before.

"How mythic." Alan looked over at Carl who was audibly grinding his teeth. "So epic."

"Yes, well," Carl began, before swallowing his pride and giving up the argument.

"The point is," Carl continued, "we have been given a quest - a job, a task - to go and hunt rabbits."

"By who?"

"I don't know."

"Why?"

"I don't know." Carl glared at Alan, who was having too much fun to stop.

"But what -"

"I don't know, okay?" Carl snapped as both Alan and Ella started to laugh. "You guys are arseholes."

"Yeah," Alan said. "So, you coming or what? I haven't eaten rabbits in ages."

He decided not to mention the previous night's embarrassment but couldn't help rubbing at his bruised wrist.

"Of course," Carl said after a second of hesitation.

"I'm in," Ella said. She ignored Carl's glare and shrugged when Alan looked at her. "I haven't had rabbit in a while and da's already working the fields."

"Fair," Alan said. "It's a free world - join the party."

**** Party Invitation Sent ****

"Err, guys did you -" Alan looked up to see Carl and Ella staring into the middle-distance, Ella silently mouthing words to herself as Carl's eyes darted back-and-forth. A second later Alan received a new message. A second after that, another.

**** Scholar Carl has joined the party ****

**** Fighter Ella has joined the party ****

A strange sensation scratched at Alan's mind. It was a little like the feeling of another person stood close beside him - no sound or touch to give them away, just a vague feeling of presence. He closed his eyes and Carl and Ella became phantom limbs whose location he knew instinctively. He stepped to the side and, sure enough, the knowledge of Carl and Ella shifted too, guiding him back to them. Judging by the sour expression on Ella's face and the bemused look on Carl's when he opened his eyes again, the others felt it too.

"Okay," Ella said, slowly, "that's weird."

"Yeah," Carl said. "At least it can't get much weirder." He chuckled. "I mean, how weird can *rabbits* possibly be?"

CHAPTER THREE

The walk down to the riverbank was quicker and more relaxed in the daylight as a group or "party". They each had their day packs and Ella even passed around a canteen full of thin barley soup, for which Alan's stomach was incredibly grateful. He and Carl laughed and joked as they went, with Alan mentioning the star that he had seen fall to earth the night before. Ella didn't believe him and he wasn't sure that Carl did either. After some of the tricks he had played on them over the years, he could understand their scepticism. Still, given how strange the morning had been he felt a bit sore that they wouldn't give his story any merit. Then again, Carl pointed out, they'd been seeing ghostly images all day. Was he that sure he could trust his senses from the night before? That stopped Alan's complaints dead in their tracks - maybe the falling star really had just been the first of the visions?

They didn't see any other villagers and Alan hoped it stayed that way - news travelled fast in the village and he didn't want his dad to find out he'd skipped work in the fields. Not until there was a rabbit or two to make up for his absence, anyway. Fresh game would fix nearly all arguments.

The riverbank was an even more unimpressive sight in the daylight. The water seemed a little higher than usual and not quite as murky but that wasn't saying much after the summer they'd had. It was still early but the sun was well up by now and Alan was a little confused as to exactly how the mysterious quest-giver expected them to hunt rabbits, which surely should be hidden in their warrens. It wasn't until he dropped down from the old road onto the dirt, and got his first good look at the expanse of grass and shrubs, that he saw the big change from the previous night. Carl and Ella dropped down beside him and quickly joined him in staring, slack-jawed, at the sight ahead of them.

"What are they?" It took Alan a second to realise that he was the one who had asked the question. Even though he knew the answer.

He just couldn't accept that these things were *rabbits*!

For a start, there were nearly a dozen of them. Then there was the fact that they were just sat out in the open, nibbling the same patches of grass over and over, without any of their natural fear. The fact that they had ghostly text floating over their heads - **<Fierce Rabbit>**, **<Anxious Rabbit>**, **<Swift Rabbit>** - wasn't even their most surprising feature. It was the size of them that really shocked Alan. The rabbits were all, well, fat. Their coats were soft and relatively clean and covered thick thighs and chubby cheeks. Instead of the single mangey beast that Alan had stalked the night before, there was a feast of docile, unaware prey right in front of his eyes.

Rabbits could be a whole new kind of weird, as it turned out.

"Pinch me," breathed Ella, "I'm dreaming."

"You're not the only one," Carl said. None of them took their eyes off of the sight. None of them dared. Alan was afraid that if he looked away, if he even blinked, the whole scene would disappear like fog burned away by the noon sun. One of the rabbits lifted its head to stare up at the three humans, then turned back to its dinner, completely uninterested.

"What are we waiting for?" Alan looked from Carl to Ella, the spell finally broken. "An invitation?" He dropped his pack by his feet and bent down to find a good stone.

"We don't know what's happening here," Ella said, her words slow. "This is … this is wrong. We need to let somebody else in the village know."

"It's a miracle," Alan said, "and we can let them know when they smell cooked rabbit." Besides him, Carl was likewise looking around for ammo. When Alan had found a suitable stone he quickly whirled it up in his sling, taking aim at the closest rabbit and letting the stone fly loose. It traced a shallow arc through the air before smacking the rabbit in the head.

And bouncing off.

For the second time in as many minutes, the three stared slack-jawed at the rabbit. A small green bar popped into existence above it, shrinking down by around a third, as the rabbit stopped chewing, looked Alan square in the eye and began to hop determinedly towards him. None of the other rabbits reacted.

"Did you -" Carl looked at Alan, aghast. "Did you just manage to piss off a rabbit that can shrug off a stone to the head?"

"I didn't - what the hell do you want me to say?" Alan scrabbled around on the ground for another stone, his heart racing. "Hit it! You hit it too!"

Between the three of them, they found another stone and, as the rabbit hopped steadily closer, Alan spun it up in his sling and let fly. The stone hit again, this time on the rabbit's flank, and the green bar shrank and turned a dull orange. It didn't shrink as much as before, however, and the rabbit kept on hopping.

"Oh screw this," Carl said, "it's just a rabbit." He dropped his slung and jogged forward, picking up speed until he was a metre or so away from the rabbit. Then he turned his next step into a kick, swinging his foot around and catching the rabbit in the side. It staggered away from him a little way - and then kept on hopping, this time turning to chase Carl. The bar shrank a little more.

The three of them froze again but this time the rabbit didn't wait for them to regain their senses. It launched itself at Carl in one great leap, somehow latching itself onto his arm as he raised it up to shield his face. Alan heard him cry out in pain and could see a burst of blood fly free. The rabbit had managed to bite down through cloth and skin and was latched on, a high, keening cry escaping through its clenched jaw.

"Get it off! Get it off get it off!" Carl fell backwards, slamming the rabbit into the ground again and again. Alan darted forward to help his friend but Ella beat him to it, reaching her brother in seconds with a rock in hand and slamming it down on the rabbit in one fluid motion. There was a sharp crack as rock hit bone and then the rabbit fell lifeless from Carl's arm. The bar above it flashed red and then shrank into nothingness.

**** Angry Rabbit killed (+10 XP) ****
**** Quest Progress: 1 / 5 rabbits killed ****

Alan reached Carl a second later, who was clutching his arm as blood seeped from between his fingers. His sleeve was in shreds and Alan realised that a bar, much like the one that had appeared over the rabbit, had appeared over Carl's head. It wasn't quite full and as Alan watched, a sliver of it disappeared. A few seconds later, another sliver vanished.

"My pack," Carl cried, tears escaping from the corner of his eyes. "There's a book in my pack, it says what to do!"

"A book? Now?" Alan jumped back as Carl swung a kick at him, before racing back to where their packs lay at the side of the old road. He carried Carl's back to him, as Ella watched on with a look of fear draining the colour from her face. The other rabbits sat still and calm, chewing the grass.

The book, when Alan pulled it out - after discarding "101 Country Recipes" and "Diary of a Fly Fisher" - was called "First Aid for Beginners". He opened it at random and tried to find something, anything, to help Carl, before the book was snatched from his hands.

"I read this the other day," Carl said, hissing as he shifted his arm and fresh blood pumped out through the rags of his shirt. Alan could see a deep cut and the silver flash of something that might have been bone. The thought turned his stomach and he had to close his eyes for a second, breathing deeply.

"There's a section on cleaning cuts," Carl said, "and a -"

His eyes glazed over.

Ella looked from him to Allan and back again.

"Carl," she whispered, "are you -"

A shiver ran through Carl and a second later he hissed, a sharp intake of breath, as he looked to his injured arm. Before Alan's eyes, the wound twitched and shrank, the muscles and skin knitting together in front of his eyes until Carl's arm was whole again, smooth and unblemished beneath the ragged shirt sleeve. Above his head, the bar filled back up and faded from sight.

"What the hell was that?" Ella grabbed Carl's arm, even as he stared in shock at it and let the book drop from his fingers. "Carl, what just happened?"

"The book," Carl said, looking down at where it lay in the dirt. "As soon as I picked it up I just knew … it taught me to cast a spell called 'Cure Light Wounds' and I just …"

He trailed off into silence.

"Power from books." Alan couldn't believe it. "That's what you said, being a school-er meant you got power from books."

"Well yes," Carl said, "and it's 'scholar' not 'school-er' but I never dreamt -"

Alan stopped listening. Even as Ella helped her brother to his feet, Alan was staring down at the rest of the rabbits in front of them. Thinking hard about the message he had seen, the description of a Lightning Disciple. He let instinct guide him, raising one arm and curling his fingers to point at a <Placid Rabbit> a dozen metres away. What had the ability been called again?

Lightning Strike.

Even as he thought the words, a spark crackled across his fingertips. His arm and hand began to thrum with power, pins and needles sinking into his flesh, and a distant sense of fatigue crept over him. Both grew, his energy draining even as the power in his hand built. After a couple of seconds, it was unbearably intense and he mentally let go. As he did so, a bolt of lightning flared out from his fingertips, shooting through the air in a zig-zag shape that struck into the ground at the rabbit's feet with a sound like a whip-crack, kicking up a spray of dirt. The animal was sent flying, slamming into the river bank a dozen metres away even as a bar above it appeared, flashed red and shrank to nothing all in a single instant.

**** Placid Rabbit killed (+10 XP) ****
**** Quest Progress: 2 / 5 rabbits killed ****

"Holy shit." All three of them uttered the same old curse at the same time, with varying levels of shock and awe.

"What the hell was that?" Ella stared at Alan, her eyes narrowing.

"Lightning Disciple," Alan said, not able to take his eyes off of his outstretched arm. "It said I could cast something called Lightning Strike. Carl chose schooner -"

"Scholar."

"- and figured out how to cure himself from a book, just like magic. And you chose -"

"Fighter," Ella said, "I chose Fighter."

She stared down at her hands, then cast her eyes around until she spotted a tree branch that was half-covered by grass. Picking it up, she gave it an experimental twirl in her hands. Then, before Alan or Carl could say anything, she charged past them both towards the rabbits. With an inarticulate cry, she brought the makeshift staff around, slamming it into the side of a **<Gentle Rabbit>**. Alan winced as he heard bones crack, the rabbit skidding across the floor a little way before finding its footing and hopping furiously back towards Ella. The bar above it was half full.

"Smash!" Ella shouted the word at the top of her lungs, bringing the wood down in an overhead swing right onto the rabbit's skull. There was a loud crash as the rabbit was driven into the ground, a small shockwave rippling out through the air from the point of impact.

**** Gentle Rabbit killed (+10 XP) ****

**** Quest Progress: 3 / 5 rabbits killed ****

"Holy shit." Alan didn't know what else to say.

"It's real," Carl said, his voice full of wonder. He was back on his feet now, watching his sister bend down to grab the corpse. "I thought it was all just phantom lights and make-believe but this is …"

"Power." Alan finished the sentence for him. "Look at what we just did! That's the last time those arseholes out at the bandit camp mess with us."

"Yeah, except they have guns and a few more brain cells than rabbits." Ella shook her head. "And what if they can throw lightning around too?"

Now there was a scary idea. Alan's stomach churned at the thought of the bandits riding in, throwing this new magic around the village. Hopefully, they'd set their sights slightly higher than a few homes and fields - especially if everyone in those homes and fields could hit back just as hard.

"Let's get this quest done first," he said, shoving the thought away. "We can worry about the bandits later."

As the words left his lips, a new quest appeared on the edge of his vision.

**** Quest Gained: Bandit Bother ****

A quick glance at Carl, and then over at Ella, told him they had seen it too.

"One thing at a time," Ella said, dropping the latest rabbit corpse with the first. "Take a look."

Alan crouched down and looked the rabbit over. It was very, very fat and very, very dead. Then he got a new notification.

**** Loot Corpse? ****

Well, why not?

**** You have gained: 5 copper ****

A number in the back of Alan's mind, which he hadn't noticed before, ticked up from zero to five. He raised an eyebrow at Ella who shrugged. He got the same messages when he examined the first corpse and - when he wove his way through the group of rabbits, none of which paid any attention to him - again when he retrieved the body that he had struck with lightning. Carl knew that copper was a type of metal but beyond that none of the three had any idea what it meant. It was a sensation that Alan was getting tired of.

Emboldened by their early success, they set their sights on finishing off the quest. Alan had gotten his breath back enough to fire off another bolt of lightning, choosing a rabbit that was a bit further away this time and only letting the power build for a moment. The bolt that struck was weaker and also less accurate; Alan hit a rock and a tree, leaving him gasping for breath and the rabbit chewing away. In the end, Ella walked over and knocked it on the head with her makeshift staff again.

**** Sly Rabbit killed (+10 XP) ****
**** Quest Progress: 4 / 5 rabbits killed ****

Ella took the final rabbit in the same way. Carl made his excuses and hung back and Alan saw him scratching nervously at his arm. This rabbit was quicker than the first few and managed to latch on to Ella's ankle before she knocked it down. Carl worked his magic again and the scrape the rabbit had left - biting nowhere near as deep as it had on Carl - gave way to smooth dark skin once more.

**** Fierce Rabbit killed (+10 XP) ****
**** Quest Progress: 5 / 5 rabbits killed ****
**** Quest Completed: Be Vewy, Vewy Quiet! ****
**** You have gained: 100 copper, 100 XP ****
**** You have reached Level 2! ****
**** Attributes Increased! ****
**** Quest Gained: A-Hunting We Will Go! ****

The messages flooded Alan's awareness at once, in a dizzying clamour for attention that he almost didn't notice. As they scrolled across his vision a wave of energy welled up inside of him, flooding every corner of his body in a warmth that momentarily wiped away every lingering bruise and cut, every sore joint and slight toothache. Even his stomach felt full, as though he had just eaten a large meal. Rather than the sleepiness that would bring, though, he felt more alert and awake than he could ever remember feeling. The sensation passed and the fatigue in his limbs returned but Alan was left smiling nevertheless.

He turned to see Ella and Carl similarly affected. Carl had his hands to his temples, a wide smile on his face, while Ella clenched and unclenched her fists, as though testing out her muscles.

"That," said Ella, "was amazing." She looked at the two of them, her face full of wonder. "Like the best night's sleep I ever had."

"Tell me about it." Carl sighed. "Think it was because we completed the quest?"

Alan thought it over. That would make sense - a reward from the quest-giver, maybe? But something else nudged at his attention - the message about reaching "Level 2". As soon as that had appeared he had felt strong, faster - just generally better. Even his head felt a little clearer - and when he tried to explain it all to Carl and Ella the words came that much easier.

"That makes sense," Carl said. "I mean, I felt the same way. Like I'd improved at something only the something was … well, everything."

"Gain experience to reach the next level." Ella said the words with a faraway stare, then frowned. "Why do I know that?"

Alan checked his memory. Ella was right. It was like a memory of a memory, knowledge that he had that he was sure he'd never had before, as though it had just appeared in his brain. That was more than a little unnerving, although he quickly dismissed the worry. He could shoot lightning now. What was there to worry about?

It wasn't the only new knowledge, though. He concentrated on the messages he had received so far that mentioned 'XP'.

**** Total XP: 250 ****

**** XP Needed To Reach Next Level: 350 ****

"So XP makes us reach a new level and that makes us … better?" Carl had clearly been working along the same train of thought. "Hey, if it feels this good every time then I'm all for it."

"You said it." Alan grinned. "You know what would make you feel even better?"

Alan lifted the brace of rabbit corpses that he had strung up, causing Carl - and, after a few seconds with a troubled look, Ella - to lose any trace of concern in favour of wide eyes and rumbling stomachs.

"Yeah, I could eat," Ella said.

"Come on, then. Once everyone sees this they'll all be down here throwing lightning at rabbits." Alan hoisted the brace over his shoulder, as the three of them set off back to the village and the promise of - at long last - a good meal.

CHAPTER FOUR

The trio traded jokes the whole way back to the village after Alan had Carl heal his wrist. The magic fizzed away the bruise, as though Alan's arm had been wiped clean with a cloth, taking the pain with it. The air was warm and getting warmer, with a sticky humidity that was beginning to cling to Alan's skin, despite a gentle breeze. There was a storm on the way for sure and Alan couldn't wait. That, and the promise of good food, put them all in a lively mood.

Michael Arton was on guard duty on the gate again, although this time he had turned up. His eyes were still red and puffy and even from a distance he stank of the foul potato vodka he made, but he was upright and had even dragged a spear out of storage. It was just an old fence post with a knife tied to the end but it would do the trick in a pinch and looked marginally imposing. Michael saluted at Alan, Ella and Carl as they passed through the gate. The three shared a glance - it wasn't like Michael to take guard duty seriously at all.

"Morning Michael," Alan said. "Late night, huh?"

"Good morning," Michael said, "and welcome to Riverford."

"… yeah, thanks, Michael." Alan frowned at the man. "You feeling all right?"

"Welcome," Michael said. "What a glorious morning it is!" A tear trickled down from the corner of one of his eyes, cutting a path through a layer of grime. Then a shiver seemed to run down him, from head to toe.

"My - my head …" Michael grasped at his head with his free hand and clenched his eyes shut, forcing out more tears.

Ah, that made sense. He was horrifically hungover. Again. Alan chuckled under his breath and heard Ella cough discreetly. The man was legendary for his ability to inflict self-punishment. The bright summer sun was hardly helping. Alan couldn't afford the time or cost of getting that drunk but if

Michael was willing to deal with the consequences Alan wasn't going to stop them. The village as a whole turned a blind eye, more from apathy than mercy.

"Be seeing you," Alan said, and the three passed on through into the village, leaving the sorry guard behind.

The village was still quiet, although Alan imagined that would change in a hurry once news of the rabbits spread. Somewhere, he could smell bread baking. He had no idea how anyone had found wheat - the granary had been empty for weeks - but supposed someone had squirrelled some away somewhere. Against the rules, technically, but the end product was usually shared around enough to quieten any complaints. Well, shared with the right people, anyway.

They'd have to share the rabbits too, but that was no problem, Alan thought. There were plenty of them, after all, and they made for easy hunting. Well, they didn't run or hide, at any rate. As long as people moved fast enough and hit hard enough there'd be a rabbit in every pot before lunchtime.

"I'm going to save a leg or two to smoke," Carl said, as they turned the corner to the siblings' home. "Nothing fancy - just something to look forward to a few months from now. The rest can go right into a stew."

Alan chuckled. Healing wounds, throwing lightning - and yet they'd spent most of the trip back discussing the finer points of cooking and eating rabbit. Let it never be said that they didn't have their priorities right. Turned out you could eat daydreams after all. Speaking of which … There was no mistaking the familiar figure of his dad up ahead, carrying a - Alan frowned. Was that a chicken? They didn't own any chickens. And why wasn't he still in the forest? He'd normally spend the entire morning there, especially now that all of the obvious food had been scavenged. Had he … had he found a chicken in the forest? Years of scraping by and now two strokes of good fortune in one day!

"Dad!" Alan cupped one hand around his mouth and waved with the other, the brace of rabbits slung over his shoulder. "Dad, we got rabbits!"

His dad didn't respond. He just kept on walking along towards the village square, a fat, dead chicken slung over his shoulder by its feet, whistling in a jaunty manner that Alan didn't recognise. He was standing taller, swinging his arms freely, acting like he didn't have a care in the world. Which, to be fair, Alan realised he had also been doing.

"Here, hold these." Alan passed the rabbits and his pack to Carl who clasped them close. There was a strange tension growing in Alan's stomach and he couldn't explain it. Something about the way his dad was walking, for all that he looked carefree. Like he wasn't comfortable in his own skin.

"Dad!" He jogged ahead, quickly catching up with the ambling pace. The tune - a melody that Alan didn't recognise - died on his dad's lips as Alan reached him and grabbed him by the shoulder, turning the two men face-to-face.

"Can I help you, squire?" Alan's dad looked at him with a bemused grin and not a trace of recognition. He was ruddy-cheeked and there was a new layer of fat under his skin, filling out some of the sallow features that Alan had seen only hours ago. Even his clothes had been mended and washed.

"Dad, what's going on?" Alan withdrew his hand slowly. "Are you - are you feeling alright?"

"Now that you mention it, I haven't been sleeping well recently." His dad's grin turned into an almost comical frown, twisting the edges of his mouth right down while the rest of his face froze in place. "Something keeps disturbing my chickens in the middle of the night. I think it might be those goblins again."

"Chickens?" They didn't have any chickens. "Goblins?" Like out of one of Carl's books?

His dad nodded and his face returned to a neutral position - all except for the eyes. The eyes remained locked on Alan and they were wide with terror. They looked like a scream sounded and Alan took a step back despite himself.

"I reckon the goblins are outgrowing the food the forest can provide. See if you can thin their numbers for me and I'll make it worth your while."

**** Quest Gained: Chicken Run ****

"Dad, what's wrong?" Alan's heart pounded in his chest, his skin cold despite the heat, sweat mingling with humidity.

A comical frown again.

"Come back when you've dealt with those goblins."

"Dad, I -"

"Come back when you've dealt with those goblins."

A thunder of footsteps broke into Alan's nightmare and he looked away to see Ella running down the street towards him. His dad took the opportunity to turn and saunter off again, taking up the same whistled tune as though nothing had happened.

"Ella!" Alan felt torn between following his dad and getting help. "There's something wrong with my dad! I think - I think he's forgotten me!"

"I know," Ella said, and Alan saw rare tears rolling down her cheeks as she reached him. "It's got our ma too."

"He didn't recognise me," Alan said, his fists clenching as the rest of him shook. "Just kept going on about chickens and goblins."

"Ma didn't recognise us either," Ella said. "Just walked straight past us on the street, said she was going fishing. Carl was going to try -"

They both jumped at the sound of a choking cry from behind them and they turned to see Carl heading for them, the copy of "First Aid for Beginners" grasped in one hand. Alan opened his mouth to ask but closed it again when Carl just shook his head, wiping away tears of his own.

"What do we do?" Ella looked at Alan.

Why was she asking him? Alan didn't know. If Carl's literally magical ability to cure people couldn't cure them of whatever was wrong, then what chance did throwing lightning around have of helping?

"We find out if anyone else is like this," Alan said, "or if there's anyone who isn't. Then we …"

What then? Alan had gone to bed the night before dreaming of falling stars and a full stomach. Twelve hours ago the world had made a dreary, depressing sense. How was he meant to know what to do now?

"… then we plan what to do next," he finished lamely. It wasn't much to go on and he could see that Carl and Ella both knew it - but the siblings clung to his words like a drowning man clung to a thrown rope. He let himself believe a little too, let himself hope.

A quick search of the village, however, offered up precious little in the way of things to be hopeful for. Everyone they met in the streets was in the same deluded state, spilling forth from homes with frozen faces, eyes still fearful or half-asleep. They spouted vague rubbish about a life in the village none of them knew. The blacksmith, Saul, told them all a lengthy tale about his time in the army. Alan knew he had never been more than two miles away from the village. The bone-setter claimed to be a turnip farmer. Even a pair of travelling merchants, who had stopped off in the village to ride out the upcoming storm, claimed to be long-time residents. And the children -

Well, Alan tried not to think about the children.

It wasn't until they reached the side room at old Samuel's house, an unofficial place for men to gather and gamble and drink, that they found anyone acting quite right. Samuel was arguing with a group of men who had brought in tables and chairs, completely demolishing his furniture, and started singing some incomprehensible song. His face was even ruddier than usual and every time the men started a new verse his moustache twitched with rage. The men, meanwhile, carried on singing and drinking as though nothing was out of the ordinary. When he saw Alan, Carl and Ella walk in acting like themselves he just about melted with relief - right up until they explained that they had no idea what was going on either.

They fished Arthur Gumley out from under a table, where he was drunk but sane, and when they reached the small chapel next to the graveyard they found old Bess Cartwright. She was trying to talk one of the Benchley twins out from behind the lectern, where they were giving an impromptu sermon on the dangers of something called blood magic. They found Elaine Gumley still out in the fields, blissfully unaware that there was anything wrong. She collapsed into a flood of tears when they explained what was happening and again when she learnt that her husband wasn't affected. When she learnt he was still drunk from the night before she chased him around the field with a hoe.

It wasn't until they were heading back into the village, the whole group of them sane and together, that Alan thought to examine one of the affected villagers closely, with the same care that he had examined the rabbits before. To his surprise, a new icon popped up over the villager's head.

<Roger O'North>
<Tailor>
<NPC>

Never-mind that the man's name wasn't Roger and they weren't a tailor - it was the last line that caught Alan's eye.

"NPC?" Carl asked after Alan stopped the group to explain what he had seen. "Looks like an acronym but I have no idea what for."

None of the rest of the group had any idea either, although that didn't stop them from discussing it long past the point at which their ideas made any sense. They examined each villager that they passed and all returned the same result. They were still discussing the letters when they reached the Gumley house. It was the one house where they knew none of the occupants had been affected, although Ella wondered out loud whether the villagers would take up new homes just like they had taken new names. For the time being, they set the bar across the door. It wasn't that they were afraid of the other villagers, as such - the NPCs, as Carl started calling them, seemed naively harmless. They were a distinctly uncomfortable sight to see, though, and nobody wanted one walking in unannounced. They gathered in the kitchen, the only room large enough to hold them all, the stove cold and dark as Alan ran through everything they had encountered that morning. He finished up by describing the star he had seen fall the night before.

"It's Old World tech," Samuel said. He fiddled with the tips of his moustache, a familiar sight in the village whenever he was worried or uncertain. Given that he was the sort of man to assume he led every village meeting or project, Alan was surprised that he hadn't twisted it all out years ago.

"You don't know that," Elaine said. A pale woman, she trembled a little as she spoke. "It could be magic. A curse." She hissed the last word between her teeth, as though she was afraid that someone would hear her, her eyes darting to the corners of the kitchen.

"What, just because of what the boys said?" Samuel grunted. "Star falling? Come on, Elaine."

"If you'd been awake, old man, you'd have seen it too," Ella said, her eyes narrowing. Alan saw Carl wince at her tone. "And you've seen the rabbits."

The rabbits in question were hanging from a hook behind the door, save one which was already being skinned and prepped outside by Bess and another that was almost finished roasting in the brick oven.

"So you found some fat rabbits? Doesn't sound like a curse to me." Samuel shook his head. "This is Old World tech, you mark my words. Every time something goes wrong round here it's our damn ancestors and their infernal machines. Name one good thing they ever did!"

31

"You mean like the houses they built?" Alan looked around the room. It was stone-walled with wooden beams and everything was built in squat, solid shapes. Every house in the village was built the same way - well, the ones still standing anyway. Even if they were getting a bit run-down.

"Fah!" Samuel snorted and waved a hand dismissively. "That was their ancestors. I mean the ones at the end - the ones who buggered things up."

There was a general murmur of agreement around the table and Alan found himself joining in despite himself. The last few generations before everything fell had been a messy time to live through, to hear it told. Entire governments, gone overnight. Generations of knowledge, lost to flood and fire. A sharp halt to mankind's advancement, followed by a slow and steady slide towards the grave. Samuel was, unfortunately, right.

"Point is," Samuel continued, "we've dealt with things like this before." He eyed Arthur. "Remember when the river caught fire?"

"Oh aye," Arthur said, slightly more with it after dunking his head in the rain barrel. "Or those windmills across the river? Sound of them used to drive off all the good hunting, 'til they collapsed. Accidentally, mind you."

"And what did we do?" Samuel leaned forward. "We waited them out." He slapped the table softly with each word. "We just need to carry on until everyone wakes up. Give them time."

"Leave my dad like that and just wait and hope?" Alan's cheeks burned. "That's your big plan?"

He wasn't surprised, as such. Life in the village - hell, life in any of the villages for miles around, he was sure - wasn't exactly a breeding ground for fresh thinking. Potatoes were harvested the same one year as the next and fish generally swam in the same waters every season. It wasn't about taking great leaps or fantastic new ideas, not like in the Old World - it was about grinding your way through day after day, month after month, year after year. But still, it was his dad. And Samuel wanted them to just wait?

"You tell me then, boy, what do you think we should do?" Samuel leaned forwards across the table towards Alan. Alan met his gaze at first, then blinked and looked away. He didn't know.

"We figure out what caused all this." Carl looked up from where he had been studying the grains of wood in the table. "Old World tech or magic or whatever it is - we find the source and we might be able to figure out a cure. It stands to reason."

"Reason? There's no reason when it comes to that Old World nonsense," Elaine said, shaking her head. "You can't bargain with it. Might as well ask the sky for a favour."

"There's no rhyme or reason to this," Samuel said, smacking his fist on the table. "You might as well ask why we were spared."

"Yeah!" Arthur pounded the table in solidarity - only when he did it, his fist clipped off of the edge, breaking a thick chunk of the wooden surface off. A small shockwave blew dust across the surface of the table, radiating out from Arthur's fist.

There was silence in the room for a long second.

"You made a character!" Alan pointed at Arthur, who was staring down at his fist bug-eyed. "Dad told me this morning - you were going round telling people you were a fighter!"

Arthur didn't respond, still staring at his fist. Carefully - very carefully - he uncurled it and placed his hand slowly back down on his lap, as though he were afraid it would go off again without warning.

Elaine raised a hand.

"So did I, if I'm honest," she said in a quiet, almost embarrassed voice. "Well, I just wanted to see what all the fuss was about. And I did always like crows, you know, so ..."

"Elaine chose Crow Sage," Arthur said, in a quiet voice, still looking down into his lap.

The table turned, as one, to look at Samuel. He squirmed under the combined gazes, his moustache twitching again and again as his face turned redder. Eventually, he broke, deflating, his proud shoulders slumping forward.

"Knight," he said, refusing to meet anyone's eye. "Bess chose Witch."

"That's it," Carl said. "Everyone who chose a class was spared. I know my ma and da refused to play along with the screens this morning - guessing your dad was the same?"

"Yeah," Alan said, "he told me to just ignore it." His stomach churned at the thought of how close he had come to being one of these NPCs. If he hadn't been impatient to see what the screen was all about, that could have been him shambling around thinking he was a tailor.

"And I'll bet you everyone else out there either slept through it or ignored it too." Carl looked grimly satisfied. "It makes sense in a way. I mean, when two strange things happen at the same time there's usually a connection."

"Two strange things?" Alan snapped his head up. "I know what caused this!"

Samuel frowned, letting angry bluster overtake his temporary embarrassment. His lip curled up in a cruel sneer.

"How would *you* know what caused this?"

"I don't," Alan said, "I mean, I don't know for sure. But I told you about last night. I saw a whole flock of stars fall out of the sky and one fell in the forest near here. What are the chances that would happen right before all this? It has to be linked. It has to be the cause."

The people sat around the table exchanged glances. It was Arthur who spoke first.

"Stars don't just fall down to earth, lad," he said, in a voice that straddled the line between kind and patronising. "They're - well I'm not sure what they are but they're way up in the sky."

"He's right," Carl said. He threw up his hands in front of him as Alan turned. "I mean, he's wrong but he's right. Stars don't fall but a meteor or something like it might have. I don't know how it would be linked to what we've seen and the NPCs but there could be something there, I guess."

"So what?" Samuel snorted. "You think that's what caused this? Some rock from space? No, this'll be something in the land, boy, some buried poison. We need to wait this out, same as I said before. Nobody's hurting, not really - I saw some of the folks eating and drinking earlier, though Lord knows where they got the bread. They can take care of themselves. We just need to make sure they don't go wandering off for a few days and wait for them to wake up."

"I'm not waiting," Alan snarled, both palms flat on the table. "I know what I saw. There are answers out there in the forest and if can find whatever fell -"

"No!" Samuel slammed the table again and it creaked but didn't break. "Now you three need to fall in line until this is through. We have a responsibility to the village! We need to act together and I will not have you running around daydreaming about magic space rocks -"

Alan didn't hear the rest of the speech. He'd heard enough to know what inaction sounded like. He simply stood, lifted the bar from the door, and walked out of the house while Samuel continued to spit and rant and Ella and Carl scrambled for their things. He passed Bess by the door, peeling the fur from a rabbit with practised hands. She called out after him but Alan kept walking.

A man was carrying a fat bale of golden straw along the road as he reached the garden gate, despite there having been no straw harvest in months. Alan stood there and watched him pass, whistling the same unfamiliar tune that his dad had been whistling earlier, until Ella and Carl caught up to him.

"He's wrong, you know." Alan jerked his head back towards the house. "Samuel."

"Samuel's a prick," Ella said, "but -"

"I know what I saw," Alan said. "I didn't dream it and I'm not waiting around if there's a way to save my dad."

"I know, mate." Carl clapped him on the shoulder. "We're with you. I'm not leaving ma or da like that any longer than I have to. Now if you say you saw a star fall into the forest then I believe you."

Alan looked wordlessly to Ella who nodded.

A great pressure spread its wings and flew from Alan's shoulders. He hadn't stopped to think how he was going to do this, let alone how he was going to do this by himself. He was glad beyond words that he didn't have to.

The moment of relief was undercut slightly by the loud rumbling of Alan's stomach. He grimaced.

"Wish I hadn't stormed out, though. That rabbit smelled amazing."

"Oh, that's not going to be a problem." Ella grinned and reached into her pack. A second later she withdrew a cloth-wrapped bundle that was still steaming slightly and giving off an amazing savoury aroma.

"You stole their lunch?" he asked.

"No," Ella said, "I took our rabbit that they kindly cooked for us. They should be glad I left them the rest. If they want more they can go to the riverbank themselves."

"She told them that on the way out," Carl said, grinning with brotherly pride. "Right to their faces. I thought Samuel was going to burst!"

"Did you also tell them that the rabbits bite damn hard now?"

"Must have slipped my mind," Ella said, deadpan. Alan and Carl burst into laughter. Ella only grinned wickedly.

CHAPTER FIVE

Alan, Ella and Carl made their way to the edge of the forest in a low mood, despite their earlier joking and despite telling themselves - often at great length and out loud - that they now had a plan. The enormity of the situation wasn't lost on any of them. Whatever had caused the visions to appear before them, whatever had given them each their powers, had also caused nearly the entire village to lose their minds. If this star, meteor or whatever it was didn't return things to normal, Alan wasn't sure what more they could possibly do.

The trip was made slightly more bearable - and slightly more confusing - by their lunch. They ate thick slices of rabbit, sandwiched between fresh bread. It was juicy and delicious and Alan would spend the next hour picking crumbs from his shirt and licking the flavour of the rabbit from his fingers. It was the best meat he had ever eaten, which was confusing in its own right given how scrawny and flavourless the rabbits usually were. What was more confusing, however, was the bread.

A man had been selling it in the village square as they had passed through, one of the traders that had been trying to wait out the approaching thunderstorm. He had offered it to them in exchange for copper - and when Alan had accepted, curiosity getting the better of him, he had felt that strange sense of quantity in his head tick down by the desired amount. The trader (or were they now a baker?) had smiled and handed over several loaves despite Alan giving him nothing in return. That had been strange. The fact that bread had been baked in a village with no wheat had been - and still was - even stranger. It was soft and white and springy and still slightly warm, not the hard, dry tack they were all used to. It was delicious. Alan just couldn't figure out where it had come from. The faux-normality of it made it even stranger than the fact that he could shoot lightning from his fingers.

Carl and Ella were going back and forth on whether there had been a Baker class listed, and whether they could just magically make bread appear out of thin air, when they reached the edge of the forest. The border was the old road, which wound its way up from the riverbank, up through the village and on to the neighbouring village a dozen miles away. The tree line had crept all the way down to the grey and white surface of the road, although the closest trees were barely more than shrubs. Still, Alan thought they looked taller and healthier than the last time he had seen them. The trees further from the road were tall and with a dense, dark green canopy that blocked out much of the light once you got deep enough inside. In the decades since the Old World fell it had apparently spread and recovered quite significantly - but now it was beginning to slowly die back again, the same as the rivers and the soil. It was as though nature had just given up.

They stepped under the canopy of the forest and Alan was immediately struck by a rich, dark scent rising from the forest floor. The earth. It smelled wet and alive, far more fertile than even the most coveted growing land that surrounded the village. Usually, the forest floor was a dry expanse of dead branches and stunted growth, especially this deep into summer, but instead, everything seemed vibrant and fresh.

"Like the rabbits," Ella said. She didn't need to say anything more.

**** Location Discovered: Riverford Forest (+100 XP) ****

In the back of his head, Alan could feel a compass-pull back towards the village, stronger and surer than memory. It was the same as the strange awareness of Carl and Ella that he had gained, as though the world was determined that he know exactly where he was and exactly where he had been.

His thoughts were interrupted by a startled shriek as Carl fell flat on his back before disappearing into the undergrowth. Alan caught a glimpse of something thick and green twisted around his leg before Carl was suddenly pulled across the forest floor away from them.

"Carl!" Ella dashed forward before Alan could say anything, disappearing between the trees in an instant. Alan cursed and raced after her, his progress slowed by the new growth that seemed to have sprung up overnight. It tangled his feet and made rocks, roots and holes invisible until the last second. It took all his awareness to keep his balance and so he didn't notice the clearing, small as it was, until he ran into it.

Only half a dozen or so metres across, the clearing was little more than the space where two trees had collapsed to the ground and not yet been replaced. Alan vaguely remembered climbing over and under their dry, rotting trunks as a child. Now, though, the trunks were barely visible under a swarming, writhing mass of vines and creepers. The frailest were little more than finger-width while the thickest resembled Alan's arm. Together, though, they twisted and braided themselves into limbs as thick as Alan's torso, hauling themselves up into a towering mass in the centre of the clearing, where Alan saw -

"Carl!"

His friend was bound tightly by the vines as they crawled around his body, suspending him several metres up off of the forest floor. His mouth was covered and Alan could see him straining against the monstrous plants.

<Forest Guardian Colony>

<Level 5>

The name flashed across Alan's mind even as one of the vines whipped out. Ella ducked beneath it, dropping to her hands and knees, but Alan wasn't so quick and the vine caught him in his chest. It was one of the thinner vines that Alan had seen but it still sent him sprawling backwards, his chest pulsing with a dull ache and a dozen small rocks digging into his back as he crashed to the ground.

Alan felt another number in the back of his mind tick down and when he focused harder it jumped to the forefront.

**** HP: 090 / 110 ****

**** MP: 100 / 120 ****

Another fake memory rose up along with it. HP was a measure of how healthy he was, while MP measured his ability to cast magic. Regardless of how he knew that or what it really meant, he got the idea - if his HP went down when he was hurt, he didn't want to see what happened when it reached zero. Alan rolled to one side as the vine smacked down again before pushing himself to his knees and sprinting for cover behind a tree at the edge of the clearing. A second later Ella dove in beside him, breathing hard.

"What is that thing?" Ella gasped, stomping down hard on a vine that crept around the base of the tree.

"It's called a Forest -"

"Not what I meant!"

"No idea." Alan winced as a vine creeping around the other side of the tree brushed against his leg. He kicked at it and it withdrew but he doubted it would stay away for long.

"We need to think about this properly," Ella said. "Make a plan. Maybe if I run round one way you can -"

Alan stepped around the tree and flung lightning wildly at the Forest Guardian Colony. His first shot went wild, slamming into a tree on the other side of the colony, but the second shot connected with the base of the creature and sent chunks of vine flying as sap and moisture instantly boiled and expanded, exploding from the beast in a spray of plant matter. It didn't scream - not that Alan had expected a plant to scream - but the vines around its base beat the ground in an angry, discordant tempo.

The bar above its head, displaying its health, appeared and dropped down to roughly three-quarters full.

**** HP: 090 / 110 ****

**** MP: 020 / 120 ****

Alan felt a deep weariness in his bones and when he called upon the lightning for a third time it ignored him. He could see Carl squirming in the creature's grasp and a new vine winding its way across his throat. Carl's struggles paused for a second then redoubled as he sensed the new danger. Alan threw up his hands again and again but all he got in return was a vine that grabbed him by the wrist and flung him at the nearest tree. His entire world went sideways before coming to a sickening, crunching halt as he hit the trunk, dropping to the floor. The vine around his wrist didn't let go, instead gripping tighter - until, with a dull thud, a hatchet came slicing down and cut straight through the plant.

"That's why I said we needed a plan, genius." Ella reached down and helped Alan to his feet, dodging back as a vine hit the ground where she had been standing. "You're lucky I packed this."

"Point taken," Alan said, wincing as he staggered away from another attack, calling for the information in his head.

**** HP: 050 / 110 ****

**** MP: 030 / 120 ****

"I'll get its attention," Ella said, "then you hit it."

She didn't wait for Alan's response, darting away from him, round the edge of the clearing, with her axe in one hand and a rock in the other. The latter she threw, striking true in the middle of the Forest Guardian Colony's trunk. It beat the ground again in a rapid pattern, then swung its vines around to follow her.

"Come on, Lightning Strike!" Alan flung both hands up in the direction of the monster again. Nothing. From atop the mound of vines, Carl's muffled cries for help turned into a choking set of gasps as the monster tightened its grip on his throat.

"Come on, come on!" Alan threw his hands up again and again, willing the power to flow forth, straining immaterial muscles. "Why won't you work?"

**** <u>Lightning Strike</u> ****

**** A high-damage magical attack that strikes a single enemy with lightning. Channelling more than the minimum mana into a casting will result in increased range and damage. Accuracy increases with channelling time. ****

**** Range: Variable (Minimum: 10 metres) ****

**** Damage: Variable (Minimum: 50 damage) ****

**** Cast Time: Variable (Minimum: Instant) ****

**** MP Cost: Variable (Minimum: 50 MP) ****

The message flashed across his vision and his mind. Words and numbers that made sense individually, but together were just a jumble. The one thing that stood out, though, was the cost. He knew what MP was now, that it rose and fell with the strange fatigue that fell across him each time he threw lightning.

**** HP: 050 / 110 ****
**** MP: 045 / 120 ****

It was nearly back up to 50. Rather than a stepped increase, like the ticking of a clock, it rose steadily as he caught his breath, water pouring into a pool. In the heat of battle, it was hard to tell but it seemed to go up by roughly one every second or so.

**** HP: 050 / 110 ****
**** MP: 048 / 120 ****

He was dimly aware of Ella shouting at him to shoot, to shoot now, as Carl choked and wheezed and strained against the vines. He dropped to one knee, took a deep breath, and raised his arm to point at the Forest Guardian Colony.

**** HP: 050 / 110 ****
**** MP: 050 / 120 ****

The lightning screamed from his fingertips, cutting a path through the air in a great cracking sound that echoed off of the trees. It tore into the monster, slightly lower than the last bolt to hit, and again the vines were boiled from the inside out, exploding in a shower of super-heated sap. This time the damage done seemed higher, however, and rather than beating the ground in a rage, the Colony flailed aimlessly.

**** Critical Hit ****

As new vines slowly began to form over the wound, Alan saw a glimpse of something white and fleshy in the centre of the column. He made his mind up in an instant, even as the sucking emptiness in the centre of him made his vision spin.

"The hole," Alan cried, "there's something in the hole! Hit it there!"

Ella paused, looking from Alan to Carl - whose limbs were shaking violently - her eyes wide. Then, with a curse that Alan heard even over the thrashing of the monster, she gripped the hatchet with both hands, ducked low and charged into the whirlwind of whipping vines. Alan saw them cut into her as she ran, lines of blood spurting out from a dozen shallow rakes. It didn't stop her, though, and Ella began to cry out as she ran, a fierce and terrifying cry that resonated in Alan's gut. Even the vines seemed intimidated, slowing just enough for Ella to burst through the last line of defence and - with a wide, two-handed swing - bury the hatchet deep inside the hole that Alan had caused.

This time the monster did scream, a high-pitched cry that made Alan wince and clutch at his head until it faded.

**** Critical Hit ****

**** Forest Guardian Colony killed (+100 XP) ****

Every vine still connected to the monster flung itself into the air, straining for the sky. Then, one by one, they fell limply to the floor. For a few moments, the repeated impacts sounded a little like rain and Alan instinctively looked up, where the storm clouds were still slowly moving in.

"Carl!" Ella abandoned the hatchet and ran for her brother, who hit the ground in a tangle of vines, choking and wheezing. Alan turned, bent at the waist and proceeded to empty his stomach of everything he had eaten that day. The drop in MP to almost nothing had twisted his guts in every direction at once. When he could stand straight again and there was nothing left to throw up, he staggered over to where Ella was helping Carl rip the vines wrapped around him away by the handful. As soon as he had uncovered his pack his hand shot inside, scrabbling around until he found his book and healing magic began to wipe away the angry red welts running down his throat.

Seeing that his friend wasn't seriously hurt anymore - and with his own vision clearing - Alan turned to inspect the body of the Forest Guardian Colony. Oddly he didn't get any hint that he could loot the corpse until he reached where the hatchet was buried. Moving aside the vines, he found a fat, white grub the size of a small child, with vines burrowing into and under its translucent skin. As he watched, the vines began to wither and fall away. He could still see the dark shapes of their roots buried under the grub's skin, wrapping and digging their way into its flesh.

Wordlessly, he handed the hatchet back to Ella as she and Carl approached. She took it with a grim nod and wiped the worst of the blood from it with a handful of leaves from the forest floor. All three looted the corpse, gaining 40 copper each.

"Anyone want to guess what that was?" Carl kicked a bundle of vines out of the way with obvious satisfaction. "That sure as hell wasn't living here a week ago."

Neither Alan nor Ella had an answer for him but they did tread far more carefully after that. There was no telling how many more of the Forest Guardian Colonies lurked in the forest and none of the three wanted to get caught off-guard again. Given that the monster had appeared out of nowhere, who knew what other sorts of monsters had appeared that were even worse? Ella hit Carl when he voiced their fears out loud and even Alan had to admit, it wasn't helping the mood.

When they came across the next Forest Guardian Colony, it wasn't as big of a surprise. This one had established itself part-way up a living tree, anchoring itself into the crook between two branches and draping its vines below. Only Carl's eye for detail spotted the threat before they blundered into it. He was still scratching at his wrist, some irritation that his magic apparently couldn't heal, and almost paranoid in his attention to every shadow. Alan couldn't exactly blame him.

They had a quick and quiet debate between the three of them as to whether or not to face the new threat. Ella voted to go around, while Carl voted to attack. Alan figured he wanted a little bit of payback against the creatures. As his friend, Alan decided to give him the satisfaction. Sort of.

So after a quick explanation of the further details he had received about his Lightning Strike ability, he stepped out into the clearing with a hand sheathed in lightning. True to what the message had said, by focusing and focusing and really trying hard to hold on to the building power, he had activated his ability without letting it loose. The pressure was intensely uncomfortable, a thousand times worse than pins and needles. In his head, he could feel his MP dropping fast, after the initial and sudden disappearance of the 50 MP minimum. Fatigue rolled over him in heavier and heavier waves and his breath came harder and harder. At the same time, he felt surer about his strike - more confident that it would go where he wanted. Just as he felt his MP drop into the single digits, and the first of the vines began to twitch in his direction, he let the power loose.

The previous attempts with Lightning Strike had sounded like the crack of a whip. This was closer to a real lightning strike. Alan felt it in his bones, a resounding and definite stamp on the surface of the world as a bolt thicker than his arm shot forward. It pierced the Forest Guardian Colony right at the base, where the grub had been on the first one, and burned straight through. Alan saw daylight on the other side and, through the ringing that gripped his skull, heard the distant crack of tree branches.

**** Critical Hit ****
**** Forest Guardian Colony killed (+100 XP) ****

"Holy shit," Carl gasped as he peeked around the tree. The monster fell from the tree ahead. With nothing to hold it together, it was just a limp bundle of rapidly decaying vines.

"Holy shit," Alan agreed.

His head spun but he managed to keep it together enough not to empty his stomach any further, if that was even possible. A few sips of water later he felt able to continue and after that, it was easy going. They were still on edge, jumping at every shadow and hanging branch, and Alan felt nauseous long after his MP had fully recovered. Nevertheless, they made good time and managed to avoid running into any further monsters. Alan guided them ever-onwards in the direction that he had seen the falling star take.

It was mid-afternoon by the time they came across the crash site. There was no warning - they simply crested a small rise and found themselves looking through a break in the trees at a scar cut deep into the forest floor. It wasn't particularly wide - perhaps a dozen strides across, all told - but it was long, stretching away from them in a great upheaval of earth and trees. The exposed soil was lighter than the dark topsoil and it clung to their shoes as they walked the length of the scar.

Each step they took was, for Alan, slightly faster than the one before. He couldn't help himself. As much as he knew Ella and Carl believed him, as much as he knew they trusted him - well, he didn't want them to have to trust him. Not on this. Not after every other crazy, nightmarish thing that had happened that day.

He could see the end of the scar ahead, a great bank of earth ploughed up behind it by whatever had fallen from the sky. Trees and rocks dotted the mound, swept up in the shockwave, and Alan was suddenly very grateful that the star had fallen the other side of the village. He didn't want to think what those sort of forces would do to the old brick walls and homes.

Still, this was it. Proof that he hadn't been seeing things. The key to curing the village. It had to be. He was jogging; now he was running, leaving Carl and Ella behind. But as they got closer and closer, his hopes started to fade. When they were a dozen metres away his heart began to pump ice-water rather than blood. The star had seemed massive and yet he could see nothing ahead. The end of the trail of destruction was marked by nothing more than a hole in the ground. He fell to his knees in front of it, not wanting to believe what he saw.

Nothing. There was nothing there. After a while, he became aware that someone had come and stood next to him and he felt a heavy hand drop once more to his shoulder.

"I'm sorry," Carl said, his voice whisper-quiet. "I know -"

"I saw it," Alan said, his voice catching. "The star that caused all of this. I know I saw it."

"I believe you," Carl said. "I mean, look around. What else could have cut the forest apart like this? Something fell out of the sky - I believe you."

"Then where is it?" Alan shook his head. "Where?"

"Maybe it burned up." Carl shrugged. "I mean, things do that when they fall from space. I -"

"- read about it in a book. I know." Alan wiped grit from the corner of his eye. The ground around them was baked hard alright, as though a great fire had raged where they now stood.

"I just wanted to think this was a way to cure the village, you know?"

"I know," Carl said. He sighed heavily. "Me too."

They stayed that way for a long while, staring at the hole where a star wasn't. Alan didn't know what else they could do, where else they could turn. Another village, maybe? But there was no reason to think anyone would know anything about magical stars that fell from the sky and granted powers and curses. Even if they could, the nearest village was a day away and the thought of leaving the village alone, vulnerable, for that long -

"Hey guys, look at this."

Ella waved over at them from the side of the scar, right where the hard, baked earth ended. When the two of them rose and made their way over they found her staring down at the softer ground, holding back a shrub with one hand.

"What are we looking at?" Carl frowned and looked down. "Hey, isn't that -"

Alan saw it too. The ground they stood on was baked hard and dry and fairly level by the star's passage. Where Ella stood, however, the earth was moist and soft and full of depressions.

Bootprints, Alan realised. Old World boots too, with hard, angular lines cut through in a repeating pattern. They led to, then from, the crash site. And where they led away, they led straight in the direction of a thin plume of smoke on the horizon.

Straight in the direction of, if rumour was to be believed, a bandit camp.

CHAPTER SIX

They passed through the forest with little trouble after leaving the crash site. It took them several hours to reach the far edge of the forest at a cautious pace, always following the pillar of smoke and broken foliage. They didn't see any more monsters but the prospect of bandits - terrifyingly real for years - weighed heavily on them. On several occasions Carl called a sudden halt, insisting that they were being followed, but each time they doubled-back on themselves to find absolutely nothing. Alan and Ella agreed with him that there were obviously other threats in the forest but privately Alan wondered if Carl wasn't just jumpy.

By the time they reached the tree line the light was beginning to fade. Below them, down a little slope, lay a stretch of old road. Beyond that, a jagged wall of metal and glass, Old World vehicles crushed down and piled high, looping around a low jumble of huts. Light flickered through the gaps in the wall - from the top of the slope, Alan could just see a fire in the centre of the space, the source of the smoke. Dark shapes moved here and there, blocking the light and talking in voices loud enough that the sound - but not the meaning - drifted back to where the party crouched.

Alan's memory and imagination filled in the shadows. The bandits - and it was only ever *the* bandits, as even bandits didn't stray too far - had last visited the village two years ago, a gaggle of mean-looking, enviably well-fed men and women with dirty rusted clubs and a single, evil-looking Old World gun. Always enough of a force to cause trouble if they needed to but never so many that the village fell to desperation and tried to fight back. It had occurred to Alan once that the bandits never visited too often for the village to cope and that they rotated between all of the local settlements regularly, if rumour was to be believed. Whoever was calling the shots had a brain in their head.

Alan heard a sharp bark cut through the air and for a split second he froze, certain that a pack of wild dogs had managed to sneak up on them. Then he realised - first with relief, then with dread - that the sound had come from the camp ahead. Sure enough, he saw a low shape pad its way over to the fire and lay down.

"You're mad," Carl said, shaking his head and looking away from the camp for the first time in what felt like hours. "You know that, right? No way we're getting in there and out again."

"Carl's right, Alan." Ella sighed. "Look, it was a nice idea but we can't just walk in and ask them to hand over … whatever it was they took from the forest. And it's not like you can take it by force."

"Why not?" Alan stared her down. "I can throw *lightning*, Ella. What's stopping me?"

"Well, to start, you can throw lightning just under once per minute once you run out of MP if what you said was accurate," Carl said. Alan had filled the two of them in on the extra details he had found out about his ability during their trek through the forest. "And that's not a lot of good against two dozen bandits with guns. Guns, Alan! You know, the sort that don't make you wait a whole minute to fire again!"

"Carl's right," Ella said, rolling her eyes. "Again."

"But they don't know that," Alan said. "I go in there and get real flashy - I've got the MP to throw off two bolts to start with - and they don't know I can't do more."

"Yeah, until you stop fighting back and throw up everywhere," Carl said. He stared Alan dead in the eye, an uncomfortably intense gaze. "Which leads to the second problem: you gonna kill them?"

"What? No, of course not!" The thought turned Alan's stomach. Kill them? Real people, not rabbits or monsters? There were limits, surely? There had to be limits.

"Well they're going to try to kill you," Carl said with a sigh.

"I could aim for their legs?"

"Oh yeah," Ella snorted, "I bet getting hit by lightning is fine as long as it's just your legs."

The three of them sat in gloomy silence for a long time after that. Alan stared down at the camp, where a few of the figures were beginning to stagger towards tents and huts. Throwing lightning was a powerful trick, sure, but he could do with a little bit of versatility right about now.

"Don't suppose you fancy pretending to want to join?" Carl asked, looking to his sister. "You know, impress them by hitting a few things real hard, go in, grab the meteor and leave when they're not looking. Bet they always want people who can fight."

"No." Ella's response was flat and hard. "If they see our faces it's all over. If they recognise us, where we come from …" She trailed off into an uneasy silence.

Alan shivered, despite the warmth. They'd all heard the rumours, of settlements that had tried to trick or cheat or stand up to the bandits. What good was getting his dad's mind back if the bandits just rode in and burned everything down a month from now?

"Then I won't let them see me," he said. He ignored the looks of concern that Carl and Ella shot him. "I'll go in after dark. They're less likely to spot me if I'm by myself and I bet they don't even set a guard."

"Yeah," Ella said, in a strained voice, "I mean, who'd be stupid enough to try and sneak into a bandit camp in the middle of the night?"

"I sneak in, I sneak out," Alan continued, "and we all camp out just inside the forest. As soon as it's light enough to see where we're going - as soon as we can spot the monsters before we run into them - we head home. Before they wake up and realise what's missing."

"That's a terrible idea," Ella said.

"I know," Alan said softly. "We need that star, though. It's the only clue we've got for fixing things and who knows what they'll do with it in there? For now, we know where it is and they won't be expecting anyone to come for it. We can't afford to wait."

Carl sighed and nodded. Ella just looked away. Alan found himself feeling disappointed - he had been hoping that one of the other two would have a better plan. So be it.

The hours passed slowly after that. There was little to do except watch and eat the last of the rabbit, the few cold scraps of fatty meat still delicious to them after months of root vegetables and grain. Alan, in particular, was grateful to get something back into his stomach after losing his lunch earlier. They had a little of the water from the canteen and Carl even found a small cluster of mushrooms - none of them wanted to risk eating them raw but Alan's mouth watered at the thought of them later in a nice rabbit stew.

By the time the sun finally dipped below the horizon, the camp was quiet. The flickering lights in the largest building still burned but the men and women who had been wandering the grounds were now largely gone, disappearing into their tents. The campfire in the middle of the camp still burned but was mainly embers now; only a few logs, watched over by the only bandit Alan could still see, provided any sort of light. Sure enough, his gut had been right - the gate into the camp hung open and unguarded. It was a supremely arrogant show of either indifference or strength; Alan supposed that one inevitably led to the other.

An unspoken part of Alan's plan fell through at that point. He had assumed - hoped - that as night fell, the star would begin to shine and he could simply follow the light to it. After all, shining was what stars did at night, wasn't it? Regardless, it didn't happen. Alan didn't share his disappointment with the rest of the group. He knew Carl would probably have something cutting to say and Ella - well, he doubted she knew any more about stars than he did but she'd no doubt side with her brother.

Still, he couldn't wait around for a better idea. Alan whispered his goodbyes to Carl and Ella and crept out of the forest, a scarf wrapped tight across the lower half of his face. The Old World road running between the forest and the camp wasn't that wide but it was utterly, totally, exposed. Despite the lack of guards, Alan's skin crawled as he crept across the hard surface, following a thin, tell-tale trail of forest dirt that was just about visible in the moonlight. His heart only stopped hammering the inside of his chest when he reached the relative cover of the crude wall, pressing his back into the jagged ring of steel.

**** Location Discovered: Riverford Bandit Camp (+100 XP) ****
**** You have reached Level 3! ****
**** Attributes Increased! ****

Alan grunted as the same wave of warmth welled up within him again, sizzling through every fibre and nerve in his body. Carl had healed the damage he had taken from the Forest Guardian Colony hours ago but this - this washed away his lingering stress and fatigue too. He suddenly felt energised and alert, as though he hadn't spent the entire day hunting and fighting and trekking through the forest. He grinned to himself as he crept through the gate - perfect timing. It wouldn't last but now, at least, it helped.

The inside of the camp was almost silent. There were a few snores from the tents as Alan crept through, a few muttered words that made his heart freeze, but that was all. He spotted the dog he had seen earlier, curled nose-to-tail and twitching slightly as it dreamt next to the fire. He paused in the shadows of the nearest tent and watched it for a few minutes but it didn't stir. The air was still and hung heavy with the dirt and grease and oil of the camp, hopefully masking his scent.

Slowly, he crept through the mess of tents. Now that he was here - only now that he was he actually among the wolves - did it occur to him that he didn't know what he was looking for. He had forgotten to ask Carl what a star looked like up close and there was no obvious glow visible. And yet -

There was a faint tickling in his mind and on his skin. It resembled the vague awareness he had of Carl and Ella, still up on the tree line, or the feeling of somebody standing very still and very close behind you. It was a lively, buzzing sensation that made his flesh tingle, like lightning but slowed down. It pressed against him from the direction of one of the nearby tents.

With little else to go on but this new sensation and his gut, Alan crept closer and closer. He stepped with exaggerated care over each rope and line, away from the fire and closer to the wall of old metal. When he reached the tent in question he circled it twice, making sure each time that the new sensation pivoted around him, always pointing inside. He could hear a faint, snuffling snore from inside and, on his third circuit, he risked a quick glance through the flaps.

A lone bandit slept there, flat on their back. One arm was sprawled behind them while the other fell across their stomach and, thankfully, their head lay at the end furthest from Alan. The moonlight didn't reach far enough inside for much detail to emerge but there was enough near the entrance for Alan to see where the sensation in his head focused.

A rod, maybe four feet long and as thick as Alan's wrist, lay at the feet of the bandit. As the bandit grunted and shifted in their sleep, one leg fell over the rod and turned it a little, causing a perfectly tapered spiked end to swing into view. The surface of the rod was metallic and reflected the moonlight well and the entire thing seethed in Alan's mind, like a constant vibration against his soul. If that wasn't the star, Alan didn't know what else it could be.

Checking left and right and seeing nobody, Alan squatted just inside the tent flaps so that they hung down his back. This meant that he blocked out all of the light and so had to wait a few, agonising moments for his eyes to adjust to the nearly pitch-black interior. When Alan could see the rod - the star? - again it was a dark shape against a darker background.

When the bandit stilled a little, Alan reached out slowly towards the rod. The bandit moved and Alan snatched his hand back, certain that they were about to wake up. Instead, they merely shifted back into whatever restless dream they were having. He reached out again just as a random kick from the bandit caught his hand and he winced at the sudden ache in his wrist.

**** HP: 117 / 120 ****

**** MP: 140 / 140 ****

Reaching around the bandit's leg - and jerking his hand back just in time to avoid another wild swing - Alan finally reached and grasped the rod. It was cold to the touch but curiously alive and vibrant against his skin.

**** You have gained: [???] ****

**** You have gained an unidentified artefact! ****

The new messages caused Alan to flinch and the movement translated down his arm, into the rod still tucked under the bandit's leg. A dark shape rose in the darkness, the bandit's arm coming up towards Alan with a confused groan. Panic took him; he tumbled back, still gripping on to the rod. The bandit cried out in half-asleep confusion and Alan reacted instinctively.

With Lightning Strike.

Electricity shot out from Alan's free hand over the figure's head, blasting a hole through the tent and smacking into the wall beyond. Sparks flew and small fingers of lightning arced off of the metal, hissing and cracking and casting flickering light over the corner of the camp. The bandit - who Alan now realised, with a sinking horror, had merely been shifting in his sleep - sprang to alertness with an inhuman speed, batting aside the tent fabric even as Alan tumbled out backwards.

The camp roared into life around him. Without waiting to see if he was followed, Alan scrambled to his feet and took off, sprinting along the side of the metal wall with the star - the rod, the meteor, whatever it was - clasped in one hand. He sacrificed stealth for speed, dashing forward as fast as he could.

**** [Scholar Carl]: Alan! ****

**** [Fighter Ella]: Alan! ****

The voices burst into Alan's mind, the shock of it causing him to stumble and trip over a guyline running from the nearest tent. Somehow he kept hold of the rod as he fell, leaping upright again even as a trio of bandits rounded the corner behind him, burning torches from the fire clasped in their hands.

**** [L. Disciple Alan]: What the hell? ****

**** [Scholar Carl]: Are you okay? ****

**** [Fighter Ella]: We saw the lightning from here, are you okay? ****

**** [L. Disciple Alan]: How are you doing this? ****

**** [Fighter Ella]: No idea. ****

**** [Scholar Carl]: Run like hell, man! ****

Alan leapt over rope and crate and rubbish as he ran, bandits hot on his heels. More and more joined the chase, winding their way through the maze of tents until Alan felt as though the whole camp was behind him. A man jumped out in front of Alan and Alan flung out a hand - lightning took the man in the chest and he went down screaming. Another bandit appeared behind the first, raising a shape at Alan. He didn't wait to see if the shape was a gun or not and flung out his hand again. This bandit joined the first on the floor - Alan spared a closer look at him as he sprang past.

<Bandit Thug>

<Level 7>

<NPC>

The bar showing the bandit's health hovered over their head and wasn't empty. It wasn't even close to empty. Alan paled and redoubled his speed, orienting himself back towards the distant presence of his friends, aiming always for the gate and the tentative freedom beyond.

The gate was almost in sight when a hulking figure came charging through the closest tent to Alan, smashing wood and canvas aside with great sweeps of their arms. They slammed into Alan before he could react, smashing him against the metal wall before throwing him back towards the centre of the camp with a wild cry. Alan raised his hands and shot off a bolt of lightning towards the figure but it missed, lighting up the night sky instead. He crashed through a tent and came to a halt sprawled next to the fire, coughing up dust and - with a dull, distant feeling of horror - blood.

**** HP: 027 / 120 ****

**** MP: 010 / 140 ****

By some miracle, Alan still held the rod and he used it to help him stand.

He stumbled a little when the pointed end sank into the ground and had to heave it free, sending shooting pains through his battered ribs. He had tied the scarf tight enough that it still masked his face, even now, but the extra effort of trying to pull air through it strained his lungs even further.

Around him, the bandits approached. They circled around him, lingering at the edge of the light cast by the fading fire, before stepping towards him in unison, slowly closing the noose. Alan saw the one who had thrown him - an enormous, muscle-bound woman with a cruel sneer - dragging the dog in on its chain leash. It strained and snarled against her control, lunging at Alan with spittle at the corner of its jaws.

\[Scholar Carl\]: Alan! We're coming to get you! **

There wasn't time. Alan could barely stand without the aid of the rod. It had a broad, flat top opposite the spike and he leaned on it, anchoring it on harder ground and just glad to have something to take the weight off of his ankle. He was pretty sure it was broken, not that it would matter once the bandits were through with him. They didn't suffer insults lightly and if they were NPCs now too … Well, there was no telling what they'd do. At least they wouldn't be able to use abilities - not that getting beaten to death was any better. At least lightning was fast.

Alan eyed the nearest bandit. If he could hit them with Lightning Strike and run fast enough, maybe he could make the others back off - but he knew that his MP, rising as slowly as it was, would take another 30 seconds to reach the minimum needed. He didn't have that sort of time. The bandits closed with fists and chains and rods of their own, cruel-looking things of rusted iron. The bandit woman with the dog grinned at his obvious discomfort and slammed her meaty palms together in mocking applause.

"Nobody steals from us and gets away with it," she said, her words thick and slow and deliberate. Alan could practically see the puppet strings on her.

"I'm sorry," Alan said, hands raised in surrender, wincing as he let his weight shift off of the rod and back onto his ankle. "I - I'm sorry, I -"

\[Fighter Ella\]: Hold on, we're almost there! **

The bandits around him took up the applause, throwing in a jumble of laughs and cheers and whistles. He saw the pleading in each of their eyes even as they grinned wider and wider, saw the primal terror in the dog-woman's stare even as she clapped.

Clap. Clap. Clap.

A memory shook loose in his head. A memory from that morning. What was it that the class description had said? He had been so caught up in being able to throw lightning from his fingertips, so amazed by the power of it all, but there had been another. He had been given two starting abilities.

\[Fighter Ella\]: Alan! **

\[Scholar Carl\]: Alan! **

"Thunderclap."

He whispered the word as the woman let the leash slip through her fingers, the dog tensing its legs and throwing itself through the air at his throat. His grip on the rod failed as his fingers uncurled themselves and - as though suddenly magnetically attracted to each other - his hands swung together, palms flat. As they met, a shockwave burst from the point of contact, passing harmlessly through his body and then slamming out in all directions in a rippling wave of force that cried out in a rolling, thundering peal of noise. Dirt and moisture were blasted free from the surface of his skin as the air itself crashed away.

The last thing Alan saw before pain and nausea and fatigue overcame him was the crumpling bodies of the bandits and their pet falling backwards, twitching, into the dirt.

CHAPTER SEVEN

Darkness. The soil at his feet. The sky above him, full of churning, rolling clouds. It had looked like a dome of boiling, inky water, shot through with ribbons of light that lived only for a heartbeat, crackling and splitting the air. No rain, yet, a fact that Alan had been incredibly grateful for. The clouds had rolled in too thick and fast for them to prepare and only this grace, this unknown period of time before the first drops fell, had given them a chance of saving any of the harvest.

To his right, Alan's dad had cut the grain with a speed born of decades of repetition, slinging it into the cart. A large plastic tarp had lain nearby, weighted down by stones, ready to be thrown over the cart the instant the rain started. Before that happened they had rushed to gather as much as possible. There had been no time for talk and not really enough time for thought. Alan simply had to let his muscles do the thinking for him.

When they had finally admitted defeat, the rain hitting the ground around them with an ever-increasing tempo, they had gathered a little less than half the field's yield under that plastic tarp. They had kept going, slower now, gathering only as much as they could dry, cook and eat in one go. They would later gorge on under-ripe grain porridge and hope that their dry supply would last them later on. The rest of the field had been ploughed back into the soil.

It had been pure dumb luck that Alan had been looking in the direction of the large oak tree on the rise when the lightning struck it. Later that night he had dreamt of a finger of light reaching down slowly, gently, to brush the tree. There and then, however, the tree had simply exploded in a burst of light and a deafening clap of thunder. The lightning's path only revealed itself in the afterimage that took nearly an hour to fully fade from his sight.

"It goes up first, you know," his dad had said over dinner that night, a large bowl of porridge bubbling away on the stove. Alan had laughed - lightning came down from the sky to the ground, everybody knew that.

"Yes, but it goes up first." His dad had grinned with his infinite patience. "Just a little - a spark so small you can't even see it. That little spark wriggles and winds its way up

into the clouds and the lightning - the real lightning - traces its way back down."

There had been a long pause after that, Alan remembered, as his dad had stared at the rug hanging on the wall. His mother's last creation.

"Sometimes you've got to give a little on faith," his dad had said, sadness in his voice. "And sometimes - not always, but more often than you'd think - you get a lot back in return."

Alan hadn't known what to say at the time, or at any time since.

"Alan!"

But after that -

"Alan!"

Alan's eyes snapped open. Darkness. Then the darkness resolved itself into the outline of two faces silhouetted against a cloudy night sky, only a star or two piercing through the approaching storm. His limbs felt heavy and there was the acid taste of vomit in his mouth again but his side felt fine, if a little stiff, and as the warm glow in his ankle faded away it took the pain with it.

**** HP: 120 / 120 ****

**** MP: 047 / 140 ****

"Hmwa -" he slurred, coughing as Ella helped him sit up. He braced himself against the hard surface of the road and took a sip from the canteen she passed to him.

"We've got to go," Ella said, her voice wracked with fear. "We've got to go now, Alan."

Confused, Alan looked around. The last thing he remembered …

The wall of the bandit camp loomed to his left; Carl and Ella must have dragged him out. The rod lay by his side, buzzing silently, and he grasped at it, clutching it tightly to his chest.

"Come on, we've got to move." Carl pulled Alan to his feet, passing him the pack with a worried glance over his shoulder. "Whatever you did, I think it's starting to wear off."

As if to illustrate Carl's point, a cry went up from the other side of the wall. That was all the impetus Alan needed to join Carl and Ella, who were already sprinting for the tree line. They dove into the forest at a reckless pace, given the near-total lack of light. The occasional shaft of moonlight managed to pierce both the clouds and the canopy but other than that, Alan had to trust to chance to see him through. As such, he fell repeatedly, feet catching on roots, in holes and - for one terrifying moment - in something that felt like a writhing mass of vines. Each time he scrambled upright and charged on, following the meagre trail created by Carl and Ella ahead of him.

They came to a halt by a small spring, water bubbling up through the stump of a long-dead tree and cutting a shallow path through the forest floor. Alan was sure he had never seen it before - and while he didn't know every square inch of the forest, water sources were important enough to be memorable. Ella refilled the canteen and Carl bent to take a drink directly - the staggered back several steps, spluttering and coughing.

"You okay?" Alan eyed his friend warily. The last thing they needed now was a bad water source making them all sick. There was enough Old World poison under the ground that it found its way up every now and then.

"The water - it tastes amazing!" Carl stared at the spring. "I was expecting - "

He stopped speaking and knelt before the stump, cupping water in his hands and taking a long, slow draught. Alan saw his eyes widen.

"Try it." Carl stepped back. "Just - try it."

Raising an eyebrow at Ella, who shrugged, Alan knelt and drank from the spring. If it hadn't been for Carl's warning, he would have choked on it too. The water was cool and tasted absolutely, totally clean. There was no smokiness to it, no oil-sheen, no bitterness. Just crisp, clear water. When the moonlight broke through for a few seconds it showed the water to be cleaner than any water Alan had ever seen in his life.

They took a few minutes to drink their fill, rotating between them as they cupped water from the spring. Ella even emptied out her flask on the ground, a waste of water that made Alan flinch, before washing it out and refilling it.

"Everything's changing," Carl said, as they stood to leave. "Not just us - not just the rabbits and whatever the vine monsters were. The ground, the plants, the water - this is bigger than just the village."

"The bandits were NPCs," Alan said. The two looked at him and he shrugged. "One of them was, anyway, and the rest seemed to be acting the same way. Not like I stopped to ask."

Carl rubbed the back of his neck with one hand, a frown twisting its way across his face.

"That's good, right? Doesn't that - wouldn't that mean that they don't have any abilities like us? I mean, we were saying when this all started -"

A distant crash echoed through the forest. All three of them looked up from what they were doing, staring in the direction of the noise. Back in the direction of the bandit camp. Alan heard nothing at first, nothing except the beating of his own heart, but after a while he heard a noise - soft and crunching, skin and leather slipping against wet bark, the rapid retreat of some small animal in the undergrowth. Someone was heading in their direction and Alan had no desire to wait around and find out who.

The three of them took off at a slow jog that soon gave way to a slightly panicked run. Alan was all too aware of the noise they were making themselves, smashing through the undergrowth and cursing as they stumbled into roots and low tree stumps. Their route took them east, south of the crash site and in a straight line towards the village. Alan didn't think - he just ran. Fear sunk its claws into him; the corners of his eyes were soon filled with twisting shapes, hands reaching out of the moonlight and shadow to grab at him. He knew it wasn't real, knew that there was no way the bandits could have caught up already - but it didn't matter. For all that Carl had said the bandits being NPCs made them less dangerous, Alan kept on thinking back to the way he had been thrown easily through the air. If this change could let rabbits bite through leather and flesh, what would it do to a group of armed thugs?

He was so caught up in his fears and attempts not to trip that Alan almost didn't catch the moment that the small, lumpy figure launched itself out of the undergrowth at Ella. She screamed, sounding more surprised than hurt, and stumbled away from it. It clung to her, however, clasping two stick-thin limbs around her upper arm and clawing at her head with two more. She smacked at it and Allan heard it scream in ragged, gibbering wails before she reached up and got a solid grip on its neck. Pulling it free, Ella swung it around and straight into the nearest tree. Alan heard a wet crunch and then it fell still.

**** Goblin Scout killed (+20 XP) ****

"What the hell was that?" Ella panted as she slumped against a tree, blood trickling down her face from a gash that the creature - the goblin - had opened up in her scalp. Carl pressed a hand against her head, healing the wound, while Alan crouched down to examine the body.

It looked to Alan very much like a half-formed child's doll, one built from rotten potatoes and sticks and dirty old straw. Its limbs were too thin and its torso, head and paws were bulbous and pitted. It was completely naked and the only decoration Alan saw was a loop of dried hide curled through one floppy, leathery ear. He looted a couple of copper from it but discovered nothing else.

A cry went up around them - the same half-formed cry that the goblin had screamed at them. Alan couldn't see where the cry was coming from but it sounded low, close to the ground, and as though it fenced them in completely.

A dark shape leapt up from the undergrowth at him and suddenly Ella was there, smacking at it with her hatchet and sending it tumbling away from them in two pulpy halves.

**** Goblin Scout killed (+20 XP) ****

"Run." Ella batted away another goblin as it leapt for her - this one hit the ground, rather than a tree, and skidded away into the dark of the night, gibbering wildly as its unseen allies rose up in chorus around them.

"Run!" Ella pushed Alan into action, even as Carl leapt forward. The three ran, the goblins' cries increasing in volume and ferocity as they gave chase. They weren't visible until they leapt, springing up out of the undergrowth with surprising strength, the moonlight highlighting their fierce red eyes and jagged teeth. Alan tried dodging them at first - when they wised up to his plan and started to come at him two at a time, he batted them away with the rod.

"Keep running!" Ella shouted, catching one goblin mid-air and squeezing until it dropped to the ground with a soft choking sound. "Keep running!"

Carl simply cursed and kept rushing forward, having gained just enough of a lead not to be harassed by the miniature beasts.

Needles of pain drove themselves into Alan's shoulder - a goblin had made it past his wild swings and dug its teeth into him, latching on through his sleeve. He slapped at it to no avail, growing increasingly frustrated as the momentum of his running made the goblin flop around, twisting and turning the teeth in his arm. As he passed the next tree he dove into it, shoulder first, smashing the goblin against it as he pushed off again and stumbled forward. His reward was an increased stab of pain as the impact drove the teeth deeper into his flesh - but the goblin cried out and Alan heard a sound like a bundle of twigs snapping and it fell away.

**** Goblin Scout killed (+20 XP) ****

The horde behind him redoubled their cries at the sight of this latest victim and Alan somehow found it within himself to push faster, blood trickling down his arm. He didn't dare turn around - just flung his blood-streaked hand out behind him and threw a lightning bolt back, completely blind. The resounding crack of it temporarily drowned out the goblins and he threw another but to no avail - although there were a few cries from the goblins they were of anger, not pain, and no message appeared across his vision to signal a fresh kill. He gritted his teeth against the sudden, grasping fatigue of the MP spent, and stumbled on.

They ran on, deeper into the forest. The trees were slightly thinner here, although still thicker than Alan remembered, and the moon had found a new gap in the clouds. There was no way forward that wasn't straight into shadows, though, and if it wasn't for the fact that they were running straight ahead Alan was sure he would have lost sight of Ella a dozen times by now. He couldn't see Carl, couldn't think straight, couldn't catch his breath - but every time he wanted to slow, a goblin swiped at his heels or jumped for him.

**** [Scholar Carl]: Argh! ****

"Carl!" Alan shouted out loud, forgetting this strange new mind-speak, and the goblins around him shouted out gibberish in response. He didn't get a better response, however, before Ella stopped dead ahead of him, windmilling her arms to keep from falling. It was too short a warning for Alan to stop, however, and he slammed into her back at full speed, knocking her forward and him to his knees. With a cry, Ella fell to the ground - and then kept falling, disappearing through the undergrowth and out of sight.

There was no time to ponder this new mystery, however, as the goblins swarmed Alan in seconds, a writhing mass of mottled flesh and needle claws that beat and scratched and bit at him. Alan cried out as he felt his HP plummet, death by a thousand cuts rushing towards him. He threw lightning and managed to blast a couple of goblins free but there were too many, all around and over him.

"Thunderclap!" He screamed the word out even as a goblin leapt for his throat, red eyes gleaming. It never landed, however; Alan's palms struck each other in front of his face and the same peal of energy from the bandit camp rang out, slamming goblins away from him in every direction. A few hit trees, hard, and fell limply to the ground; most disappeared into the undergrowth in a rain of soft thuds.

**** Goblin Scout killed (+20 XP) ****

**** Goblin Scout killed (+20 XP) ****

**** Goblin Scout killed (+20 XP) ****

Silence, in the forest.

"Jump down!"

Ella's voice was pained but firm; it seemed to come from below him. Alan crawled forward, still covered in blood, passing a twitching goblin that had fallen in the dirt. His hands pushed apart shrubs then found empty air; he pulled himself to the lip of what turned out to be a narrow crack that ran through the forest floor. Below, a few metres down, he saw the worried faces of Ella and Carl looking back up at him, lit by a soft, blue glow that seemed to come from everywhere and nowhere. There was a pressure coming from the crack, like wind without wind, and the hairs on Alan's arm - at least, those that weren't plastered down with blood - stood on end.

"Quickly," hissed Carl, "before they wake up!" He brought his foot down hard on a goblin that had fallen into the crack and the small monster fell still.

**** Goblin Scout killed (+20 XP) ****

Alan looked around. The forest was dark and still for now but he knew that wouldn't last. His mind conjured a hundred goblins, scattered around him like fallen leaves, ready to pounce up as one at any second. Not to mention the Forest Guardian Colonies. The bandits. Whatever other horrors lurked in the dark. He scrabbled forward, ignoring the pain of every cut and the deep wounds in his shoulder, pulling himself into the crack and falling through in an undignified heap. Ella caught him as he fell, as though he weighed very little, and smiled at him as she set him down on the ground. Carl was quick to stoop down and heal him, Alan's wounds knitting back together in an itching, stinging wave of energy.

**** HP: 120 / 120 ****

**** MP: 013 / 140 ****

Alan's head was gripped in a tight headache, the sensation of almost running out of MP now worryingly familiar to him. Even so, he had the presence of mind to push himself back against the wall, hiding under the rim of the crack. The light was dim but constant, a soft glow that seeped out of thin-air and painted the world in washed-out shades of blue. Still, it was better than unreliable moonlight - not that this was the time for good lighting. Alan pressed himself flat against the rock, as Carl and Ella ducked down beneath a few shrubs that had grown over the rim and down. Above them, they could hear the scattered sounds of the goblins rousing themselves, chattering voices high-pitched and questioning. There was none of the previous bloodlust or pain - just confusion.

Alan locked eyes with Ella and tried to mouth out a message - then had to resist the urge to smack himself in the forehead.

**** [L. Disciple Alan]: Wait them out. ****
**** [Scholar Carl]: They're gonna find us down here man. ****
**** [Fighter Ella]: Not if we stay still. ****
**** [Scholar Carl]: They're gonna find us! ****
**** [Fighter Ella]: They won't! ****
**** [Scholar Carl]: They will! ****
**** [L. Disciple Alan]: Did you hear that? ****

The mental chat fell silent and Alan could see the others look up. He strained his ears and for a second heard nothing but the usual chatter - then he heard it again. The sound of heavy footsteps jogging through the forest, distant but getting closer. Multiple sets, although it was hard to tell with how closely their rhythms matched.

**** [Fighter Ella]: The bandits? ****
**** [Scholar Carl]: Must be. ****

Whatever or whoever it was, the goblins had clearly heard it now too. A great screeching cry went up, followed by a stampede of tiny feet brushing through the forest floor. Looking up, Alan saw a swarm of goblins leap over the crack, silhouetted as vague blobs against the night sky and canopy. The sound of the goblins faded into the night and Alan finally breathed deep. Wherever the goblins had come from, whatever they were or used to be, it seemed like they hated the bandits just as much as they hated Alan, Carl and Ella.

**** Skill Increased: Stealth (Level 1) ****

"What now?" Alan flinched at the sound but Ella's voice was low enough and the goblins were far enough away. He shrugged.

"You get the new message too?"

Ella nodded. Carl nodded. Alan sighed.

"We really need to figure this out, whatever it is. I'm tired of wandering around not knowing what the hell is going on. I'm tired of having to figure everything out as we go. I just wish we had a little help."

**** Help function currently unavailable. ****

**** Warning: database rebuild in progress. Some features may be disabled during the rebuild period. ****

**** Please contact an admin or moderator for further assistance. ****

"Great," spat Carl, "more questions."

"Look," Ella said, "we can figure this out later." She paused, her face twisted into a frown. "Maybe. But we need to get out of the forest before something else tries to kill us. And, uh -"

She looked back up at the crack above them and the near-shear walls that ran up to it.

"We need to get out of this hole," she said. "And I don't think we can climb."

Alan agreed. The walls were hard rock rather than soft earth and the sides were annoyingly free of any handholds. It looked as though the ground had simply been cut through and pulled apart, leaving a flat, almost glossy ascent. Carl grabbed at one of the shrubs that had grown down over the side but it ripped from the earth when he pulled on it.

Alan sighed. What he wouldn't give for a good, simple length of rope.

"We could try walking out." Carl looked at Alan and shrugged. "Seems to run into a tunnel down that way," he said, pointing, "and da always said there were tunnels and caves under the forest. Might find a way out or, I dunno, some rocks or something we can pile up."

Carl looked to Ella, who mimicked his shrug. "What else can we do?"

They chose a direction at random and followed the crack in the earth. The bottom of it was smooth stone with only a faint dusting of dirt; it made for surprisingly easy going. After a few hundred metres the earth overhead arched and covered their path, blocking out the sky. The ravine - now a proper tunnel - twisted its way down into the ground, the same diffuse light still casting a blue twilight ahead of them. The air was cool and still and smelled strongly of damp and their footsteps sounded very loud to Alan, now that they were trapped by the rock.

They had walked for maybe ten minutes or so when the ceiling began to slope down towards them, levelling out just above Ella's head. The walls took on a rougher appearance and they soon came across thick wooden beams jutting out from the floor, seeming to prop up the ceiling. The ever-present light was joined by lit torches on the walls that spat and hissed and cast dancing shadows on every surface.

"This is ..." Carl shook his head. "Has someone been living down here?"

"Could be." Alan looked closer at the torches. They were slotted into loops of metal bolted directly into the walls and gave off no smoke. If someone was living down here, they had the time to light long stretches of tunnel for no real reason. They would have to be entirely self-reliant; Alan had never heard even a hint of a rumour of a forest tunnel dweller.

He stepped forward to take a closer look at the nearest torch and this took him across the threshold of the first set of wooden posts. All at once, a low gong rang out in his ears and a burst of text flashed across his vision.

**** Location Discovered: Riverford Mines (+100 XP) ****

**** You have entered a dungeon! ****

CHAPTER EIGHT

A piercing cry echoed down the walls of the tunnel towards them, the torches flickering wildly in its wake. The cry was painful to listen to and Alan clasped his ears while he waited for it to fade. When it did, finally, cease there was still a faint echo that took minutes more to die off.

"Well that's not good," Alan said. He squeezed the star rod. It wasn't exactly a weapon but after that cry … well, even being able to shoot lightning from his fingers, he felt a little safer with a good, solid club to hand.

"You think?" Carl cast his eyes around and picked up a fist-sized rock from the floor.

"What's a dungeon, Carl?" Ella asked. "Tell me it's an Old World word for 'place where everybody has a really good time'." She had her hatchet out and while her face showed no traces of fear her voice was sharp and clipped.

"It's a - well it's a place where people used to be locked up." Carl eyed the tunnel ahead. His face had traces of fear aplenty. "It's an old Old World word. We're talking centuries old."

"Locked up?" Alan took a tentative step forward, then another. "Why?"

"For crimes," Carl said. "Or just, you know. To get rid of them."

"Damn it," Ella sword under her breath. "Come on, let's head back. Maybe the other way had a tree root we could climb or something."

Not taking her eyes off of the darkness ahead, she backed slowly up the tunnel. She had only gone a few steps, however, when Alan heard her curse again. Looking back, he saw that a thick wall of mist had sprung up behind them across the breadth of the tunnel. Ella placed her hand up against the mist and, as Alan watched, shifted her body weight against it. She didn't move. When Alan approached and tried, he found the mist as cold and as solid as the rock walls, lit from within with the same washed-out blue glow.

"Great." Carl pulled his arm back as if to throw the rock at the mist, then thought better of it. He caught Alan's eye and shrugged.

"If it goes through, I've lost my only weapon. If it bounces off, I've just thrown a rock at myself. Lose-lose."

"Yeah, sounds about right." Alan hoisted his pack back on to his shoulders and redoubled his grip on the rod. "Come on, then. Looks like we've got no choice."

Again, he thought bitterly. His new-found abilities were beginning to lose their charm, even without the curse that had fallen on the rest of the village. What good was throwing lightning if -

He paused, turned, and threw a lightning strike at the wall of mist. It sank into the depths of the swirling wall and was lost without a trace. Carl flinched and Ella shot him a filthy look, doubtless due to his lack of warning.

Right. What good was throwing lightning if it didn't fix anything?

The tunnel ahead sloped downwards and twisted around to the left. They progressed slowly at first, their pace picking up slightly as the tunnel continued with no sign of any danger. Alan stood a little straighter, stepped a little more confidently, and saw Ella's grip on her hatchet loosen. Slightly. Which made it all the more disarming when a rock under his foot shifted as he stepped down and a second later a large log came swinging down from the ceiling, smacking into his side with an awful crunching sound that sent pain racing through his body as he slammed against the opposite wall.

**** HP: 023 / 120 ****

**** MP: 140 / 140 ****

**** Affliction: Internal Bleeding (2:00)****

What followed was a harrowing few minutes of blood, pain and the awful, wrenching feeling of his own insides being snapped back into place and bound together. For a blessed few moments he was unconscious - then he was awake, coughing up blood as Ella held him down and Carl poured healing into him. Even when Carl fell back, pale and drained, Alan still couldn't move without sending pain coursing through his side.

**** HP: 015 / 120 ****

**** MP: 140 / 140 ****

After everyone had lain where they were for a long while, taking great care not to touch anything at all, Carl rolled over and - very carefully - began to heal Alan again. This time the healing was to parts of Alan that were closer to the point where the log had hit. He felt his muscles writhe and reform under his skin, which itched like hell when it closed back up. Eventually, all that remained of the damage was a large amount of dried blood and the knowledge that Alan would relive the event in his dreams for many nights to come.

"Nobody. Touches. Anything." Alan spoke slowly, partly due to his body's lingering insistence that he couldn't breathe and partly to drive the point home. "That nearly wiped me out. Took me down from 120 HP to about 20 in one go."

"Wait," Ella said, "you only have 120 HP?"

"Yeah," Alan said, "why, how much do you have?"

Ella just shook her head and helped him to his feet, looking grim.

"Enough that I'm going first," she said, "but not so much that I won't be watching my step."

Alan wasn't going to argue with her. Not after learning what it felt like for your ribs to worm their way back through your insides and snap back into position.

They slowed back down after that, allowing Alan to catch his nerves, Carl to catch his breath and Ella to keep a close eye on the floor. They found another three suspicious patches of rock, plus one tripwire strung across at ankle-height. They stepped over all of them, Ella triggering the last with her hatchet just to be safe. A pile of rubble fell from a hole in the ceiling, just as she snatched her hand back. Carl didn't like his sister being in harm's way and said as such. She offered to let him go first and, when he declined, told him to put up or shut up. Alan had laughed but he had been the only one.

They came across the first open space before they realised it, stepping carefully around a corner and finding themselves in a small cavern. There was a light layer of mist on the floor, which was at least level and not sloping further down. The room was roughly circular and about twice as broad as the old road that ran through the village. Alan could see another tunnel on the far side but it quickly twisted a corner and cut off any further view.

"This is different," Ella said, coming to a halt and peering out at the mist.

"Think it's good different or bad different?" Carl raised the rock behind him, ready to throw.

"When is it ever good different?" Ella asked.

Carl didn't say anything. It wasn't like Alan had a comeback either; near-enough every change over the past 24 hours had been bad. When Ella stepped out into the room there was a split second where he thought the floor would drop from under her. Instead, all that happened was that the mist was sent swirling away from her legs on breezes that Alan couldn't feel. It just seemed to melt into the floor, revealing a growing circle around Ella and, when they stepped forward, Alan and Carl too.

"Maybe it's nothing," Carl said, "maybe it's -"

His next words were cut off when a dark shape dropped from the ceiling, knocking him to the ground. Alan turned and kicked it away from him even as more dark shapes thudded to the ground all around them. The first one - the one he had kicked - staggered back a little before turning beady eyes on him and hissing through a mouth full of chisel-tip teeth. A rat. Alan had never seen a rodent of such unusual size, coming as it did up to his knees, but the simplicity of it was slightly refreshing after the horrors of the Forest Guardian Colonies and the goblins. Rats were simple indeed - they ate the village's grain, fought back when cornered and carried filth and disease. Alan didn't hesitate in the slightest before raising a hand, pointing and firing Lightning Strike at it.

He missed.

The lightning crackled off of the stone floor, sending up a small cloud of steam where it flash-boiled a puddle, but doing little more than startling the rat. The creature's health was barely depleted - until Alan darted forward, made as if to grab it by the head and fired off a second bolt of lightning as it leapt for his hand. This struck point-blank and slammed the rat back against the wall. Its health dropped to zero and the body fell, steaming, to the ground.

**** Large Rat killed (+20 XP) ****

Alan's celebrations were cut short when pain shot through his thigh as a second rat leapt for, and clamped on to, his leg from behind. Shouting, he fell to his back and swung his leg up and then down, smashing the rat against the floor. He did it again, and again - the second blow dazed the rat as it loosened his grip but he kept going until it fell still under him.

**** Large Rat killed (+20 XP) ****

A little way away Carl was struggling with a rat that had leapt for his face, using both hands to hold the rat back as it bit and clawed at him. Alan took a second to line up a kick and made sure his boot connected right at the side of the creature's skull, resulting in a heavy crunch and the rat falling to the floor.

**** Large Rat killed (+20 XP) ****

**** Skill Increased: Unarmed (Level 1) ****

"Thanks," Carl said, taking the offer of a hand up from Alan and climbing to his feet. His eyes widened. "Ella -"

"- is doing just fine," Ella said. Alan turned to look at her. She was covered in spatters of blood and there was a scrap of fur caught on the edge of her hatchet, which could have come from any one of the several dead rats that lay at her feet. The mist had melted away completely, leaving the cave floor completely clear. Alan checked the corner of his vision and saw several messages corresponding with Ella's kills.

"Shit," Carl said softly, looking at the corpses. "You did all this?"

"Not bad, huh?" Ella said with a terrifying grin. "It was pretty easy too, like I -"

Her grin disappeared, replaced by a confused frown.

"- like I knew exactly what to do," she said. "Like I'd been doing this for years. My body just moved on its own. It was as easy as chopping firewood."

"That's good, though," Alan said. "Right?"

"But how, though?" Ella looked to Carl for answers. As she always did. "I mean, how can my body remember how to do something I've never done before?"

"Wouldn't be the strangest thing," Carl said, shrugging. "I mean, compared to goblins and giant rats -"

"Large rats," Alan corrected.

"- and throwing lightning around." Carl shrugged. "I mean, you chose fighter. You know how to fight."

"Hmm." Ella's tone said that this discussion wasn't over but she didn't push it. Instead, she just bent down and began to loot the corpses around her. Alan did the same, grabbing a few copper from each of the first two. But when he got to the third …

"Holy -"

"- shit."

He looked over at Ella who was looking over at him, eyes wide and all worries temporarily forgotten.

When he had looted the last rat he had received the usual copper. It was a number at the back of his head ticking up - it wasn't real, for all that he had bought some bread back in the village with it. But there was something else, too. The last rat had - for want of a better word - melted, trickling away into cracks in the stone, to reveal a dagger buried inside. A dagger. It was as long as his arm and made of metal - he had no idea what sort - polished to a mirror shine. Despite presumably having been swallowed by the large rat, it was perfectly clean of any blood or grime and had a leather-bound handle that fit comfortably into his grip.

**** You have gained: 35 copper, Iron Dagger ****

Ella, meanwhile, had made a similar discovery. But when Alan walked over to show her the dagger, fielding endless questions from Carl with variations of "How the hell should I know?", she hadn't found a dagger. Instead, she cradled a metal club the length of Alan's leg, with a thick, bulbous end covered in spikes and cutting edges. It was, Alan noticed, longer than the rats had been. There was no swallowing that.

"It's a mace," Ella said, turning it over in her hands and correctly guessing Alan's imminent question. "It's pretty basic but it has a good balance. Plenty of reach. Doesn't have the cutting power of a sword but you can crush a whole lot of bones with it. It's all about the strength of the wielder - well, skill too."

"How do you know what a mace is?" asked Carl, putting just a bit too much emphasis - consciously or unconsciously - on 'you'.

"I don't know," Ella snapped, whipping her gaze to her brother. She stood and Alan suddenly appreciated just how long - and threatening - the mace was. "It's like I've always known. Like someone's been messing with my head, putting memories in. I know what a mace is and a flail and a damn naginata! Someone is doing this to us and I'll bet you anything in the world that same person knows how to lift the curse on the village. Probably put it there. If they can fill my head with knowledge about old, Old World weapons I've never seen before then they can fill ma and da's heads with new lives and take out the real ones."

A tear broke free from the corner of her eye and cut a path down through dried blood and dirt, as her grip on the mace tightened.

"She forgot us, Carl. What if I forget you? What if you forget me? It's in our heads, Carl - how are we supposed to fight back against that?"

"I won't." Carl reached out and grabbed Ella gently by the shoulders. "Hey, look at me - I won't forget you. You won't forget me. And we'll fix ma and da and ..."

His voice trailed off.

"I won't forget you. I promise."

Alan let them have a moment, then coughed gently. "Here," he said, passing the dagger to Carl. "You take it."

Carl hesitated, then took the dagger and tucked it into his belt. He nodded silently at Alan, who nodded back. What else needed to be said? There they were, knee-deep in dead rats the size of dogs that melted into weapons. Sometimes it was better to let the moment do the talking.

"Come on," Ella said, sniffing and smearing grime across the back of her hands as she wiped away the tears. "Let's get moving. I just want to see them again, even if they don't see us."

Alan reached out to her but Ella had already walked away, her mace slung over one shoulder. Seeing Ella with her mace and Carl with his dagger, Alan felt out of place without a proper weapon of his own. At least he had the star rod. If it could survive falling out of the sky he doubted a few rat skulls would give it any trouble.

The tunnel onward was much the same as the one before, crudely hacked walls supported by broad wooden beams. It didn't slope down any further, however, which lifted Alan's spirits a little. They'd need to start climbing eventually if they were going to make it back to the surface but at least they weren't sinking any lower.

"Is that it, then? The meteor?"

They had been walking for a few minutes when Carl spoke up. The two of them were hanging back a little, letting Ella take the lead again. Carl had sheathed his new dagger and was eyeing the star rod. Alan hesitated for a second then nodded and passed it over to Carl, who took it with wide eyes.

"Doesn't look like any star you ever told me about," Alan said. He couldn't help but let a little smugness into his voice.

"Meteor, not star," Carl said. "Well, meteorite now. It doesn't look like any of those, either. They're supposed to be chunks of rock and metal, usually quite small by the end I think. This is ... this is crafted. This isn't natural."

"Think it's like the dagger," Alan asked, "or the mace?"

"What, made out of rats?" Carl turned the rod over and over. "It could be. Well, made out of something, anyway. Maybe it didn't look like this when it fell - not like we know how any of this works. But if it is the cause of all ... this ... then it'd be strange for it to be changed by it too. If you say it fell from the sky before the changes happened then it'd be even stranger to think that it was created later."

"It's an artefact if that helps." Alan saw Carl's look and shook his head. "No idea what that means - I just got a message about it. It's an unidentified artefact."

"I mean, yes I suppose it is, but I guess the message meant something specific." Carl passed it back. "I'll take a longer look at it if - when we get out of here. I'm a scholar now, right? Pretty sure that's the sort of thing we're supposed to know about."

"Hey, we get out of here, you can take as long as you want looking at it." They walked in silence for a little while before Alan spoke next.

"What was your second ability?"

"My second ability?" Carl winced and looked - to Alan's surprise - embarrassed. "Yeah, I got screwed on that one."

"What do you mean?"

"It's called 'Scribe'," Carl said. "Lets me take the books I can use for spells and make my own version, cram them all together in one spellbook. I think it said something about making new spells too, eventually."

"Why's that bad?" Alan asked. It sounded great to him - better to only have to carry around one book rather than a dozen.

"Because you need a book to do it in," Carl said. "A new, clean, blank book. That and something to write with. When's the last time you saw anything like that on any of the merchants' carts? And can you imagine what it'd cost?"

Well, that made sense. Alan had never even seen a sheet of unused paper, let alone an entire book of it. The ones Carl had for reading were valuable enough - what this 'Scribe' ability was asking for might as well have been imaginary. Still, stranger things had happened in the last 24 hours.

"Cheer up," Alan said, patting his friend on the back. "Who knows? Maybe the next rat you kill will turn into a book?"

Carl laughed a loud chuckle that echoed down the corridor and caused Ella to turn her head and stare daggers at them. Carl quietened down but chuckles still escaped him - and Alan - for a long while after that.

CHAPTER NINE

They faced two more rat chambers after that. Each was roughly the same: a mist-covered circle that only became clear as they walked in, with large rats emerging from cracks and crevices in the walls and ceiling to attack. Each time there were roughly half a dozen rats - slightly more in the second chamber and slightly fewer in the third. All three of the party reached Level 4 after the second, which helped immensely with the third. Although the last chamber had fewer rats they were larger and meaner and smarter, darting in and out of reach instead of committing to one, absolute attack. The increased reach of Ella's new mace caught more than one by surprise, as did Alan's Lightning Strike. Knowing the rats were coming ahead of time, he channelled the spell as they entered the chamber and nailed the first rat to poke its head out with perfect accuracy. He was rewarded for his foresight with another iron dagger. He gladly stowed the star rod away now that he had a proper weapon.

The floor of the tunnel began to slope upward after that, much to everyone's relief. It was only gradual but every step took them closer to the surface. At least, that was what Alan hoped. The unspoken fear among the three of them was that the tunnels would never reach the surface; that there was nothing that could be done to escape. A dungeon was a place where people were locked up, according to Carl. Alan didn't know what they had done to deserve that but then there were a lot of things in his life right now that didn't seem exactly fair.

They took a rest after the last of the rats. None of them wanted to spend any longer in the chambers than they had to but the tunnels seemed safe - well, apart from the traps. They had come across a half-dozen more, managing to avoid - or deliberately trigger - each one as they went. When they found a long, straight section of tunnel with no traps and nowhere for the rats to crawl out of, they stopped halfway along. They had only meant to stop for a little while but when Carl fell asleep within seconds of sitting down against the rock wall, they had to face facts. The level up energy was exhilarating, yes, but it had been a very long and very busy day. Alan judged it to be a little after midnight but they had no way of knowing for sure - until he thought about it hard enough and a small icon appeared in the corner of his vision and told him it was, in fact, 0:45 in the morning.

They slept in turns after that. Alan and Carl at first - then, a couple of hours later, Ella shook Alan awake to take over. It wasn't enough sleep - he woke into a choking cloud of weariness that seemed even greater than when he had closed his eyes - but after a little while, sat against the wall and keeping an eye on both ends of the tunnel, he felt the benefit. It wasn't energy as such - more like the absence of fatigue. It was better than nothing.

The two hours passed slowly. There was nothing to do, really, except watch over the sleeping bodies of his friends and try not to imagine every shadow was about to come alive and eat him. The air was still and damp, as before, and cool but not cold - they had all slept in worse. A little after the first hour had passed, according to the handy new clock that he had discovered, a thought struck him - he had never taken a close look at Thunderclap. He put out a mental call for information and was rewarded with another vision.

**** <u>Thunderclap</u> ****

**** An area of effect spell, centred on the caster, that knocks back and stuns enemies. Knock-back force and stun duration vary depending on enemy size and level. ****

**** Range: 7 metres ****

**** Damage: 1 damage ****

**** Cast Time: Instant ****

**** MP Cost: 25 MP ****

No surprises there. It had done exactly what the description said. Although the damage was tiny compared to Lightning Strike, it had saved his life twice now and he made a mental note to pay it more mind in the future. There was no telling what other sorts of monsters were lurking around now and he was grateful for a way to - hopefully - stop them getting at him. He winced at the memories of everything that had tried to sink its teeth - or worse - into him over the past day.

He also took another look at the star rod - the meteorite, Carl had said. It still fuzzed around the edges of his awareness, still showed up in his mind as an unidentified artefact, still refused to do anything at all when he poked and prodded and examined it. There were markings on the surface, a webbing of straight lines that split off at right-angles and wove their crooked way up and around the length of it - not grooves, exactly, but with a slightly different shine and feel. Just another mystery, for now, and he found himself having to work a little harder to convince himself that this would somehow save the village. What else did they have, though?

He passed the rest of his watch in contemplative silence. Carl didn't appreciate being woken up - having fallen asleep before they even agreed to stand a watch - but Alan showed him the clock and fell asleep before Carl could do much in the way of arguing. This sleep lasted even less time than the first - or, at least, that's what it felt like. When Carl shook him awake he had to crawl through the fog of half-sleep again, only really rejoining the world when he accidentally tripped over a rock. The clock showed that it was very early in the morning but Alan knew the sun would be up. They shared a few words and a little more of the canteen of water and set off again.

The next chamber they came to was nothing like the previous three. Instead of being circular, it was long and rectangular, maybe the length of Alan's house. A single rat, no larger than the others, sat in the middle of it and a long length of rope spanned the ceiling, disappearing down at one side of the room into a pit cut into the floor. The other side hung down a little way, suspending a flat wooden platform over a similar pit.

"Well this is suspicious," Carl said.

They stopped just outside of the new chamber, weapons drawn and Alan's hands raised. The rat held its ground, staring at them and twitching its whiskers but making no move to either flee or attack.

"Bet you there's more rats in the pits," Alan whispered, "just waiting for us to go in."

"An ambush?" Ella smiled. "An ambush by rats? Yeah, why not. You want to risk it?"

"What else can we do?" Alan pointed at the far wall, where a tunnel was visible. "We have to go through. But let's make things a little easier first."

He began to channel lightning into his hands. The rat immediately squeaked and dashed forward and was rewarded with a strike straight into its face that singed fur and sent it skidding across the floor.

**** Large Rat killed (+20 XP) ****

The three of them waited. Nothing happened. The body lay still. The pits in the floor remained dark and mysterious. There was no sound, no chattering horde of rats, nothing. Ella took a tentative step into the room and Alan held his breath as she crossed the entrance - then let it out again as nothing happened. He felt his shoulders relax and heard Carl sigh with relief next to him.

"Guess we were owed an easy one," Ella said, reaching down and looting the corpse. It didn't melt away into an item - after the first two, none of the rats had. Either there had been something special about them or it just wasn't a common occurrence.

"Nothing down the pits?" Carl was keeping his distance.

"Dunno, it's pitch black down there." Ella peered down into one of the pits before walking over to one of the torches on the wall and pulling it from the band of metal that held it in place. She dropped it down the pit with the platform suspended over it and watched it fall.

"Nothing," she said, "just a long drop and a hard landing."

Walking over to the other pit she repeated the process, holding the torch closer to the edge as it fell so as not to light the rope. This time she frowned and Alan heard a soft thud - followed a second later by a more distant thud.

"There's something down there," she said, "something held by the rope. Torch hit it first then bounced off. Let me try and pull it up."

She placed the mace carefully on the floor, gripped the rope in both hands, then pulled. Alan saw the muscles in her arms - and was it his imagination, or were they more well-defined than before? - tense and strain and Ella grunted with the effort. The rope didn't move. It didn't even more sideways. It might as well have been made of rock. After a few seconds more of straining at the rope, Ella released her grip with a frustrated sigh.

"Guess it's nothing."

"So someone just ran a rope across the ceiling like that for no reason?" Alan shook his head. "A magic rope that just hangs there like that? Why? There's got to be something to it."

"I don't think anyone built this place." Alan and Ella both looked to Carl, who shrugged. "I mean it. Mines are supposed to be about digging up rocks and ores out of the ground. You seen any digging equipment? Anything to carry rocks? So far it's just a long, winding tunnel through the hillside. It's not a mine."

"But the message said -"

"I know what the message said. But look around. It's ... it's too simple. Like you described a mine to a kid. Just tunnel and room, tunnel and room. There's rats to fight and that's about it. It's like someone started building a mine and gave up half-way through."

"Or isn't finished yet." Alan looked down at the floor. Someone had certainly gone to a lot of trouble to flatten it out. Oh, there were bumps and grooves here and there, a few pebbles, sure. A faint coat of dirt and rock dust. But it didn't look, or feel, used.

"Same thing." Carl shook his head. "Point is, everything we've seen so far is a single path and it's starting to head up. I say we keep going and leave the mysteries for later."

"I would have thought you'd be all about the mystery," Ella said. "Or are you just annoyed you're having to get your hands dirty?"

"Just hungry, that's all." Carl patted his stomach as he and his sister made for the tunnel. "I dreamt about those rabbits, you know. I could sure go for a big bowl of rabbit stew right about now."

Alan followed them on, turning Carl's words over and over in his head. Not about the stew - well, partly about the stew, but partly about the mine. It was true, he reasoned, that everything so far had been like - like a painting that hadn't been finished. Nothing to do except walk and fight, walk and fight. So then why was the rope there? If everything had been created with the bare minimum of effort, why was the rope there?

He looked down at the body of the rat and an idea came to him.

"Give me a hand!" He crouched, wrapped his arms around the dead weight of the rat, and tried to pull it up. The rat was a lot heavier than it had looked, though, and he only managed to get the front half up off of the floor.

"What are you doing," Ella asked. "Want to bring it with you or something?"

"The platform," Alan gasped, shrugging off his pack and trying to get a better grasp around the rat's middle. "Help me get it on the platform!"

"The platform?" Ella squinted at the wooden boards that hung from the visible end of the rope, then her eyes widened. "Oh. Oh!"

She trotted back to Alan, dropping her pack and mace on the floor. As Carl looked on, clearly thinking his sister and friend had lost their minds, Ella reached down and grabbed the rat by the tail. Alan had to stagger back a step or two to keep from falling as Ella lifted the body with ease. Trying to ignore her smug grin, Alan helped her to guide the body over to the wooden platform, which hung at waist height over one of the pits. Together, they manoeuvred it onto the boards and - with a coordinated nod to each other - let the weight drop.

With a rasping creak, the platform began to drop down into the hole, pulled down by the weight of the body. Looking up, Alan saw that the rope ran over a couple of small metal wheels, which squeaked as they turned, pulling the other end of the rope up out of the opposite pit. After a few seconds, during which the three of them grabbed their things and moved to the other side of the room, the rope ran out as a wooden bucket, banded with metal, rose into view and came to a shuddering halt. Pulling lightning into his palm, just in case, Alan stepped forward and peered over the rim.

Inside the bucket was a small leather pouch, what looked like a metal dinner plate and a small blue crystal, wrapped in a thick leather cord and attached to a long loop of string.

"You lucky git," Carl said, looking to Alan with a wide smile. "There's no way you knew that would happen."

"I just thought about what you said," Alan said, chuckling as he dismissed the lightning and reached in to grab the spoils. "Everything we've seen in here so far has been the bare minimum, so why the rope? It didn't make sense unless we were meant to do something with it. You're just lucky I didn't make you climb down to get it instead."

"Yeah, good luck with that," Ella said. "He never was good at climbing."

"Thanks for the love and support guys, really."

"Any time. Now, who wants a …" He peered at the dinner plate, a name flashing into his head. "… a buckler. Who wants a buckler?"

"Me," Ella said, reaching over and taking it from him, "seeing as I know what it is and I'm guessing you two don't." She didn't get any disagreement from either of them.

Alan peered at the crystal.

**** You have gained: Necklace of Energy ****

**** Necklace of Energy: grants bonus of 20 to maximum MP. ****

Alan whistled appreciatively. Given his MP seemed to go up by 20 every level, that was quite the bonus. He slipped the loop of the necklace over his head and felt his skin tingle. His head cleared just that little bit more and he felt marginally more rested - although that wasn't saying much, given how little sleep they'd had.

"And I'll be taking that," Carl said, plucking the leather pouch from Alan's hand. He gave it a quick shake and raised an eyebrow when a muffled jingle came from within. He pulled it open and Alan saw his face fall as the bag - and whatever had been within it - melted away into a trickle of dust and sand that slipped through his fingers. Carl looked up at them with defeated eyes.

"Got two hundred copper," he said.

"Cheer up," Ella said, slapping him on the back. "Just think of all the bread you can buy with that!"

"Oh yeah, magic bread," Carl said, trudging away towards the tunnel. "Just what I need." The disappointment in his words was undercut slightly by his stomach choosing that second to growl loud enough for Carl and Ella to hear, sending them both into a fit of laughter as they followed Carl out of the cave and into the tunnel beyond.

They didn't have far to go after that. The tunnel curved up and around, spiralling up a tight circle. Alan was sure that they were almost to the surface when the tunnel levelled out again, running straight ahead and into a new - far larger - cavern. Mist obscured the floor once more and the far wall was only just visible in the gloom. Rocky spurs jutted up from the floor and down from the ceiling, giving the appearance of a gargantuan mouth. The torches inside the cavern were unlit, and only the vague, blue glow gave any shape to the darkness.

"It's a trap, right?"

They stopped just at the edge of the tunnel. Alan looked to the others for an answer to his question but they just shrugged.

"There's bound to be rats," he said. "Dozens of them. I mean, look at the size of the room! We're supposed to just walk in there?"

"Only way out is through," Carl said. "Unless you saw a second tunnel that I missed. I say we rush in - there's nothing we can do out here and the more we wait, the more we worry."

"If there's rats, there's rats," Ella said, mace in one hand and the buckler in the other. "If there's too many, we run back here to the tunnel and make them come at us a few at a time."

She paused and her eyes took on a faraway look.

"Huh. Just levelled up a skill called Tactics."

Alan stared into the shadows and mists of the chamber ahead. He could see precious little of the floor and even less of the ceiling; he didn't want to think about the legion of rats that could be hiding among the stone and the shadows.

"You sure about this?" Alan gripped his dagger tight.

"Hell no," Ella said. "You?"

"No."

"That makes three of us." Carl looked as though he was about to say something, then stopped, shaking his head.

"Well then," Alan said. "Let's do this."

No time like right now, he thought, as they stepped into the chamber. The temperature of the air instantly dropped several degrees and Alan saw his breath begin to form clouds in front of him. The mist around them melted away as before, revealing an ever-larger circle of loose stones and branches. As Alan stepped closer, however, the branches took on a bleached-white colour and the rocks morphed into skulls, grinning up at him.

"Oh come on," Carl hissed, stepping carefully around a set of ribs, "we're so screwed."

"Just keep an eye out for rats," Alan said, his voice low, "and get ready to run. It doesn't matter how many there are, if -"

He stopped. His legs fell still; his words died on his lips. A peculiar sensation ran up his spine. It was primal - old, older than even the old Old World. It felt like a razor being run slowly and carefully up his back, cutting between his shoulder blades without drawing blood until coming to a halt just at the base of his skull and pressing there, just hard enough to make itself known. Alan's mind flashed back to the rats and the goblins and even the Forest Guardian Colonies and wondered if this was what they felt; if this was what it was like to be hunted.

Turning, as if drawn by rope, Alan found his gaze drawn instinctively up. For a moment he couldn't see it - and then, there it was, a mammoth shape nestled in the dark of the cavern ceiling. As Carl cried out a warning and Ella turned to see what the danger was, a long, thick tail unwrapped itself from around a rocky protrusion and dangled down into the light. Four great limbs flexed and released, causing the monstrous bulk to drop from the ceiling and slam into the floor. The impact threw up dust and a wall of air, causing the three of them to stagger back and shield their eyes. When Alan could stand to look again, heart picking up pace, he found himself staring into eyes the size of his head.

<Giant Earth Rat>
<Level 10>
<Dungeon Boss>

CHAPTER TEN

"Don't move."

Carl's voice was low and - amazingly - calm. Alan wondered how the hell he was managing that. Then he looked to his side and saw the white-knuckle grip Carl had on his dagger. His friend wasn't calm - he was terrified out of his mind. He just wasn't wasting any energy on panic which, Alan thought, was just as well. It was a long way to the tunnel behind them and he didn't fancy their chances at getting back to the entrance tunnel either. Not with several tons of rat in the way. It towered over them, the largest thing Alan had ever seen, clad in a thick coat of dark fur that looked more like rock than anything else.

"If it doesn't think we're a threat it might not attack." Carl took a slow, wobbling step back. "Just back off real slow and it might not bother with us."

The giant rat apparently had a sense of humour because it chose that moment to snarl at them, sounding more like a bear than a rat, and charge. It covered the ground between them in a few seconds and only Ella's quick reactions stopped them from being bowled over. She shoved Carl to one side and Alan to the other, lowered the buckler in front of her and braced. At the last second, as Alan was still sprawled on the floor wondering what the hell had just happened, he heard her cry out a single word.

"Hold!"

The buckler glinted as though caught by sunlight and Alan saw her stance deepen. Then the rat was upon her, smashing into the small plate of metal that Alan now realised was a shield, and driving her back. Somehow Ella kept her footing, sliding across the floor as the giant rat scrabbled for purchase and slowly lost its momentum. By the time Alan had made it back to his feet Ella had been forced back almost halfway to the exit tunnel. The rat seemed momentarily shocked by its charge being halted - a moment Ella used to take a step back and crack it across the jaw with her mace.

The rat reared back and screamed, clawing at the blood that began to gush from several shattered teeth. Alan saw its health bar appear and drop - but not by anywhere near as much as he had hoped. Still, he knew how to remedy that. He called lightning into his hands and threw it, striking the rat on its flank with a whip-crack of light. The rat screamed again and a dark patch of burnt hair blossomed across its side but its health bar barely moved. Alan didn't wait for it to turn on him; he threw again and again and each time the lightning hit but to little effect. The power seemed to flow across the rat's hide before sinking into the earth below and disappearing. Alan sank to his knees, the sudden expenditure of nearly all of his MP taking his breath away.

When Ella cried out it was almost too late; Alan looked up to see the rat - visibly pissed off, even if it wasn't hurt - barrelling down on him. He tried to stand but his legs still shook from the cost of the repeated casting. He collapsed to the side at the last second, avoiding the rat's charge until its tail whipped around and caught his arm, knocking him back and sending the dagger flying from his hand. He landed on his pack and felt something break; he only hoped it wasn't the star rod.

"Hey!" Alan saw Carl running towards the rat, shouting and waving his arms. "Hey! Over here!"

"Carl no!" Ella began to charge towards the rat, which had come to a halt and was turning its glowering eyes to Carl. It advanced cautiously this time, clearly not trusting the humans to stand still, lunging and snapping with a jaw full of fangs as Carl dodged back out of its reach. Then it howled and scrabbled at its face again, blood spilling from its snout, and Alan saw a glint of metal in the dark fur. Carl had managed to stab his dagger down at the last second, embedding it in the monster.

And still, its health barely fell.

Then Ella was there, barging Carl aside and bringing her mace up and around in a wide arc that caught the giant rat square under the jaw. It staggered back a little with the blow but not far enough. Ella turned, using the momentum of the first swing to spin her around for another strike - this one down, the head of the mace smashing into the hilt of Carl's dagger, driving it down into the rat's snout. Even from a dozen metres away, Alan heard a sharp crack of bone.

The giant rat reared back and screamed. Alan had thought its first scream had been bad enough but this was on another level entirely. It rose in pitch and volume until his ears rang and then it kept going, driving into Alan's skull until he could feel his teeth rattle in their sockets and he fell to the ground, clutching at his ears. He couldn't think, could barely breathe - and then the cry cut off and Alan found himself on his back, a thin trickle of blood flowing from his nose.

Above him, the fangs of rock biting down from the ceiling of the cavern trembled, like trees in a strong wind. Then Alan saw a puff of dust from the base of one as, with a terrible crack, the rock broke free and plummeted towards the ground. A second later Alan heard another fall, then another, but he was already up and running. He felt the first pillar impact the floor before he heard it, the rumble shaking his footing even as he felt small shards of stone pelt against the back of his neck and head, his pack providing a little bit of protection.

The second impact was closer and knocked him over once more. He curled tight, clutching at his legs as half a dozen pillars of rock slammed into the ground, filling the air with a storm of rock shards and great billowing clouds of dust. When he staggered up again, coughing and wheezing, it was into a world turned dark by the rock dust, blocking even the ever-present blue glow. He thought he saw the huddled figure of Ella, or perhaps Carl, a little way off - but when he got closer he saw that it was just a large boulder. It melted into the floor in front of his eyes and was gone.

The rat roared. The force of the sound blew the dust away and the rat emerged, a bloody, scraped mass of teeth, its fur plastered close to its body by blood and dust. Alan could see dozens of cuts across it - the rocks had fallen far closer to it than to him, after all. Its health was lower. Not by enough.

Alan mentally probed his status and found some of his MP had returned. For lack of a better option, he fired lightning towards the beast, which was snuffling around in the retreating dust, one eye a pulped ruin, searching for its prey. This time, however, the lightning did not arc across the rat's body and into the earth. Instead, it curved and struck it clean on the snout, crackling against the dagger still buried in its flesh. The rat screamed and convulsed and this time Alan saw its health fall significantly - then again a second time as the rat caught the dagger by one claw and ripped it free, chunks of seared flesh splattering to the ground around it.

For all that the giant rat had just ripped itself open, Alan felt worse than it looked. He coughed, sending a shooting pain through his chest, and when he wiped the back of his hand across his mouth it turned a crimson red. The swipe from the rat's tail, the falling rocks, being repeatedly driven to the ground - he could feel it taking a toll on him and he couldn't see Ella or Carl anywhere.

**** HP: 037 / 130 ****

**** MP: 036 / 180 (+20) ****

He heard a rough grinding noise cut through the battlefield. When he looked up he saw the source of it - rocks jutting back through the cave roof, scraping against each other as the fangs regrew. The rat saw it too and was momentarily distracted - then the two of them locked eyes and the rat roared again. It wasn't as loud or as piercing as the cry that had driven Alan to the floor but a quick glance up let him see that the new rocky fangs were twisting and shaking all the same.

Which gave him an idea.

He bent low and picked up a chunk of rock that hadn't melted away, flinging it at the rat with as much strength as he could spare. The rat wasn't visibly hurt - although it did flinch at the impact - but it narrowed its eyes and began to charge towards Alan, picking up speed. He nervously watched the beast approach, trying to measure the time and the distance and figure out the best moment to act. He tried to subtly slide sideways, hoping the rat would turn to follow, but found his legs had lost all strength in the face of the oncoming rat.

It suddenly hit him that he'd only get one shot at this. If it worked, though, it was the only shot Ella and Carl would need. He ripped the pack from his shoulders and flung it to the side as the rat charged closer and closer, picking up speed even with its cut and torn legs. There was nothing between them save the thinning dust clouds and a rapidly shrinking distance. This was it. Alan watched the rat charge closer. He could do this.

He couldn't do this. Terror and imminent death gave his legs new strength and he dove to one side, ducking low beneath the swinging tail this time, as the giant rat passed him. He fell on his arm and he felt something crunch ever-so-softly and pain sprang up inside of the limb. He cried out then, his scream muffled in the dirt. Any second now the rat would turn and spring back at him. Any second now -

A fierce cry rang through the cavern but rather than the shrill and needling cry of the giant rat it was raw and human. Ella! Alan saw her emerge from the cloud of dust, trailing it behind her like a cloak, with her mace clutched in both hands. She drove it into the side of the rat and the blow glanced off of its thick hide but grabbed its attention. She swung again as it turned, aiming for the ragged wound along its snout, but the rat was faster - sharp teeth clamped down on her arm and squeezed until she cried out and the mace fell to the floor.

But she had bought Alan the time he needed.

He had been channelling Lightning Strike since Ella emerged, holding it and holding it as his palms flexed and itched and burned with the power. With the rat distracted he let it fly, straight and powerful and aimed up at the ceiling. Alan saw the bolt crack against the rock, which splintered and shattered under the powerful blow. Even as the bolt faded, and the pervasive blue glow was once more the brightest light in the cavern, the fang of rock that he had struck the base of twisted, shifted and fell through the air, stabbing down towards the dungeon boss. Alan watched with satisfaction as it drove straight into the rat's spine, burying itself in the monster and forcing the air from it in one choking, pained scream that set the other rocks shaking and let Ella fall back, clutching her arm.

Then it ceased. The rat slumped, pinned to the ground by the fallen rock, and fell still. The bar showing its health dropped to nothing and faded away.

**** Dungeon Boss: Giant Earth Rat killed (+500 XP) ****
**** Dungeon Cleared! (First time: +500 XP) ****
**** You have reached Level 5! ****
**** Attributes Increased! ****
**** Ability Learnt: *Static Shock* ****
**** <u>Achievement Earned: Environmental Activist!</u> ****
**** *Through careful study (or blind luck) you have learnt to use the terrain to your advantage in a fight.* ****
**** *Damage you trigger from environmental sources against enemies is increased by 25%.* ****

The rush of energy that signalled levelling up swept through Alan and he was gripped by a coughing fit as blood and dust were forced out. His head cleared a little and when he stood up he felt surer on his feet, at least for the time being.

"That was crazy," Ella said, panting as she leaned against the giant rat's corpse. Alan simply stood, drinking in the sensation of being alive and whole. He didn't say anything but the fight had scared the hell out of him in a way that nothing ever had. Not the large rats. Not the bandit camp. The only thing that came close was seeing his dad stare at him, utterly devoid of recognition, wearing an expression that wasn't his own.

"Where's Carl?" Ella's head snapped up and she cast her eyes around the cavern. "Carl!"

**** [Fighter Ella]: Carl! ****
**** [Scholar Carl]: Calm down, will you? My head's killing me. ****

Carl came stepping through the dust, his dagger held loosely in one hand. It was almost entirely red with blood and the smell coming from it reminded Alan too much of roasted meat. This wasn't a situation he wanted to feel hungry in.

"Is ... is that it?" Carl asked. "It's definitely dead?"

"You saw the message." Alan smiled and stood straight, then instantly regretted it. While levelling up had rekindled a little energy in him, his arm was useless and he felt as though his insides had turned to knives. He welcomed the healing hands that Carl laid on him, despite the uncomfortable feeling of his bones shifting back into place.

"And we cleared the dungeon." Ella tapped the corpse idly with her mace, deep in thought. "Think that means that there are no more monsters?"

"Maybe," Alan said, slowly. He didn't want to just assume - the last thing they needed was to be ambushed by more rats when their guard was down.

"Then maybe we can get out!" Carl's eyes gleamed through the dust and blood and grime. "I never thought I'd miss the village but here we are."

"First things first." Ella bent to touch the giant rat corpse, then gestured for Alan and Carl to do the same. Once he had retrieved his dagger and made sure nothing had happened to the star rod, Alan placed one hand against the hide - with a not-insignificant amount of fear that it would jerk to life as he did so. When it didn't he let himself relax a little, then focused his attention on the loot.

There was the usual reward of copper, along with silver this time - fifty of the former and one of the latter. The vague awareness in the back of his mind ticked up again - the two were obviously related. If the new baker in the village would give him bread for a few coppers, he couldn't wait to see what he could get for silver.

But then he noticed the next part of his reward and forgot all about bread.

**** You have gained: 1 silver, 50 copper, 1 Giant Rat Tooth, 1 Mana Potion (Common Quality), Belt of Storage (Low Quality) ****

Alan wasted no time in examining his rewards.

**** Mana Potion (Low Quality) (Held: 1) ****

**** Restores 150 MP over 3 seconds ****

The first was a small glass bottle of a curious blue liquid, sealed with a cork. At first, Alan thought the liquid inside was frothing and it was true that there were miniature bubbles forming in it. Then, however, he realised that the bubbles drifted sideways rather than up. As he turned the bottle around to examine it closer the direction of the bubbles shifted - he quickly realised that they always flowed towards him, regardless of where the bottle was or how it was held. Grinning, he tucked it into the top of his pack. That would come in handy in an emergency.

**** Belt of Storage (Low Quality) ****

**** This magical belt can hold far more than its size suggests. Items stored in the belt will take up only half their original volume and weigh only one quarter their original weight for so long as they remain in the belt. ****

Alan thought his eyes would escape his skull, he was staring at the belt so hard. It was a long strip of leather with an unusual buckle, a twisted knot of silver and copper, and a couple of pouches hanging either side of his hips. Each pouch was about the size of his fist and secured with a small brass clasp. It made his current "belt" - really a ragged strip of old fabric - look pathetic. He quickly swapped it over, marvelling at the way it fitted him perfectly - he could swear it had shrunk down a little as he looped it on.

"Very sharp."

Alan looked up to see Ella grinning at him. She had a wide grin on her face and a new ring on one of her fingers. It was only a simple band of wood but it glimmered slightly when he wasn't looking at it directly. Ella caught him looking and held it up.

"Jealous?"

"Of a ring?" Alan snorted. "No chance. Give me something useful over something decorative any day."

"You mean like your necklace?" Ella laughed as Alan's hand went to the crystal strung around his neck and his cheeks blushed.

"That's different," he said. "It gives me a higher maximum MP."

"Yeah, and this -" Ella waggled the finger with the ring on it. "- gives me a bonus to my strength. What does your belt do - apart from hold up your trousers?"

"Well," Alan said, letting a sickly smugness slip into his voice, "just watch."

He cast his eyes around for a large enough rock to demonstrate, before remembering the other part of his loot. The rat's tooth was one of the big, flat fangs that had stuck out of the front of its snout. It was lighter than it looked, had dropped out of the corpse's jaw with ease and - more importantly - was just the right size to show off his new belt's ability. Holding up the tooth for Ella to see, Alan reached down with his other hand, opened one of the pouches and placed the tooth into a space half its size. Or tried to, at least. The tooth wouldn't go in. Which was hardly surprising, given that the pouch was half its size. Ella didn't look impressed.

"Wow, it's a belt." She rolled her eyes. "I mean, a belt with pockets. Very impressive."

"No, it should -" Alan tried, again and again, to ram the tooth into the pouch, with no success. Then he bent down, picked up a rock off of the floor and dropped it into the pouch. It remained the same size and weight as before. He stood there for several seconds, staring at it, before taking it out and trying it in the other pouches. No change. When he looked up, Ella had already turned away to speak to Carl, who was holding up a tattered strip of fabric for her to see. Alan looked back down at the belt, examining it closer. When the same description as before popped up he mentally waved it away.

Why was he having more trouble accepting that his new magical belt wasn't actually magical than he'd had with anything else over the past 24 hours? It was the betrayal, he realised - a bit dramatic, sure, but this was the first thing they'd found that wasn't as fantastical as he had been told. The giant rat might have just been a rat but it had at least been giant - this was just a belt with a fancy name.

Oh well. He tried to push his disappointment down inside of him. At the end of the day, he had a new belt. There was nothing wrong with a new belt. With any luck the next monster they fought - and Alan didn't doubt that their fighting wasn't truly over - would be carrying a good pair of socks and some shoes. By the time the three of them had gathered their things and finished a short-lived but extremely lively argument over whether or not to carve the giant rat up for meat (Alan caved when Carl asked if he was sure it wouldn't melt inside of them after they ate it), he had forgotten that he was even disappointed in the first place.

The exit tunnel turned a corner a little way in and then began to climb up. The climb was steeper and steeper with every passing metre until the relatively smooth floor turned into a series of broad steps. Carl was the first to feel the breeze from up ahead but Alan felt it a second later. After the still air of the mine, it was a welcome relief and everyone's pace began to pick up. They sped up even more when the dim glow of the air and the flickering shadows of the torches gave way to sunlight and the wind began to blow Carl's cape - for that was what the strip of fabric had turned out to be - wildly behind him.

They emerged from the tunnel into the dim sunlight of mid-morning, the sun almost hidden behind the twisting, churning black clouds that now stretched from horizon to horizon. The thought of the driving rain that was doubtless coming couldn't dampen Alan's mood, he was so happy to see the sky - any sky - again. The air felt tense and electric - it was like fingers running down his spine and the taste of cold water on a hot day rolled together as one. There was a storm on the way and it would reach them within a day. He just knew it. He let his inner child jump and shout at the thought of seeing real lightning on display. Somehow it felt more meaningful, now that he could conjure lightning of his own.

**** Dungeon exited ****
**** Dungeon resets in 11:59:59 ****

The tunnel exit behind them sprouted a mist barrier, the same as the one that had appeared over the entrance. Apart from that, the scene around them was the same as it ever was. Alan recognised where they were - one of the low hills that just poked up through the forest canopy. The trees below formed a rich green carpet, not the patchy cover that he remembered, and he knew for a fact that the tunnel they had emerged from hadn't been there the last time he climbed up the hill, but otherwise, it was a familiar sight. It was one of the highest points for miles around and a common escape when he had been younger.

Nobody said anything. Alan had expected Carl to cry out in relief but his friend just smiled and nodded, seemingly to himself. Alan knew how he felt. The memories of the escape from the goblins and the fight with the rats - both large and giant - clawed at his mind and he knew he'd take a while to sleep easy. But the victory? Oh, that memory made it all worthwhile. They had given the bandits the slip, hidden from the goblins and conquered the dungeon and Alan had never felt more powerful in his life than he did right now.

Not even when he held lightning.

CHAPTER ELEVEN

The trip back to the village was uneventful. They were close enough to the old road that the trees - as lush and thick as they had grown, even since they had entered the dungeon - were still relatively thin. They managed to avoid a Forest Guardian Colony after Alan spotted it in the distance, its vines waving just a little too much for the beast to remain hidden. They had neither the energy to fight nor the will; for all that they had emerged triumphant from the dungeon, the knowledge of what they would be returning to hung over them. Knowing just how thin their hopes really were knocked the battle urge right out of them.

They crossed the old road with weary feet and - at least in Alan's case - a deep sense of foreboding. His companions didn't seem any more enthusiastic. Carl's shoulders had slumped more and more with every step closer to home, while Ella was practically dragging the mace along the ground. Their fears were confirmed when they entered the village and came across Ella and Carl's mum carrying a fishing line and a bucket full of fat, silvery fish. She nodded at each of them in a friendly greeting but Alan could tell that she wasn't in control. He eyes, rather than screaming, now seemed dull and glazed. Defeated. Ella reached out a hand to her as she walked away but Carl pulled his sister gently back.

The insult was driven deeper when they entered the village square and found it had been transformed into a marketplace, low wooden benches set up either side of a central path. Various villagers stood behind each stall, chatting pleasantly to each other and waving to Alan, Carl and Ella as they passed. The stalls were laden with vegetables and fresh fish and tanned rabbit hides. It was the most food any of them had ever seen and on any other day, it would have been like something out of a beautiful dream, far outstripping even the sight of the countless fat, docile rabbits from the day before. The familiar faces in unfamiliar roles turned the dream into a waking nightmare. Alan didn't even stop to wonder where all of the food had come from - they just kept walking.

When they reached the junction at the other side of the village square they finally paused. Alan realised he had no idea where they had been going; now that they had to choose a path, he wasn't sure what to do. The Gumley house was in one direction; his own house and Carl and Ella's in another. The thought of walking into the house and seeing his dad not there - or worse, there, rising to ask this strange young man why he had barged in - turned Alan's stomach. He couldn't go home. Not yet. Based on the way Ella and Carl were looking down that road, he was sure that they felt the same way. Wordlessly, they turned left, towards the house that they had stormed out of the previous day.

The smell of rich, roasting meat wafted down the street towards them as they approached the house. The house itself seemed different somehow but Alan couldn't quite tell what it was - until he realised that the walls were straighter, the roof less patchy and the windows crack-free. It still looked like a house that had been built, according to his dad, over two hundred years before - just without the two hundred years of weathering that had happened since. Looking around - really looking, not the usual half-aware glance of familiarity - he saw that most of the houses were showing similar improvements. The street lamps, meanwhile, had disappeared altogether.

The front door was open and they let themselves in. The house was quiet but the smell of good cooking grew stronger; reaching the kitchen they found Bess carving thick slices of meat from a roast chicken. The sight and the smell reminded Alan's stomach that they hadn't eaten since the rabbit the day before - and he'd lost most of that by draining his MP too low. Bess looked up just as his stomach rumbled and for a second Alan thought she'd heard it, before realising that the three of them hadn't been exactly subtle with their entrance. Bess beamed at them, placing the carving knife down on the table and wiping chicken fat-smeared hands down her apron.

"Oh I'm so glad the three of you are alright," she said, moving around the table and engulfing Alan in a hug. "You gave us all quite a scare when you ran out the other day, you know. We've been worried sick about you - I searched the whole village for you and couldn't find you anywhere!"

Bess was a couple of decades older than Alan's dad - making her one of the oldest villagers, depending on who you asked - and the thought of her worrying, let alone traipsing all over the village, sent a shard of guilt stabbing through him. He hadn't stopped to think about how Elaine or Bess - or even

Arthur or Samuel, despite their bluster - would react. They were a village of seven non-crazy people now, after all. He hugged her back, squeezing firmly, as she gently scolded him. After a moment she let him go, moving on to Carl and then to Ella.

"Look at you all - why you're absolutely filthy! And Carl, what are you wearing?" Bess tugged at Carl's new cape and he laughed sheepishly.

"Well, it's a -"

Then Carl's stomach rumbled and this time everybody heard it. Within seconds Bess had somehow got them all sat in chairs around the table, their packs stacked neatly by the door and a plate of roast chicken placed before them, all before Alan could realise what was happening. Bess didn't stop there - a jug of deep-brown gravy appeared, as did a large porcelain bowl of peas and boiled potatoes. There were even jugs of water, as clear and cool as the spring they had found in the forest. In less time than it had taken them to navigate the new village market, the table was laden with food and - after a silent nod from Bess - the three of them dug in enthusiastically. It was, Alan thought as he speared a tender chunk of chicken and ran it through the gravy with his fork, a form of magic in its own right. He idly wondered if this was a class ability.

"Eat up," Bess said, smiling and making up two more plates on the sideboard. "Arthur should be back soon. He'll be so glad to see the three of you - why, he's been out looking for you all morning!"

"'Ank 'ou," Alan spluttered around a mouthful of potato. He flinched when Bess's eyes turned icy for a second and swallowed carefully before trying to talk again.

"Thank you," he repeated, Bess's glare thawing out. "Really, this is delicious. And we've …"

He trailed off, looking to Ella and Carl. How much of their story should they share? It wasn't like they'd done anything wrong, as such, other than stirring up the bandit camp into a frenzy. Not that they'd gotten a good look at his face, anyway, masked behind his scarf. The only light in the camp had been the campfire. Although he'd been thrown close to it, he doubted the guards would have seen anything other than a dark silhouette against the flames, their night vision ruined by the light. Not to mention the lightning he'd been throwing around.

Still, he decided to leave that part out. He didn't want Bess to worry any more than she already had.

"… we've had a long night," he finished lamely. "But we've found what caused all this!" He gestured towards his pack where the rod was stashed.

"Alan …" Carl started, a worried look in his eyes.

"It's what fell from the sky," Alan said firmly. "It's too much of a coincidence for it to not be related; we just have to figure out how it … did what it did, then get it to undo everything."

"Maybe not everything," Ella grunted, wiping the last of the gravy from her plate with a slice of chicken. "I could get used to the food, anyway."

"The point is, we can get the village back. I can get my dad back." Alan looked to Ella and Carl. "We can get all our families back."

Bess sighed and shook her head, pushing a potato around her plate with her fork.

"If you say so, dear," she said, staring down at her plate. "It's all just so much - I just don't want you all to go getting your hopes up over … whatever it is you found. Not if it might not work."

"It will work," Alan said. It had to. Even though he still didn't know what the hell they were supposed to do with the rod.

The kitchen fell silent for several minutes. Nobody seemed to want to be the first to break the silence; everyone just stared at their food as they ate. Alan ate as much as he could but quickly lost his appetite; it was the best meal he'd had in a long, long time but a knot of nervous tension began to fill up his stomach until he couldn't face any more. When he pushed his plate away Bess just sighed again.

"Samuel's down by the river," she eventually said. "Elaine too. I imagine they'd be getting rather peckish round about now." She looked at the unclaimed food, then back to Alan. He got the hint.

"I'll go fetch them," he said. He pushed his chair away from the table and stood, waving at Ella and Carl to sit back down as they rose to join him. "You guys keep eating. I'll finish mine later."

"Oh, only if you don't mind," Bess said. "I don't want to bother you when you look so tired."

Alan put on a smile and tried to ignore the hidden worry in her words. He felt tired - he had no doubt that he looked it. He knew he'd fall asleep if he just sat there with a full stomach, even if he had only finished half his plate. He debated taking his pack with him for a moment but in the end, didn't bother - who was going to steal it?

The drizzle began as he walked back through the village market. He'd have avoided it if he could but it was the quickest route down to the river. Better the devil he knew - he'd rather pass straight through, head down, than run into one of the villagers unexpectedly on a different route. At least here they mostly ignored him, except for whenever he passed too close to a stall. They ignored the light rain completely, grinning away with dead eyes as the water ran down their face. For his part, Alan tugged his collar up and tucked his head down. It was just a light summer shower for now. He'd be safe indoors before the real storm hit later.

Once he passed the market, the low level of chatter fading away behind him, the village fell quiet again. As such, he heard the commotion from the front gate from several houses away and - when he recognised the voices of both Elaine and Samuel - picked up his pace.

There were four people facing off at each other across the boundary of the village gate, three inside the village and one outside. The first was Michael Arton, still stood in the shelter of the gate, his tattered clothes replaced with a smart leather vest and trousers. There was a long pole in his hand, tipped with a blade, and he had found - or made or conjured or whatever the hell it was called - a shiny metal helmet. The effect was moderately imposing - until Alan realised the man was paying no attention to the confrontation, staring straight-ahead and leaning on his new weapon. Next to him were Samuel and Elaine, a brace of rabbits slung over their shoulders. Both of them were talking in strained voices with the man stood across the threshold.

Alan's blood ran cold at the sight of that man. Clad in leather and with a length of metal pipe looped through his belt, the man leered at the villagers with a slick grin on his face and a casually disrespectful slouch to his posture. His arms were scrawled with blotchy black tattoos and Alan knew that if he got close enough he would smell smoke and oil and grease. This man was one of the bandits from the camp. The man was one of the men he had fled from the previous night.

This man was here to hunt him down.

Visions of the campfire fight burst across his mind. The flash of light on metal; the feeling of powerlessness as he was picked up and thrown through the air. The endless circle of eyes staring at him from the darkness, the horde of bandits closing in on him. He couldn't let them know where he was. He couldn't let them come for him, for his friends, for the village. And now the bandit was looking past Samuel and Elaine, looking towards him, and -

"Lightning Strike!"

The words left him before he knew what he was doing. Lightning shot from his outstretched arm, crackling and twisting its way past Samuel, past Elaine, past the uninterested figure of Michael Arton and the gate, slamming into the bandit's chest and sinking through their clothes and skin in a smoking cloud of scorched flesh. The bandit staggered back, the smirk contracting into an agonised snarl - and then Alan's lightning struck him again and again. The bandit wavered, staggered forward and fell, limbs twitching as they thudded to the ground in a steaming heap.

**** Bandit Scout killed (+150 XP) ****

**** Faction Reputation (Riverside Bandits) lost! ****
**** Faction Standing (Riverside Bandits): Enemy ****

Alan let his arm drop to his side, sweat breaking out on his forehead as the effort of casting three strikes in a row broke through his adrenaline and panic. The sudden realisation that this had been a real person slammed into him and he vomited roast chicken and boiled potatoes onto the street. When he had nothing left he stepped closer to the gate. Elaine had sunk to her knees and Samuel wheeled on Alan as he approached, his face devoid of its usual reddish tinge.

"What the hell did you do?" Samuel said, every word escaping his lips as a gasping, spluttering wheeze.

"I saved us." Alan pointed a shaking finger at the bandit. "He was - I -"

"He was about to leave," Samuel said, his fists clenching and relaxing over and over. "He wasn't going to do anything to us!"

"He saw me," Alan said, his voice starting to rise. "He would have brought the whole camp down on us!"

"Why?" Samuel's face was rapidly regaining its colour. "You damn fool, they were looking for you weren't they? You're the one who pissed them all off!"

"I didn't mean to," Alan said, letting the old excuse escape on reflex.

"You idiot!" Samuel's face was red and his voice had lost its uncertainty in favour of rage. "They didn't know it was you! They were asking about someone who could shoot lightning but they didn't know it was you! They've gone to every village in a day's travel looking for a face they couldn't even describe and you've led them straight to us!"

"But I - no, I got him." Alan stammered. "I stopped him! It's fine, I swear, they'll never know and I -"

He was interrupted by a roaring, snarling sound that reverberated through him and turned his blood to ice. From down the road, beyond the curve of the hill, the sound of an Old World vehicle screeching into life faded into the distance.

"They never travel alone," Samuel roared at him, close enough now that his spittle hit Alan's face and Alan was sure the man was going to hit him. "You know that! We all know that! So well done boy, you've just pissed off the bandits and told them exactly where you are! You've stolen from them, you've killed one of them, and now we're all going to pay the price!"

Elaine looked up Alan from the ground by the gate, while Michael Arton stared impassively ahead. Her face was pale with an unsettling green tinge and tears ran down her cheeks as she spoke in a soft, mournful voice.

"You've just doomed us all."

CHAPTER TWELVE

The air around the kitchen table was bleak.

After Elaine had been noisily sick behind a bush and had nothing more in her stomach to lose, she had helped Alan and Samuel to move the body of the bandit out of the road. There was nowhere for them to store it and they had no desire to bury it but at the same time didn't want to leave it out to insult the bandits or attract scavengers. In the end, they had dragged it down to the river and dumped it into the water. Alan had felt a twinge of guilt at doing so, given how clear and deep and fast-flowing the river now was. He told himself that it was fine, that the river would carry it away and any pollution would set in downstream. He told himself that he hadn't really just killed another person, that it had just been a bandit. Just an NPC - and besides, it wasn't as though he had looted the body. He told himself that the NPC villagers were, of course, a different matter.

He told himself a lot of things that didn't help.

By the time they made it back to the house, Bess had set the plates of food aside in the warming draw of the oven; it still took her only a couple of minutes to have them all sat around the table, eating and drinking. The food helped a little, although Alan noticed that Elaine didn't have much of an appetite. He did - something he would look back on later and marvel at. He felt as though he could eat forever and took solace in the richness of the gravy and the fatty crackle of the chicken skin. There was no conversation; Ella and Carl had picked up on the mood of the returning trio without anything needing to be said.

When the food was gone Alan finally started to talk. Once the first few sentences left his mouth he found he couldn't stop, until he had told Bess and Elaine and Arthur - who had reappeared smelling faintly of ale - and

Samuel everything. Every cryptic clue they had been given by the system, every trick and nuance to their new powers that they had discovered. When he described the size of the rats in the dungeon Elaine shuddered; when he showed them the rod, placing it on the table, the four who had remained in the village recoiled slightly. None of them had any difficulty believing that it had fallen from the sky but none recognised it either. Alan finished his tale with the recollection of what had occurred at the gate.

He sat back in his chair when he was done. For a long time, nobody spoke.

"Can't we just give it to them?"

Arthur was the first to speak. His eyes hadn't left the rod since it had been placed on the table but his body was pushed back in his chair, keeping as much distance as he could.

"We can't." Alan shook his head and gestured at the rod. "It's our only clue for turning everyone back."

"You don't know that," Samuel said. "You've got no idea what that thing is or whether or not it can help."

His voice was soft and low, the quietest Alan had ever heard the man. Although he had eaten the food with gusto and relaxed afterwards with a contented smile, his moustache now drooped at either end.

"I say we give it to them," Samuel said. "Even if that thing can help, what good's a magic cure we don't know how to use?"

"It won't do any good handing it over," Elaine said quietly. Her plate was still half-full and she would, occasionally, pick at the leftovers. "When you killed that man …" She shook her head, not looking Alan in the eye. "They won't take that. It doesn't matter if we give the rod back now. Maybe if that was all you'd done and maybe if we had the entire village backing us up they might call it a day but you killed one of them. They'll want blood."

"My blood." Alan slumped in his seat.

"Oh I don't think they're going to be particularly picky dear," Bess said, patting him gently on the shoulder.

"No," Alan said. She was right, he knew that; the bandits had always lived and died by their reputation. If word got out that you could steal from them and just give their goods back if caught, it was all over for them. No more intimidation, no more bribery. They'd want to teach a lesson. They'd been brutal enough when challenged before; Alan didn't want to see how they behaved now that they were NPCs.

"So we give them the thing and the boy," Arthur said, glaring at Alan. He waved off a twin pair of narrow eyes and angry snarls from Ella and Carl. "They get their stupid toy, they get their blood revenge, we all get to live."

"Pretty sure Alan doesn't," Carl said. Alan noticed his fist tighten around the dinner knife. "Pretty sure you just want to throw him to the wolves and pretend like you're a hero."

"Yeah," Ella said, leaning in towards the older man. "It's not gonna happen, get it?"

A tense moment stretched between them all. Although he, Carl and Ella were technically outnumbered by the other villagers, Alan wasn't particularly concerned. They had youth on their side, not to mention a scant few hours' worth of experience in fighting. The others seemed to realise that because, after a pause that lasted just a little too long for comfort, Samuel cleared his throat and looked away.

"It's on the table," he said. "Look, the important thing for you three to remember is the rest of the village. They may be … bewitched, but we still owe it to them to keep them safe. I will not allow them to come to harm because of your foolishness, you understand?"

"Oh we understand," Ella said, pushing back from the table and crossing her arms. "Whatever it takes, right? Whatever price we have to pay? You just want to take the easy path out."

"Well what would you suggest then?" Samuel spat, turning his stare on Ella. "Run away? Good luck getting that lot to follow you. They think it's a bright, sunny market day right now. It's just as well they're all under stalls or they'd catch their death of the cold and rain. We can't take them anywhere and even if we could, then what? The bandits come back tomorrow or the day after that - the one who came to the gate made it clear they're not going to give this up. So you tell me - what do we do?"

"We fight," Alan said.

Arthur was the first to break the silence, wheezing with quiet laughter that quickly grew in volume. It echoed off of the walls around the boundary of the room. Everyone else sat in silence. Carl and Ella scowled at Arthur. Elaine turned pale and stared down at her plate, fiddling with the edge of her sleeve. Bess just sighed, while Samuel's face grew even redder and his moustache twitched. Alan stared defiantly at him, to little effect.

"We fight the bandits?" Samuel said, through gritted teeth. "I thought you were stupid for antagonising them before, boy, but now I think you must be mad too."

"Samuel, please," Bess said. "He's just frustrated. He doesn't really think we should fight those awful brutes."

"Yes, I do," Alan said, his voice flat. "I think we should have done it years ago; now we've got an actual chance of winning, even if it is just the seven of us. Look at these powers we've got now, look at what they can do!"

"No," Samuel growled.

"I can shoot lightning bolts from my hands," Alan said, ignoring the red-faced man. "Lightning! Carl can fix injuries just by touching you, I've seen it! And you've all seen what Arthur and Ella can do, how strong they are! Well, I've seen Ella in a fight, a real one, and it's like watching a force of nature! Everything we can do now, all the power we have, it's all designed to make us better in a fight. I say we let the bandits bring the fight to us."

"No!" Samuel stood up suddenly, slamming his chair back as he leaned over the table and pointed a stubby finger at Alan. "They are killers, boy. Killers! And for all your fancy little magic tricks might impress you, those bandits won't be impressed by anything other than brute strength and blood. They have guns, Alan, real honest-to-god guns! There are dozens of them and they are coming and they are pissed off and it is all your fault! Stop hiding in your daydreams and take some damn responsibility for your actions!"

The air fell still, charged with the tension of the fight and the gathering storm outside. Alan felt the hairs on the back of his arms stand up straight and he couldn't tell whether it was due to the real or metaphorical electricity in the atmosphere. He stared Samuel down.

"Now you're going to go wait by the gate," Samuel hissed, "and you're going to take that damn … thing with you. And when the bandits turn up you're going to go with them and you're going to beg them for mercy. I doubt they'll have much for you, mind, but it should keep them distracted long enough for them to forget to be angry with the rest of us."

"Make me."

At those two words, Ella and Carl pushed their chairs back and slowly stood straight. Carl drew his dagger from his belt; Ella simply clenched her fists. Both of them stared at Samuel, who never took his eyes off of Alan.

Arthur broke the new stalemate by lunging at Ella around the corner of the table, his chair clattering backwards. The man had the height and reach advantage, as well as lean muscles honed by decades of hard living. Ella still avoided his grab easily, stepping back then darting forward when he began to fall forward. Within seconds, she had him pinned over the table, pressing his face into the wood and pinning his arm behind his back. Arthur let out a muffled cry and struggled against her grip but he might as well have been fighting stone; Ella's stance never wavered and she turned her gaze back to Samuel.

"You -" Samuel spluttered. "You petulant child! You will give yourself in, boy, or so help me I'll -"

"You'll what?" Alan stood up slowly, taking his time while never breaking eye contact. "It's a new world, old man." He spat the last two words. "We're stronger than you now and there's not a damn thing you can do to make me give myself up. The rules have changed. You need to change too - we all do."

"You'll pay for this," Samuel said. He finally looked away and the tension in the room dropped slightly as he slumped. "We'll pay. The rest of the village, your families …"

"Maybe," Alan said, "but not to you and not to the bandits. Now, we -" He pointed at Ella and Carl, then back to himself. "- are going to go stop them. If you're not going to help then you can at least stay out of our way."

He turned his back on the table and - for a second - was sure that the older man was going to lunge for him, just as Arthur had lunged for Ella. The second passed; he heard only silence from behind him. With a nod to Ella, who released her grip on Arthur, he bent down to pick up his pack from against the wall. Carl and Ella did the same; the other four sat silently, watching. The only other words exchanged were from Carl as he stepped through the kitchen doorway, thanking Bess for the food. Alan didn't hear her reply.

They walked through the drizzle to the marketplace and stood there for a long few minutes, watching the villagers going about their perverse, staged routine. Alan caught sight of his father a few times between the crowd and looked away each time. The sight of the other villagers was still unsettling but the sight of his father hit him in a raw spot that he hadn't known he had. The villagers just grinned and acted away, trading shiny, strange coins for all manner of goods that they had no right to have. The rain dripped down their faces, over and around wide eyes that didn't react to the liquid, whenever they stepped between their covered stalls.

"Alan."

Alan looked down to see that Carl had laid a hand on his shoulder; a second later his sister mirrored the action on Alan's other side. All at once, the enormity of the situation broke through his anger and frustration and he took one deep, sobbing breath. His tears mingled with the rain and disappeared.

"I'm sorry guys," he said. "I'm sorry I dragged you both into this, I'm sorry I went into the bandit camp, I'm just - sorry."

"Yeah, you screwed that one up," Carl said. He grinned when Alan looked to him, a flash of white teeth. "Like, big time."

"Pretty sure I told you then it was just going to end badly," Ella said, taking her hand away and using it a second later to thump him in the shoulder. "Didn't think it would go this badly, though."

"It's impressive, in a way," Carl said.

"Like, really, impressively bad," Ella said, her grin matching her brother's.

"Guys, I …"

Alan trailed off, not sure what to say.

"So now you've just got to unscrew it," Carl said. "No idea how you're going to manage that, though."

"I thought you were supposed to be smart," Ella said. "What, no master plan squirrelled away in that head of yours?"

"Hey, I'm book-smart," Carl said, "not - not whatever-this-is-smart."

"I was talking to Alan."

"Ouch."

Alan laughed and the noise startled a few of the closer villagers; they grinned and waved and turned back to their fake trading a second later. Alan, meanwhile, laughed and laughed, while the rain continued to drizzle down in an irritating mist.

"Not sure I'm whatever-this-is-smart either," he said eventually. "Not even sure that's a thing. But you're right - I've got to fix this. I need a plan."

"We need a plan, you mean," Ella said. "We've got your back on this."

"You sure?" Alan blinked at her. "I mean, I've done very little recently that's turned out good. You sure you trust me?"

"We're sure," Carl said. "Wouldn't be trust if we definitely knew you could do this; that's the whole point. I've known you my whole life, though. You've always been there for us."

"I've helped you chop wood, you mean." Alan shook his head. "That's nothing. This -"

"That was everything," Ella said firmly. "You did whatever you could to help us out, even if it was just a little. This is the payoff, when it really matters."

Alan had nothing to say to that. They just stood in the drizzle, looking at the villagers blissfully unaware of what was heading their way. Everyone Alan had ever known or cared about was within the village walls. He had no intention of giving himself up to the bandits. He doubted that would even work; they'd all heard tales of what the bandits did when they were pissed off. Even if the village was blameless it was close-by and it was defenceless.

That had to change.

"How long do you reckon we've got?" Alan asked.

"It depends." Carl shrugged his shoulders. "They'll come by road, make a big scene with their bikes, and that means going all the way around the forest."

"They'll all come together," Ella said. "You know they always want numbers on their side and I bet they don't know there's only seven of us who can fight back."

"Which means they'll have to wait for everyone they've sent out to scout the local villages to get back to base," Carl said, finishing his sister's line of thought. "I mean, assuming the still care about stuff like that. Splitting up to scout seems … I don't know. Smart."

Alan knew the word he would have chosen instead of 'smart'. Human.

"It could take a while, I mean," Carl said. "Depends how widely they've spread their net."

"They'll all be due back today, though," Alan said. "Back before sunset, so they set off tomorrow morning. Can't imagine they're early risers but even with having to go round the forest, they won't take long to get here."

"A day." Ella folded her arms. "We've got the rest of today and tonight. From sunup tomorrow they could arrive at any time."

"And we have to be ready when they do."

Alan thought back to the argument with Samuel and Arthur. He'd said it in the heat of the moment but he supposed it was true: this strange new system to the world had made them stronger. They could fight now. The only question was whether they were strong enough to fight two-dozen bandits at once. The one at the gate had been an NPC, as had the big one in the camp; with any luck they all were. If some of them had powers too …

"Hey," Carl said, "I know that look. Stop jumping to whatever worst-case scenario you're dreaming up." He smacked Alan on the shoulder with far less force than his sister had done. "We don't have time to be pessimistic."

"You're right," Alan said, grinning. "We've got work to do."

"So you figured something out?"

"Yeah, I figured it out." Alan hefted his pack on his shoulder. "We can't rely on the others. If we're going to make a stand it's just us. We need to get stronger. A lot stronger."

CHAPTER THIRTEEN

"Lightning Strike!"

A flickering bolt of light briefly connected Alan's outstretched hand to the body of the rabbit chewing at a clump of grass. A second later the rabbit's body was flung, steaming, across the grassy riverbank and into the waters beyond. The river, which had been a muddy trickle a few days before, quickly swallowed the rabbit up in a strong current of crystal-clear water that bore it away and out of sight.

**** Calm Rabbit killed (+10 XP) ****

"Showoff!"

Alan looked up to see Ella grinning at him. A second later she turned and swung her mace in a curve down and around towards a rabbit angrily hopping towards her, catching it in the stomach and driving it through the air. It disappeared into the river, following the first rabbit with a splash.

**** Angry Rabbit killed (+10 XP) ****

"You're one to talk!" Alan grinned and clapped mockingly; Ella answered with a sweeping bow. A nearby rabbit, apparently seeking vengeance, chose that moment to leap for her outstretched arm. Its powerful legs propelled it through the air in one motion and it latched on to her arm with its teeth. By the time Ella had beaten it loose, swearing up a storm as she bashed at it awkwardly with the mace in her other hand, her arms was streaming blood from a dozen cuts.

**** Hungry Rabbit killed (+10 XP) ****

"You're both idiots," Carl said, clearly taking his time in wandering over to his sister, book in hand, and healing her wounds in a soft glow of gold light. "I thought we were taking this seriously? You know, because of the whole going-to-be-killed-by-bandits thing?"

"It's fine," Ella said, her grin gone. "It barely dented my health." She flexed her arm tentatively, and her face relaxed when none of the wounds opened up again.

"Yeah and it wouldn't have got you at all if you'd been paying attention," Carl said, snapping the book closed with one hand and wiping his other on Ella's shirt; blood streaked down it one a pink smear.

"It's a rabbit," Alan said. "They're hardly dangerous, now. Just makes it hard to take them seriously."

"Then why are we even here? I thought you said we needed to get stronger; you think this is making us stronger?"

"Yeah," Ella said, "this isn't exactly what I had in mind when you said you wanted to practise fighting."

"We're getting experience, aren't we?" Alan turned lazily and shot another lightning bolt at a rabbit a little further away. The bolt flew wide and struck a rock to no effect. The rabbit happily chewed its way across the riverbank, paying no mind to the bright lights or loud noises that had almost killed it.

"Yeah, I see the messages," Carl said. "That's not my point. We've got what, another 10 hours of daylight? Do you really want to waste it for ten experience a rabbit down here when you know we could be getting more in the forest?"

Alan knew his friend was right. The rabbits died quickly enough and posed basically no threat; Ella's arm aside, they were slow and easy to dodge as long as you paid attention. For every one that they killed, another hopped almost immediately out of a crude tunnel burrowed into the riverbank. There was no risk of getting seriously hurt, no risk of running out; the reward, however, left a lot to be desired. Still, the thought of venturing back into the forest …

"We don't need the forest," Alan said. "We just have to keep grinding away here, slow and steady."

"We don't have time for slow and steady," Carl said. "We barely have time for fast and reckless. We need to go back to the forest."

"As much as I hate to give him the satisfaction, he might be right," Ella said. "This is too slow."

They had been taken by surprise by the first Forest Guardian Colony because they hadn't even thought that there might be dangers in the forest. They had almost blundered into one after that; how many more had they avoided by sheer luck when they had been fleeing the bandits and the goblins? Alan didn't want to think about the horrors they could have literally run into. He was sick of other people getting hurt because he wanted to rush into danger.

"I'd really rather not," Alan said. "We'll be fine here."

"Why don't you want to go back?" Carl frowned. "Getting stronger by killing off monsters - that was your whole plan. I mean you said that bandit at the gate went down easy but there's going to be a lot more than one of them tomorrow. We need every edge we can get."

The bandit. The one he'd killed in a blind panic. The one who would have just … gone away, if he'd held his hand. The reason - well, one of the reasons, all of them his fault - why they were in this mess to begin with. He hadn't thought. He'd been so reckless.

"Because," Alan started, his voice a little higher and louder than he had meant it to be. When the rest of his rebuttal failed to come to mind he shut his mouth and straightened himself up. "Because." The second time around he said it with what he hoped was confidence and finality; given the way Carl and Ella looked to each other, then back to him, he doubted it had worked.

"What's going on man?" Carl asked.

"Nothing," Alan said. "Besides, do you really want to get grabbed by another one of those guardians?"

Carl rubbed absently at his wrist, something Alan had seen him do several times since they had left the dungeon. The skin there looked red and inflamed, as though Carl was rubbing it raw. Alan could only imagine what those memories must be like.

"Well no," Carl said slowly, "but we need the experience. You know that."

"Fine," Alan snapped. "You want lots of quick experience? Rabbit barbecue, here we go!"

Taking a deep breath, he gathered the lightning in his hands. He held onto it for as long as he dared, feeling the constant drain on his MP and the growing, fizzing intensity under his skin. When he felt his stomach churn and his MP dropped into single digits he turned and hurled the mass of power into the mouth of the rabbit warren. The bolt was as thick as his waist and boomed through the air, echoing off of the clouds and the trees. When it entered the warren the ground shook a little under his feet and he clasped his worryingly numb hand under his armpit, trying to squeeze some feeling back into it.

The message he had been hoping to see didn't appear. Instead, the warren entrance slid into itself, rocks falling in and earth collapsing. A great cloud of dust shot out of the gaps and settled over the nearby rabbits.

**** Spawn Point disabled ****

**** Spawn Point re-enabled in 23:59:59 ****

A slow clap echoed through the new silence; he turned to see Ella punching Carl in the shoulder, bringing it to a halt. Alan flushed a crimson red and looked away. This was exactly what he had been afraid of, exactly what - A sharp pain shot through his skull as Ella clipped him across the ear with the back of her hand and Alan felt his health bar dip a little. He stumbled back and held his hands up to ward off further blows but Ella just stood there, arms crossed, staring at him with a frown on her face.

"You done feeling sorry for yourself?" She sounded bored when she spoke and behind her, Alan saw Carl wince and look away. Alan had heard enough from his friend about Ella's lack of patience when it came to pity-parties growing up to realise that he spoke from experience. Whatever happened next, Alan was sure he wasn't going to enjoy it.

"I don't feel sorry for myself." Alan shook his head a little, partly for emphasis and partly to clear the ringing in his ears from where Ella had struck. "I feel sorry for you guys."

"Well I'm touched, really," Ella said, still sounding bored. "But your dad's in the same state as our parents. We've got it no worse than you."

"That's not what I meant," Alan said.

"I know," Ella said, "but it's the one damn thing you have any right feeling sorry about us for."

The fire behind her eyes flared up and she took a step forward; Alan took a matching step backwards, then again when Ella's accusatory finger stabbed in his direction.

"You didn't cause this, Alan," she continued. The words, which should have sounded comforting and reassuring - and might have done, from any other mouth - were harsh and damning. "This is bigger than any of us and we don't have time for you to take this whole damn thing onto your own back!"

"It's my fault the bandits are coming for us," Alan said, finally stopping his feet from retreating any further. "My fault the village is about to be attacked! Because I didn't stop and think! Ever!"

"None of us did," Ella spat, "not really. If we had, there's no way in hell I'd have followed you anywhere near the bandit camp."

"Yes you did," Alan said, "you always do. You're cautious and Carl -" He waved a hand at his friend, who was trying very hard not to pay attention to the argument. "- Carl doesn't need to stop to think. I do and I didn't and now we're all screwed!"

"We're your friends, Alan. You don't stop and think about helping your friends, you just help them. That's the whole point!"

"Well I'm stopping and thinking now," Alan said, "and I'm through acting on instinct. Every damn time I've done that over the past few days it's just made things worse. The bandits -"

"The bandits are tomorrow's problem." There was a slowly growing note of steel to Ella's voice, a build to finality. "Today's problem is why you're suddenly treating us like we're made of glass and afraid to go after those monsters in the forest."

"Because I'm sick of risking your lives when we know nothing about any of this! I'm sick of you being in danger because I'm not strong enough to make up for all the times I've rushed us into danger!"

There. He'd said it.

"Look," Alan said, the words rushing from him before Ella could speak up. "Look, this was fun, right?"

He looked from Carl to Ella and Ella to Carl, getting a slow, hesitant nod from the latter.

"Back when it was zapping rabbits and good hunting and weird quests, it was fun! But now my dad's a ghost of someone else and so's the village and they're all so vulnerable and we've got the attack coming, I …"

He trailed off. Looked down at his feet. Ignored the pressure of Ella and Carl looking at him until Ella sighed and spoke.

"Look, I get it," she said, her voice soft and low. "You're scared. I'm scared, Alan, believe me, I'm scared. I'm scared of the bandits, I'm scared of ma and da getting worse, I'm scared that I'm just going to run and leave the village for the bandits. There's nothing stopping us from just legging it and not looking back. But we chose to face this."

"She's right," Carl said. He had drawn close again and reached out a hand to Alan, resting it on his shoulder.

"I know you," he said. "And yeah, jumping in the river's easier if you do it too quick to think about it. You don't back down, though. Not even when you've got to stare danger in the face and watch it come to you."

"We can't risk it," Alan said. He felt like he was pleading his case to his two best friends. "I can't risk you guys."

"We risk more if we stay out here," Ella said, "wasting time and kidding ourselves that we can kill a few rabbits and get ready to take on the bandits. If we had the rest of the village on our side, maybe, but we need to get more powerful and we need to do it soon. I'll face the forest again during the day but not at night. Not in the dark. *That's* reckless. We need you to make smarter choices, Alan, not slower ones."

"We trust you man," Carl said. "We trust your gut, even if you don't."

Alan laughed bitterly. "When did I become the one in charge?"

"It just happened," Carl said. "Life's like that. It happens when you're not paying attention."

"Come on," Ella said, resting her mace back over her shoulder. "We've got weird forest monsters to kill."

The absurdity of the statement finally broke through the cloud hanging over Alan's head. He laughed, brushing off Carl's hand and stooping to pick up his pack from where it had fallen against his leg. What did they have to lose? The world was upside down, bandits were bearing down on them and the village was under a curse. If their future looked bleak, why not go down swinging? They could at least do better than rabbits.

Time to go kill some weird forest monsters.

CHAPTER FOURTEEN

The forest was dark as they approached it, darker than it should have been during the day. Even taking into account the clouds overhead, which blocked out all but a faint, ink-washed glow of sunlight, it was too dark. It was as though a curtain hung across the boundary, thin and lacy and casting the interior in a soft twilight. Each tree was at least half again as tall as they had been the day before and thicker too, the bark rough and gnarled and appearing far older than it should have. There was a faint smell in the air, earthy and green and alive. It held the richness of both abundant life and natural decay, both tantalising and foreboding.

Ella held an arm out, barring Alan's path as they approached and he couldn't help but grin as she peered in between the trees. No matter the need for action - and no matter how she had scolded him for his loss of momentum - Ella had never let herself be fooled the same way twice. When she was satisfied that the hanging vines and branches were exactly that and nothing more she gave a satisfied nod and the party stepped through. They would find the monsters on their own terms.

Well, that was the plan at least.

They still managed to, quite literally, trip over the first Forest Guardian Colony they found, its tentacle vines hung loosely through a bush that Carl pushed through. He went down in a flurry of limbs and curses and only the fact that the monster seemed as surprised as they were prevented him from being ensnared. Alan cast Thunderclap almost reflexively, sure that he could feel more vines creeping through the undergrowth towards him, sending leaves and earth and tentacles slamming back. Ella spotted the main body of the beast before it could gather its wits and charged it, smashing it to a pulpy mess with her mace while Alan helped Carl to his feet.

**** Forest Guardian Colony killed (+100 XP) ****

"That's what, ten rabbits' worth? I hate to say I told you so, but …" Carl grinned and Alan shoved him down again as he trailed off into laughter. Point taken.

They kept moving after that, following the boundary of the forest as it curved down alongside the old road. The brighter light of the outside world was just about visible through the trees and helped them stay at roughly the same depth; Alan wasn't entirely sure it was safer as such but at least it made their escape route more obvious. He wasn't too worried about coming across another Forest Guardian Colony - at least not by itself. It was what would happen if they came across two or more at the same time that worried him.

Or the goblins. He shuddered at the thought of their ratty little claws and limbs, their unnerving cries.

The second Forest Guardian Colony they came across was a little more alert than the first. They only avoided blundering into it when Carl stopped short between two trees and turned back to Alan and Ella. He opened his mouth to say something and then disappeared, lassoed by a tentacle around his waist and pulled back faster than Alan or Ella could react. It took several minutes of dodging vines and throwing lightning bolts semi-blindly at anything that moved before they hit the main body with a lethal amount of damage. It took several more minutes to help Carl down from the upper branches of the tree he had landed in, long loops of vine still coiled loosely around his shoulders.

**** Forest Guardian Colony killed (+100 XP) ****
**** You have reached Level 6! ****
**** Attributes Increased! ****

"I'm going first from now on," Ella said, helping her brother free himself from the tangle.

"Be my guest," he spluttered, awkwardly wielding his dagger as he cut the monstrous plant matter free. "I'm getting pretty damn sick of them always going for me. At least I've figured out the pattern."

"Pattern?" Alan perked his ears up at the sound of that. Whatever order Carl had been able to project onto the chaos that was now their lives was welcome news.

"Nothing big," Carl said, "but the colonies? Always in a clearing, always with something for the maggot body to hide in. I figured it out just before that one got me."

"You saw it coming?" Alan was seriously impressed; he hadn't noticed a thing.

"Well no," Carl admitted with an embarrassed grin, "but I knew there was one around."

"Nice work," Ella said. "I'm still going first."

True to her word, Ella took the lead after that. With Carl's realisation to work with, they moved slightly more confidently through the forest. Now that they knew what to look for they spotted multiple clearings as they went, none of them very large. The first one they approached was empty, as was the second, but the third was draped with hanging vines and had a jumble of moss-covered rocks at the centre. There was even a small gap just visible under the rocks, with vines trailing back into it. They halted several paces away from the border and Alan hit the base of the rocks with as much lightning as he could stomach in one go. They never even saw the Forest Guardian Colony itself; the hanging vines seized then fell limp and the familiar message flashed across their vision.

**** Forest Guardian Colony killed (+100 XP) ****

In the space of a bit over an hour - plus the time it had taken them to get to the forest from the river - they had gained more experience than an entire morning spent grinding through the local rabbit population. Carl's pride aside, they hadn't even taken any damage. Alan's gut told him to relax, that they had made the right choice. His head, however, still wasn't sure and he was glad that Ella still insisted on marching carefully between the trees, buckler raised and eyes open.

Over the course of the afternoon, they levelled up twice more that way. With the knowledge to watch out for gaps and clearings in the trees, they managed to avoid blundering into any more traps. Once that danger disappeared - or at least lessened enough for Ella to walk with her buckler lowered and Alan's stomach to unclench slightly - the writhing masses of tentacles quickly lost their terror for Alan. Carl still hung back behind the rest of the group and Alan couldn't blame him for it - out of all of them, he had had the worst luck in being pulled up close by the monsters. A little residual wariness was only natural. The group nevertheless moved smoothly from encounter to encounter, roaming down the edge of the forest and then - when they had strayed a little too far from home for comfort - heading further in and reversing their course.

They fell into a simple routine; if at all possible, Alan would fry the Forest Guardian Colony at the heart of each clearing from a distance. If the main body was too well hidden - or if he missed - he would charge in and cast Thunderclap, stunning the tentacles long enough for Ella to rush past and pry open the rocks or logs that hid the maggot. After that, Carl made quick work of it with his dagger. Ella could have done that but Carl insisted. As far as Alan could tell the insistence was born from a mixture of Carl's desire for revenge and an unwillingness to just sit on the sidelines. They took a few scratches along the way but nothing that Carl couldn't heal up in a matter of seconds.

What Carl couldn't heal was the fatigue and hunger that eventually began to creep into all of them. Although he carefully avoided spending too much of his MP at once - being, by now, all too familiar with the sucking, gut-churning emptiness of running out - Alan's stomach began to complain as the sun dipped lower. They still had a few hours of sunlight left but the gloom of the forest, coupled with the heavy clouds overhead, meant that it was dark enough for the forest to become a more threatening place to traverse. They made a slow retreat towards the village, taking extra care in placing tired feet on uncertain surfaces.

The rain began to fall once more as they left the cover of the trees and by the time they reached the village, it was true rain, rather than the half-hearted drizzle of that morning. The market, when they reached it, had also changed. The sea of tents and stalls was gone, leaving only a few vendors huddled under canopies around the edge of the square. The spell that had gripped them seemed to have allowed them to notice the rain and the villagers that remained outdoors cursed and dashed between puddles just like anybody would. If it wasn't for their eyes, which flickered between dead glossiness and terrified stares, Alan wouldn't have been able to tell that they were puppets at all.

They found a stall still selling food - one of the out-of-town merchants, now trapped handing out hot fish skewers and buttery roast potatoes. Alan gladly sacrificed a few of the imaginary copper coins that they had collected over the course of the day to fill his stomach once more and the three of them sat under the covered entrance to the town hall as they ate, watching the last of the traders pack up and hurry off through a veil of rain.

"Think it's enough?"

Carl put a voice to the question that had been haunting Alan's mind since they had left the forest. From the way Ella shifted uncomfortably, he guessed it had been on her mind too.

"It's got to be," Alan said. "Unless I run or give myself up."

"You gonna do either?"

"No," Alan said. "It wouldn't work."

Carl nodded, still staring out into the rain. Beside him, Ella licked her fingers clean of the last of the butter and few scraps of fish that remained. A low rumble from overhead echoed off of the walls of the town square and

Alan looked up expectantly but it died off again to nothing. The only sound was that of the rain, hammering down onto the paved road.

"You guys could run," he said. "The bandits don't want either of you. Hell, you could probably take your parents with you even if you did have to tie them up. Figure this whole thing out when your lives aren't on the line."

Ella snorted. "Yeah, no."

"We're in this with you," Carl said. "Besides, even if we could get them out of here - what about everyone else? What about your dad? What about you?"

"Face it," Ella said, "you're stuck with us. You die, we die."

Alan nodded slowly. He wasn't that surprised. He didn't like it but there wasn't much about their situation that he did like so why should this be any different?

"Promise me you'll run if we lose, though." He nudged both of his friends in the back, forcing them to turn and face him. "If the village burns and the bandits win and there's nothing we can do about it - promise me you'll run. Promise me you won't just stay and die."

"Only if you do the same," Carl said softly.

Alan found he couldn't.

They sat in the silence of the rain. The sun was still technically up but it was an early twilight that would stretch on for a couple more hours by Alan's guess. Too dark to march safely around the forest - certainly too dark to fight - even if the rain wouldn't soak them through. Too light to sleep, though, and far too light for him to feel secure that they had done all they could do.

"Think I'm going home," Carl said. "Try and get some sleep." He didn't sound sure of himself but he stood up anyway, stretching out his back. "Big day tomorrow."

Ella nodded and rose to her feet. "I'll come too," she said softly. "If ma's there, I ..."

She trailed off into silence, staring into the rain and only snapping back to the moment when her brother coughed. The two siblings looked down at Alan where he still sat on the stone step.

"Go," he said. "Get some sleep. We'll meet back here first thing and ... figure it all out."

Nobody commented on the uncertainty in his voice. Carl and Ella just nodded, shouldered their packs and disappeared into the rain. Alan sat there a while longer, watching as the dark shapes of his friends sprinted through the twilight and the rain and out of the square. He sat there for longer than he meant to, trying to sort the jumbled mess inside his head.

Would he run? He'd fight the bandits, sure, but if it was hopeless? If there was nothing more they could do, nothing they had the power to accomplish, if all they could do was add their bodies to the pile? If even their deaths meant nothing?

He wasn't sure. Maybe it would make more sense in the morning. Maybe what he really needed was some sleep. After all, what more could he do? The weather and the low light made fighting more monsters impossible. The forest was a maze of dangers even during the day - his willingness to go in and train with Ella and Carl didn't blind him to that fact. Between the Forest Guardian Colonies and the goblins and the dungeon -

The dungeon!

He thought back to the message they had seen as they had exited it early that morning. It had been twelve hours; surely that meant they could enter again! It was underground, so the rain wouldn't matter, and there was plenty of light. Sure, they'd only get one more shot at it if the same timer applied as last time but it might just be enough to bump them up another level! Except …

Except the dungeon was a fair distance away, through the rain and in the middle of the forest. He could call Carl and Ella back, sure, but the thought of asking any more from them than they had already given - than they had already promised to give tomorrow - sat poorly with Alan. And if their parents were at home, this was probably the last chance they'd have to see them - even as strangers - before the bandits arrived. He couldn't rely on them all the time. They'd saved his life too many times over the past couple of days. Ella, in particular, kept throwing herself between him and danger and that hurt more than the monsters would. He needed to do this alone, to face the consequences of his recklessness. To have the power to back up his actions. That's what his gut told him.

He stood up, thinking about the dungeon. A cool sensation in his head told him the direction and distance; not as far into the forest as he had feared. The mad panic they had been in the first time they had stumbled over it had thrown his sense of direction for a loop. He didn't think it was far enough in to have to worry about the goblins, which had seemed to cluster closer to the other side. He knew how to spot the Forest Guardian Colonies now and there was still just enough light to risk it, so long as he didn't have to fight. If there were other monsters they hadn't shown themselves through a whole afternoon of the three of them marching noisily around.

He could do this alone. But first …

He concentrated on the ties between him, Carl and Ella, the strange bond that designated them as a party, and tried to make them break.

**** Dissolve party: yes/no? ****

"Yes," he whispered and felt the distant awareness of his friends' positions and welfare drift out of his mind. Hopefully, they wouldn't notice. Hopefully, they were too busy trying to get to sleep. Either way, he didn't want them to notice him sneaking off alone. He didn't want them to worry.

The rain showed no sign of letting up; so be it. He gathered his nerves and stepped out of the cover of the town hall's entrance, footsteps kicking up water as he started to sprint towards the edge of the village. He could do this.

He could do this.

CHAPTER FIFTEEN

Alan slipped inside the dungeon entrance, not looking back as the sound of the rain thudding into the forest floor was cut off. He knew if he turned he'd see the same wall of mist as the last time, blocking his retreat.

**** You have entered a dungeon! ****

The dash through the forest hadn't been quite as wild as he had feared. The canopy above had blocked most of the rain, collecting it and funnelling it down into more coherent streams that trickled from branches and twisted down tree trunks. If anything it had made spotting the clearings - and the monsters that lived there - far easier, the sound and sight of the heavier rainfall visible even at dusk. Alan had steered well clear, guided by the pull towards the dungeon in his head, and had only begun to worry about monster attacks as he had drawn closer to the dungeon entrance. Regardless of his good fortune in avoiding them, he had no desire to try and fight in the treacherous twilight.

The entrance had appeared out of the gloom as he had approached it, another sign of the shifting state of the world. Rather than the jagged ravine that they had tumbled into last time, there was now a clear patch of forest that had been cut back and built over. Metal tracks ran into a clearly artificial tunnel that led down into the earth, built up with more of the wooden beams and lit by more of the odd lanterns. Wheeled carts lay scattered about the entrance while picks and shovels fell haphazardly around them. Alan thought back to what Carl had said the night before - whatever force had made the dungeon hadn't given up yet.

Inside the entrance, the tunnel was more similar to what they had seen last time but built up further. The track continued down the centre of the floor - that, at least, was new. The air still felt the same, the light still shone a little too evenly to be explained by the lanterns but everything else felt more … real. Lived in.

Alan didn't waste too much time marvelling at the changes that had been made. He cast Thunderclap, the shockwave blasting his body - and clothes - free of the rain and dirt from running through the forest. At least he wouldn't catch a cold. With the certainty that came from experience - and a wild hope that the dungeon hadn't changed too much from the last time in terms of layout - he moved forward at a purposeful pace. The tunnel twisted and turned much as it had before but it passed far quicker now that he wasn't moving as cautiously as they had the last time. He slowed only when he came across the suspicious patches of rocks and the tripwires that had caused them so much misery before. Ironically, the more sculpted appearance of the walls and floors this time around made the traps stand out that little bit more and he stepped over them with ease.

The first room he came to confirmed his hopes about the overall structure of the dungeon. Although it had changed in appearance, with more elaborate support beams and scattered tables and cutlery, the important part remained the same: rats. This time there was no mist on the floor, letting him see the two rats at the far end of the room with ease as they plodded back and forth in a slow loop.

He didn't wait for them to spot him. He held the first lightning strike for just long enough that he was confident it would hit, then hurled it forward to scorch one of the rats. The second perked its head up at the sudden disintegration of its companion and - easily spotting Alan - charged forward. A second strike took that down too, its body falling to the ground before the sound of the first strike had finished echoing off of the tunnel walls.

**** Large Rat killed (+20 XP) ****

**** Large Rat killed (+20 XP) ****

Easy.

Alan wasn't about to forget what had happened the last time they had walked into the chamber, however. Raising his arms above his head, he sprinted from the tunnel to the far end of the room, vaulting over the two bodies on the ground. Behind him, he heard a series of thuds as the rats that had been clinging to the ceiling fell at him as he passed; when he turned to look back they were still getting their bearings. He didn't waste any time, charging back in and triggering Thunderclap. The force of it flashed out, smacking the rats - as well as the rest of the contents of the room - into the walls and then bouncing back. In the confined space the effect was brutal and the rats fell twitching to the ground. They weren't dead yet but it only took a quick slash of Alan's dagger to finish them off.

**** Large Rat killed (+20 XP) ****
**** Large Rat killed (+20 XP) ****
**** Large Rat killed (+20 XP) ****
**** Large Rat killed (+20 XP) ****
**** HP: 170 / 170 ****
**** MP: 151 / 260 (+20)****

Alan slumped against a wall, panting, as he waited for his MP to refill. He waved away the messages about his loot - coins only - and stared down at the scene of destruction in front of him. The wooden furniture had been reduced to splinters and much of it was now embedded in the bleeding bodies of the rats that lay scattered around the room. It hadn't taken more than a minute but the monsters - which had given him, Carl and Ella so much trouble before - were down. Defeated.

"Hell yes," Alan whispered to himself. Although he didn't want to admit it - because it would mean admitting to himself how reckless he had known tackling the dungeon by himself was - that had gone far, far better than expected. Not a single one of the rats had gotten close enough to even think about attacking him. Most of them hadn't even seen him coming. When he had recovered both his MP and his breath he set off again down the tunnel, this time with a small spring in his step. There were still plenty of rats left to kill.

The second chamber was affected in the same way as the first; the mist that had covered the ground was gone, revealing a broad, square-ish chamber where the track split three ways; dead ahead, where the tunnel disappeared off into the distance, and to either side, where new tunnels had sprung up and appeared to have immediately collapsed. Rubble and debris blocked both paths, stripping away the illusion that the dungeon was more than a straight line towards the humongous boss at the end. There were no rats immediately visible in Alan's line of sight but when he repeated his tactic of running straight across the room to the far exit they came crawling out of cracks and crevices in the walls and ceiling. He cast Thunderclap again, knocking the rats back and shaking the lanterns on the wall, but this time there were more and by the time he had finished three with his knife there were four more scrabbling their way towards him. He cast Thunderclap for a second time and the force knocked the rats back momentarily - as well as nearly deafening him - but they were up and after him again within seconds. Lightning Strike took one of them, leaving three to force him back into the tunnel he had come out of. With no other options, he ran.

The rats were fast but he was faster and the distance opened up; when he dared pause he stopped and turned and fired Lightning Strike blindly back down the tunnel. He got lucky; one of the rats collapsed, steaming, to the floor as the last two advanced remorselessly. Their eyes glowed red and they got close enough - at least until he turned to run again - for Alan to see foaming spit at the corner of their mouths. He made it a little further before his side seized up with stitch; bent double, he slammed shoulder-first into the tunnel wall. Alan fired back down the tunnel while choking down air but this time he missed and the first of the two rats slammed into him, bowling him over and skidding past him down the tunnel. The other rat leapt for him on the ground; Alan barely managed to get his hands up in time to seize it by its scrabbling front limbs, using all of his strength to hold it back and away from him. He conjured lightning; there was no need to aim when he was physically holding his target and the rat screamed as it died, thrashing about for one last moment as he heaved it to the side. The stench of burned fur so close to his face made him gag and spit on the floor, suddenly yearning for the clear air of the forest.

That left one. One rat that leapt at him from behind as he tried to stand up, sending him sprawling to the ground, on his front this time, and latching on to his shoulders. Only the thick bulk of his pack kept it from tearing great gouges in his back as it kicked at him. His MP was low, too low to cast Lightning Strike again. He couldn't hold it off long enough for his MP to recharge; each rabid swipe cut the air a little closer to his neck.

"Thunderclap!" Alan screamed into the rock floor. His arms twitched but there was no room for them to meet; one was pinned under him and the other was twisted back behind him. The rat was too heavy to push off, clawing and biting and kicking at him. Alan bucked and writhed, trying to dislodge it, and while the motion stopped it from getting a solid hit in on him it didn't shake it free. His hand twisted back, found its vile, slimy tail whipping around and grabbed on but he didn't have the strength to squeeze, not hard enough to do it damage. Every second it clawed away more of his pack, every second it got closer to his neck. There was no plan, only pure instinct. He needed something new, he needed -

"Static Shock!"

He forced the words through his mouth, into the dirt, and his free hand flared with a sudden rush of pins and needles. The rat on his back screamed and fell limp in response. His stomach churned, his MP dangerously low, but not badly enough to stop him rolling away from the rat. It lay rock-still on the floor of the tunnel next to him, every limb clenched, eyes wide-open in animalistic fury. He didn't wait for it to start moving again, driving his dagger straight into its throat. When the kill message appeared in the corner of the vision, joining all the others that he had ignored in the rush for survival, he waved it away. It wasn't important. He focused instead on the new ability.

**** <u>Static Shock</u> ****

**** A melee-range spell that targets a single enemy at a time, stunning them with a shocking bolt of power. Stun duration varies depending on enemy size and level. ****

**** Range: Melee ****

**** Damage: 1 damage ****

**** Cast Time: Instant ****

**** MP Cost: 25 MP ****

I really need to start checking new abilities as soon as I get them, he thought.

When he could stand again without immediately pitching forward in a dizzy blur, he pulled himself to his feet using the tunnel wall for support. He didn't wait for his MP to regenerate further; by the time he made it back to the chamber, stopping to loot each rat that he passed, it was back to full. For his troubles, he had gained a bundle of XP, a couple dozen copper and another dagger. He dropped it into his pack, next to the star rod.

He didn't rush to the next chamber. He didn't stop and he didn't slow - he was still moving far faster than they had the first time through - but he didn't rush either. His stomach settled more with every passing second and his breathing grew steadier; he knew what was ahead and he would meet it in time. After the last chamber, he had a few more ideas about how to tackle the rats. At least there would - should - be fewer.

The next chamber was covered in jagged blue crystals running in veins along the walls. Even from outside of it, there was a distinct blue glow that reflected back into the corridor. Alan didn't take any chances this time. He had lightning ready in his hands when he stepped in and threw it at the first rat to poke its head out of the cracks between the crystals. He got the second the same way; by that time three had wriggled free and stalked towards him, spread out and watching him with more intelligence and malice than the average rat. Alan took a few steps back into the tunnel mouth as they came and threw a lightning bolt at one; it jumped out of the way at the last second, the lightning sinking into the greedy earth. When they passed into the mouth of the tunnel Alan darted forward, clapping his hands together with the power of thunder and flinging the advancing rats back. They recovered far quicker than the previous rats had but not quick enough - Alan had already sunk his dagger into one and grasped at the other two with hands fizzing with power. Static Shock locked up their limbs, giving him plenty of time to retrieve his dagger and finish them off.

The rats melted away into nothingness after he looted them for more copper. MP - and confidence - restored, Alan picked up the pace towards the boss. As terrifying as it was - and his heart was already beginning to beat faster just at the thought of it - he needed to face it soon. Carl had been right. Alan had always faced danger and bad news head-on before he had time to start worrying. He didn't want to allow himself that time now.

The single rat in what Alan thought of as the scales room died before it even saw him, lightning searing it in an instant. Without Ella, it took significantly more work to lug its body up and onto the hanging platform - or, rather, the wooden cage, just big enough for a person to fit into, that had replaced it. The pulley system - more substantial now, with tarnished brass wheels and thicker rope - dutifully pulled up a metal bucket full of goodies. Alan quickly pocketed a couple of vials - one health potion and one mana potion, according to the description - yet another dagger, this one with a serrated edge down one side of the blade, and an ornate bundle of cloth; unfolding it, Alan realised it was a hooded cloak. Whatever fabric it was made of was soft but tough and dyed a dark moss green. Remembering the chill of the boss cavern the last time around he wasted no time in pulling it on, grateful for a little extra warmth. He was slightly disappointed when he realised that it was just a nice cloak and nothing more - then he smiled to himself. A week ago he'd have given his left arm for a good, well-made cloak. If nothing else, it'd keep him dry on the way back to the village.

He only rested briefly by the entrance to the boss rat's chamber, steeling his nerve while he peered in. The mist here was still present, although thinner, and the chamber had been reshaped into a broad hall, half-finished with support beams and clear-cut walls near him but extending into unfinished cragginess on the far side. Blue crystals were shot through the walls and ceiling once more; on this side of the room, they had been cut flat to the walls and polished smooth, while those on the far side jutted out in sharp angular shapes. Looking up, Alan could just see the hanging rocks nestled in the darkness of the roof. There was no sign of the boss.

Well, not until he ran in screaming anyway.

The screaming wasn't strictly necessary but the primal terror that had faced them the first time reared its ugly head as he crossed the threshold, digging its claws into his spine and turning his legs to jelly. The scream banished it in a wave of adrenaline. Lightning flared around Alan's fists as he ran, holding it in his left hand while his right gripped the small vial tight. He only stopped running when he heard the boss crash to the ground behind him, screeching and wailing. The dreadful sound had a new dimension this time around, setting the crystals in the walls to ring in agonising sympathy.

Alan turned and, in a split second, fired. He had been channelling Lightning Strike for long enough that the bolt flew almost perfectly straight, right down the open, screaming gullet of the boss. The giant rat spasmed, limbs flailing as its health bar dropped drastically and it rolled over, paws twitching in the air, its rocky fur scraping up a cloud of dust and dirt from the floor. Alan peered up into the darkness but couldn't see any of the hanging rocks directly above it. He didn't have time to look for long, though, as the boss rat flipped itself over again, standing on shaking legs and staggering towards him. It kept its head down, eyes staring daggers at Alan while faint wisps of steam escaped through its nostrils.

Alan's stomach sank. He had really, really been hoping that the increase in level since the last time around would mean that the first strike would finish it off. Still, there was no sense worrying about that now. He ripped the cork from the vial and downed the blue liquid inside in one go. It tasted sour and burned slightly as it poured down his throat, the burning quickly turning into a fire that raced through every nerve of Alan's body in an instant before fading away again. Only a faint afterglow remained, his stomach calm, as his MP shot back up to full.

Alan fired another strike of lightning at the rat, aiming for its massive red eyes, but the power just flowed across its fur and down into the earth. He channelled one more strike as the rat approached, hoping it would open its mouth again - but it had obviously learnt from the punishment he had already dealt it and kept its mouth closed. Not wanting to waste any more MP, Alan aimed for its eyes again but the rat dodged sideways, finding new strength in its legs. The bolt struck near its rump and Alan groaned as the lightning again flowed down into the earth. The rat let out a muffled scream all the same, having the willpower to keep its vulnerable mouth clamped shut even in the midst of pain. Alan saw why.

The base of its tail was badly burnt and blistered, right where the long, rocky fur that covered the rat's body gave way to the fine, almost invisible hair covering its tail. While the rat fixed its eyes back on him and bounded forward in ever-greater strides, Alan came up with a plan.

He flung himself to the side as the rat charged at him, ignoring the pain that shot through his ribs as he slammed into the ground. The rat skidded to a halt behind him and - turning incredibly quickly, given its bulk - charged back again. Alan flung himself to the side again, and then yet again as the boss rat made a third pass. All he needed was one chance. It was a stupid, risky chance but if the rat just behaved -

The fourth time he didn't fling himself quite far enough to the side and the rat's shoulder clipped his foot, spiralling him across the floor and grinding one arm raw. The fifth time he dodged it fully, the pain fuelling him, but his leg gave out on the sixth and again the rat knocked into him, sending him flying across the cavern. The sole saving grace was that it flung him into the carved side, where the floor was smoother although no softer.

Alan reached into his belt for the health potion vial but the boss wasn't about to give him the chance to heal. It reared up on its hind legs and slammed down again, narrowly missing Alan and sending shards of rock and dirt flying through the air. He cast his eyes up in desperation but the roof above was smooth and finished, with none of the hanging rocks that peppered the cavernous side. The rat stomped towards him and he scrabbled back, sure that it was about to come crashing down on him. Everything he had done, everything he had gambled and risked, everything he still needed to do, ruined. Why had he come here alone? Didn't he know his friends better than that?

The rat peered down at him as though it could read his thoughts, hissing ragged breaths through its scorched jaw. Then it twisted and turned, swinging its tail around to whip at Alan. Alan's heart leapt. He'd been waiting for this.

As the thick, meaty tail smacked into him he curled his body around it, clinging on even as the air was driven from his lungs and his ribs cried out in protest. He could feel the short tail hairs pressed into his cheek, feel the soft and unprotected flesh underneath. He didn't have the air or strength to say it out loud but in his mind, he screamed it.

Static Shock.

The lightning stabbed into the rat's tail, worming its way in and up through the boss monster's body and seizing it from the inside out. The giant rat convulsed then stiffened, the motion flinging Alan free as his arms lost their strength. He fell to the ground and skidded a little way before coming to a halt. He had to fumble a health potion from his belt and into his mouth - it tasted sweet and warming - before his body found the strength to stand. He couldn't stop now. He couldn't even afford to slow down now.

Slowly at first, then faster, he raced for the rat's head. He had no idea how long the stun would take to wear off; already the big monster was beginning to stir, ears twitching and clawed toes curling. By the time he reached its front legs, he could see the tendons writhing under its furred skin, see it straining to close its jaw. By the time he reached its head, it was starting to shake, limbs jerking and straining against the paralysis. It tracked him with its closest eye as he approached, vile and red and full of hate.

He didn't give it a chance to act on that hate. He brought his dagger arcing down in a two-handed plunge straight into the eyeball. It sank in with a disgustingly firm resistance and he felt the body strain, heard a scream escape its lungs through a clenched windpipe. He channelled lightning for as long as he dared then, still gripping the dagger by its hilt, fired the bolt down into the beast. The lightning rode the metal blade and cooked the giant rat from the inside out, its health bar vanishing in seconds. The beast couldn't thrash, still held by Static Shock, and so Alan only knew it was over when it finally fell limp and the message appeared across the bottom of his vision.

**** Dungeon Boss: Giant Earth Rat killed (+500 XP) ****
**** Dungeon Cleared! (First time solo: +500XP) ****
**** You have reached Level 9! ****
**** Attributes Increased! ****

Alan slumped against the cooling body, barely noticing when it began to dissolve away into sand that trickled through the cracks in the floor. He forced himself to close his eyes, to breath, as the roaring, crashing tide of blood beat through his veins, adrenaline and pain mixing together and shaking him wildly. His wounds had closed, thanks to the potion, but he still ached madly all over once the warm afterglow of levelling up began to fade. Not that it mattered. He had done it.

His rewards fell out of the last of the mess that had been the Giant Earth Rat. A ring - polished copper set with a red stone - lay on the ground next to a pair of fine leather gloves. There was an emblem stitched into the back of the gloves with silvery thread - when Alan turned them around he saw it was a trio of rats, tied together at their tails and rearing away from each other. He shuddered. Now there was a horrid thought. He didn't want to imagine what *that* meant. He'd worry about both of his new items in the morning. Hopefully, by then his head would be a little clearer. He stashed the gloves in his pack and slipped the ring into a pocket on his belt, then stood wearily. His MP was low, his health was full and he was absolutely exhausted. He tried to think back, to work out how long it had been since he had last slept and realised that it had been the first time in the dungeon, over twenty hours ago. He had fought the giant earth rat twice in a single day and he had the deep, bone-level weariness to prove it.

Laughing at the absurdity of it, he rose to his feet and set himself in the direction of the exit. Though his bed was not far now, he wasn't home yet and there was still the matter of the forest to navigate. He put one foot in front of the other and staggered on.

CHAPTER SIXTEEN

Alan woke to a scream.

Reacting even before he had opened his eyes, he rolled to one side. That just resulted in him tangling himself further in the bedsheets and falling off of the mattress, slamming shoulder-first into the floor. The layers of padding that he had just involuntarily wrapped himself in prevented any real damage but he still cursed as he pulled himself free, trying to work out who was in danger.

A woman stood in the doorway to his bedroom. Through bleary eyes, Alan recognised her as a Sheila, one of the women who worked the field next to his dad's. They had spoken every now and then, usually about the latest failed crop. What the hell was she doing in his house?

"Thief!" Sheila gasped, finally stopping her screaming. "Intruder! I don't know what you think you're doing in my house but I'll have the guard on you for this! Guard! Guard!"

Memory and realisation hit Alan like an angry giant earth rat. He'd been so tired the previous night that when he'd left the forest he'd made the rest of the journey half-asleep. He hadn't thought to look through the house when he had staggered in. He hadn't thought to check who lived here now.

"Sorry," he said, holding up his hands in apology. "Wrong house!"

That hurt to say. The house was right - it was Sheila who was wrong. He saw it in her eyes that she knew the same but that didn't stop her from stepping back as though she had been slapped, face turning pale and her cries turning to shocked gasps.

"The wrong house?" she spluttered. "Why, you cheeky little sod! If you think I won't -"

But Alan didn't hear the rest of the threat. He scooped up his pack and barged past her, Sheila shrinking away from him as he ran from the room and the house. He traded one kind of oppressive atmosphere for another; as he stepped outside, Sheila still shrieking away from upstairs, he could feel the pressure of the storm bearing down on him. The clouds seemed low enough to touch, thick and black and rumbling in a never-ending grumble that he could feel in his bones. Fine weather to fight for your life in.

It was light enough out, despite the clouds, that he knew he had overslept. He could blame his little night-time dungeon adventure for that. He still felt tired - especially now that the adrenaline from his sudden awakening was wearing off - and every part of him ached. A quick check of his HP showed him that he was fully healed, at least. The health potion hadn't been quite as thorough as Carl's magic, no matter what the numbers said.

He didn't bother trying Carl and Ella's house. He headed instead for the town hall, dodging his way through yet another market that had sprung up. The streets were full of villagers and the majority of the faces that he passed were dominated by a set of glassy, glazed-over eyes. One or two still showed terrified awareness but the majority were dull and lifeless. He tried not to think about what that meant for them; for his dad. Normally he would have pushed it out of mind, concentrated on the task at hand. Unfortunately, that wasn't any more pleasant a prospect.

Dodging between the crowd, Alan reached the covered steps to the town hall. Ella and Carl were nowhere to be seen - but then Alan heard a pointed cough and wheeled around to see them looking up at him. Both of them carried small bundles wrapped in cloth and both of them stared at him - Carl in confusion and Ella in suspicion. Ella was wrapped in a long cloak that bulged strangely round her.

"Sorry, I slept late and -"

"Why?" Ella chucked her bundle at Alan and he caught it awkwardly, peeling aside the rough cloth to see leather and the glint of metal. "Up late? Nice cloak by the way. New?"

Her tone made it clear that she knew the answer. Her body language made it even clearer what her real question was. The past few days had changed her. Normally Alan knew she would have stood with her arms crossed and a mean scowl on her face - he'd been on the end of enough lectures about skipping fieldwork to be all too familiar with that routine. Now, though, her hands flexed by her hips, inching their way towards the bulge of the heavy mace that hung from her belt under the cloak.

"... promise you won't get angry?"

"Sure," Carl said, shrugging.

"No," said Ella.

Carl looked to his sister, who stared at Alan.

"Come on, really?"

"If he has to ask then there's no way I'm not gonna be angry," Ella said. "He did something stupid again. I just want to know how stupid."

"You don't know that," Alan said, trying to muster up a little hurt confusion. "Maybe I -"

"You cut the party link so we couldn't tell where you were going, which means you didn't want us to know. Which means it was to do something stupid. Am I wrong?"

"Well, no," Alan said, holding the bundle as a barrier between him and Ella. "But in my defence, I -"

"Where?"

Well, there was no getting out of this. Time to start the day as he'd probably end up finishing it - by meeting the pain head-on.

"… I went through the dungeon again."

The air around them filled with the manically happy chatter of the market and the distant rumble of thunder. Alan waited for his friends to react, bundle still ready to shield him, but they just stood there, staring at him. Carl's jaw dropped slightly but he didn't say anything. Ella's face was completely blank and still.

"Well," Carl said eventually, choosing his words slowly, "that was -"

"Suicidal," Ella snapped.

"I was going to say dumb," Carl muttered.

"No, it was suicidal," Ella said, growling between her teeth. "You should be dead now, Alan, rat chow."

"But he isn't," Carl said. "He's fine! Not a scratch on him!"

"Actually," Alan said, "I could use some of that healing magic if you get a chance."

Carl's expression soured.

"Oh you stupid idiot," he said with a sigh. "Hold still."

He dropped his bundle to the steps, placing one hand on Alan's arm and reaching into his pack with the other. Alan felt the now all-too-familiar glow of the healing magic flow through him. His health might have already been full but this wiped away some of the lingering aches.

"Thanks," he said, but Carl just shook his head and muttered under his breath in response.

"So, what," Ella said, "you just forgot everything we talked about yesterday? You disappearing isn't going to help. Getting eaten by rats underground won't look any different to the bandits than you running away."

"I wasn't trying to get eaten," Alan said, "I was trying to get stronger. You said it yesterday, we needed to take risks if we were going to level up enough."

"Yeah, smart risks," Ella snapped back. "As a party. Not running headfirst into the night towards a series of fights that nearly took us all out when we faced them together, let alone when it was just you! What were you thinking?"

"I wasn't thinking, okay?" Alan shouted. A few of the villagers in the market glanced over before turning back to their wares. "I was going by my gut, just like you said!"

"I never told you to run off and die by yourself!" Ella roared. This time her hand actually did go to her mace and for a second Alan was sure that she was going to pull it free and swing at him. "I wanted you to stop constantly second-guessing yourself, not turn your damn brain off!"

"Well what does it matter?" Alan clenched the bundle of cloth and leather tighter. "I don't even know how to fix my dad! What does it matter what happens to me?"

"Shut it!"

Alan blinked, refocusing on his surroundings.

Carl had stepped between the two of them, arms outstretched while his sister glowered at Alan.

"Seriously, there's no time for this." Carl stabbed one finger at Alan. "You need to get your head on straight because there's a whole lot of bandits who want to take it clean off. You can't help your dad if you're dead."

"And you!" He turned on his sister. "You need to ... well, you've actually got a really good point."

He glanced back over his shoulder at Alan.

"She's right, man, that was real stupid of you."

Back to Ella.

"Now's not the time though," he said. "You can kill him if we survive this."

"Oh I will," Ella said, flashing Alan a terrifying grin.

"Great, fine, whatever." Carl sighed and lowered his arms. Alan noticed a clean linen bandage poking out from under one of his sleeves. "Don't suppose fighting a giant rat by yourself gave you any clues on how to use the star rod?"

"None," Alan said. "I guess I figured we were never going to get it to make sense overnight. No point worrying about it, given the ... you know."

"Murderous horde of bandits?"

"Yeah," Alan said, rolling his eyes, "thanks, Ella."

"Fine," Carl said, "for now, maybe we think about how not to get murdered by said horde?"

"Well you two can get dressed for a start," Ella said.

Alan turned his attention back to the bundle in his arms. Pulling the cloth back fully, he found a sheet of thick leather that had been polished to a glossy shine and cut into shape. As far as he knew, nobody in the village had ever seen a cow in good enough health to provide such a fine piece of hide but there it was. He turned it over in his hands and peered closely at it.

**** Leather Breastplate (Low Quality) ****

With a little help from Carl - and a lot of help from Ella, who took a sadistic delight in pointing out that they were trying to put it on upside-down - Alan worked his way into the armour. It fit snugly across his body, secured in place by metal buckles at the side and across the shoulders. Also in the pack were plates for his arms and legs - low-quality leather vambraces and greaves respectively. The plates of leather weren't too heavy and were surprisingly manoeuvrable once he got used to them. He, in turn, helped Carl strap on a similar set. By the time they were done they looked …

Well, they looked ridiculous. Having said that, Alan was sure that he wanted the armour for the next time they faced down any rat bigger than normal.

"Market?" Alan raised an eyebrow at Carl, who nodded.

"Found someone selling them while we were waiting for you," he said. "No idea where they got them from."

"Same place they got the bread, I guess. Don't suppose they had … I don't know, weapons? More magic rings?"

"No, that's the first thing we wondered too" Carl laughed. "Pity. I could do with another dagger; one's fine but I keep worrying I'm going to lose it."

Alan thought for a second then dug around in his pack, pulling out the spare dagger he had looted the night before. He went to toss it to Carl, thought better of it, and instead handed it over handle first. Healing magic or not, they didn't need any stupid, self-inflicted injuries right now.

"Thanks," Carl said. "The leather armour, though - that's not the craziest thing we found for sale."

He leaned in close with a conspiratorial whisper.

"Wait until you see what Ella's wearing," he hissed.

"I heard that," Ella said. Alan thought he saw a smile flicker across her face. "I was going to keep this a surprise until the bandits showed up but since you're so eager …"

She shrugged the cloak back and over her shoulders in one fluid motion. As it slipped to the ground Alan understood why it had looked so odd on her. Her torso was clad in a thick metal shell, like his own breastplate but forged from a dull grey iron. Her arms and legs were covered in thin rings of the same metal, interlocked like fish scales. The metal was plain and without any fancy detailing and gave off the impression of rugged, honest utility.

"Nice, right?" Ella laughed at Alan's bug-eyed expression. "Iron breastplate, mail shirt and chausses. Set me back a pretty serious amount of copper but who cares about that? I'd like to see a bandit get through this!"

She banged one fist against her chest with a dull clank, an infuriatingly satisfied look on her face. Alan still thought he saw a flicker of fear behind it but said nothing; instead making an appreciative grunt and looking back down at his own armour. It didn't look anywhere near as impressive but he didn't envy Ella having to carry the weight of all that metal - not that she was showing any signs of being slowed down.

Alan looked up to the sky and saw the sun just starting to rise above the houses that lined the town square. He concentrated and pulled up the clock. 09:32. Late enough that it was no longer too early for the bandits to arrive. Any minute now …

"Stop worrying about it," Ella said. She must have seen his expression because her own firmed up again, serious and still. "We don't have the time."

"She's right," Carl said. "While you were off being an idiot last night we were doing a little bit of research."

"Research?" Alan tugged at the bottom of his breastplate, smoothing out the thin shirt he had underneath.

"Yeah," Ella said. "You remember what happened last time you asked for help?"

"Oh yeah," Alan said. "The base - the rebuild that was - something about an … admin?"

"Yeah," Carl said, "that. Well, Ella here tried again last night after we - when we had the house to ourselves."

There was a lot to unpack behind his words and none of it was good.

"Whatever the rebuild period was," Ella said, "it's … well, it's not over but it's further along. I found -"

"Pages and pages of information!" Carl exclaimed, his eyes lighting up. "A whole library of different articles on all sorts of things about what's happened! Not everything, sure, but so much! I've never seen so many words written down in one place before, Alan! It was amazing! This whole … whole framework, this system -"

"It's a game," Ella said flatly.

Carl shot her a sharp look, as though she had just ruined some big surprise, and shut his mouth.

"What's a game?" Alan frowned. "The … the bandits?"

"Everything," Ella said. "The magic, the monsters, everything. Some great big game that the Old World people used to play with their computers, only … real. From what I read and what Carl put together -"

Alan saw Carl grin to himself, despite his surprise being ruined.

"- we should all be in a - a sort of shared dream inside a computer," Ella said. "Everything would look and feel real and there'd be adventures and monsters but no real pain; we'd be able to wake up whenever we wanted and go do whatever it was that Old World people did."

"But this is real," Alan said. "Look, we've both had the bruises to prove it. My dad -"

"Yeah, this is real." Ella's expression softened, just a fraction. "It's all jumbled up but this is real. Mixed up with the game but still real. It's like … whatever did this, whatever's in charge, the system is still figuring it out. It started with the easy stuff first and now it's getting more complicated. The longer it has to work, the more everything is going to change. I think."

"You think?"

"Yeah, I think." Her expression turned frosty once more. "There's too much information to dig through in a single night and I still don't understand what half the words Carl used meant but I did the best I could, okay?"

"Okay, okay!" Alan held his palms up in surrender. "I get it. Does it help us beat the bandits?"

Ella's shoulders slumped.

"No," she said softly, "probably not. But if we get through today, maybe it'll help us figure out what's going on."

"Maybe fix it?" Alan asked hopefully.

Ella looked to Carl, who shrugged.

"Maybe," she said. "Maybe."

"Well," Carl said, breaking the silence with a cough, "I might have something that'll help. I -"

His words were cut off by the resounding toll of a bell; far deeper and louder than the village's old church bell could manage. It rang out only once but lingered for longer than was reasonable. Alan could feel it in his bones but after a second he realised he couldn't actually hear it; the sound entered his head directly, bypassing his ears and resonating deep within him.

**** Settlement Event Started ****

**** <u>Riverford Village: Invasion!</u> ****

***** An enemy force has been detected en route to Riverford Village! *****

***** Defeat the enemy force or persuade them to stand down to remove the threat to the settlement. *****

**** Time until invasion begins: 00:09:59 ****

Alan knew from the way Ella and Carl flinched that they had heard the bell and read the message too; that didn't surprise him. What did surprise him was the instant change in the behaviour of the villagers in the market. Even before the bell had stopped echoing around his head, every villager began to pack up their stalls with impressive efficiency. Wares disappeared into baskets, stalls broke down into bundles of cloth, and within seconds people began to stream out of the square, all of them heading in one direction.

"Where are they going?" Alan said. He didn't even bother asking whether this was the bandits arriving; even his luck wasn't bad enough that some other force would try to invade on the same day. He spotted his dad in the crowd and, barely thinking, shouldered his way past Carl and Ella, diving into the stream of bodies. People flowed around him but it was still tough to reach his dad through the throng, and they were almost out of the village square by the time Alan managed to grab his shoulder.

"Where are you going?" he yelled, straining to make himself heard over the din of hundreds of footsteps in uncanny synchronicity.

His dad looked back at him with wild eyes, eyes finally matched by the look of horror on his face. There was recognition there, and concern too, but Alan didn't dare let himself think that the control over his dad had been broken.

"Bandits are coming," the thing with his dad's body gasped, "we've got to get to shelter! We'll be safe in the church! Come on!"

In that moment, Alan's heart broke a little in a way he hadn't known it could. The panic in his dad's voice, the concern - even for a stranger - and the thought of running from the fight with him; it all beat him down just a little too far. He let himself be carried along by the crowd for long enough to feel guilty about it, the way one felt guilty about wasting daylight in bed or using good water to wash. Only the distant sounds of Ella and Carl shouting his name anchored him in place. The river of people broke around him and his dad was swept away. By the time his friends reached him, Alan was stood alone in a silent street, the villagers gone.

To their credit, neither Carl nor Ella asked him if he was okay. When he told them, in dull, mechanical terms that the villagers were seeking refuge in the church, they only nodded.

They passed a few stragglers on the way to the village gates, villagers who had been out towards the walls and now raced to the church with a grim determination. Each of them met the group's gaze; none of them offered to stay and fight. A few warned them to take refuge in the church but none of them waited around to see if their advice was heeded.

Rounding the corner of the last house before the wall, Alan was shocked to see that the village's defences had been upgraded considerably overnight. Where there had previously been crumbling stone and mortar from an earlier age, kept intact in places by strong-willed crawling ivy, there were now stout wooden posts of impossibly uniform logs sunk deep into the ground. Solid, utilitarian ladders were spaced evenly along the walls and led up to a walkway that looked to be at least a couple of paces deep. The gateway – which for as long as Alan had lived had been a tired metal pole that nobody had dared lower, for fear that its rusted hinge would snap clean off – was now a broad archway, covered by an interlocking grill of thick wooden slats studded through with metal clasps. There was even a small hut off to one side, in which Alan could see a gently steaming mug sat on a low table.

"Did either of you do this?" he asked – but saw immediately from his friends' gawking that they hadn't.

"I wish," Ella breathed. "I mean, there were articles in the guide about building your own houses and things but I didn't see anything like this."

"I saw something about settlements," Carl said. "It mentioned basic defences but I never …" He trailed off. "This is good, though. I mean, it is good, right?"

"Better than nothing," Alan said. Through the thick grille across the gateway, he could just make out dark shapes and smoke, with the latter drifting above the walls along with the harsh, choking rumble of Old World vehicles.

"Way to be optimistic," Carl muttered.

"Ask me how optimistic I'm feeling tomorrow," Alan replied. "Think we should … go up there?"

"One second," Ella said. She closed her eyes and furrowed her brow and before Alan could ask what they were waiting for a message popped up in front of him.

**** Party Invite received from Fighter Ella ****
**** Accept: yes/no ****

"Yes," he said softly. He caught Ella's eye as she looked back up and nodded solemnly to her. She nodded back, her jaw set in determination.

"I don't suppose we're waiting for the others?" Carl sighed. "I mean, I know what they were like yesterday but I guess I hoped they'd be here. At the end, I mean. Even if it was just so Samuel could tell us they were right."

"… I don't think so," Alan said sadly, shaking his head. "I hope they're somewhere safe."

Despite the animosity between their groups, he realised that he genuinely meant it. He had no idea where "safe" was any more but at the very least he hoped the four older villagers were far, far away. He couldn't find it in himself to wish them ill. Not now. It was amazing what a bandit invasion did for one's priorities.

"Well then," Carl said, "no point waiting. Let's go say hello. At least we'll know what we're dealing with."

As it turned out, when Alan made it to the walkway and poked his head above the top of the posts – which had been neatly sharpened into perfect spikes – the answer was nothing good. Or, as he heard Ella mutter under her breath, "utter shite".

A small army of bandits faced them from the road below. "Small" was debatable – there shouldn't have been more than a couple of dozen of them but every time Alan tried to count them he soon lost track; the only count that mattered was that he, Carl and Ella were desperately outnumbered. "Army", though, felt all too appropriate. While Alan had been expecting a disorganised mob of bandits, the riders below were organised into terrifyingly neat rows; four abreast and curling back behind the turn of the road.

Each of them was dressed in an outlandish mixture of leathers and furs, studded through with rusted metal in all sorts of improbable - yet intimidating - places. They were armed with knives and poles and ugly clubs of metal and wood twisted together. The sole point of light in it all was the conspicuous absence of any of their dreaded guns. Each bandit sat astride one of their old world vehicles; battered, lean shapes that hung low to the ground with a wheel at each end and great antlers rearing up for the bandits to grip. They looked like beasts caught in mid-leap; as Alan stared at the nearest, he was sure that its rusted metal surface was writhing slightly, like muscles corded under skin.

"Think they're here for us?" Carl asked. Alan didn't turn to look but could practically hear Ella rolling her eyes.

"What are they waiting for?" Ella hissed through clenched teeth. "Why aren't they doing anything?"

Alan concentrated on the system message that had announced the invasion. The counter was at just over ninety seconds.

"I don't think they can do anything yet," he said. "I think it's like you said - this is a game, sort of. Games have rules, right? And the rules - whatever it is that's sending us messages - won't let them start until the timer runs down."

"They're NPCs, then," Ella said.

A quick peek over the wall allowed Alan to confirm that they were, in fact, NPCs. They ranged in level from five to nine, none of them stronger than him - but the strongest outranked Carl and Ella and that was before you took the sheer number of bandits into account.

"We've got a plan though, right?" A sliver of worry broke through Carl's voice as he turned to his sister. "Come on, you were going on about having a plan earlier."

"Stick together, fight them in small groups, run if there are too many." Ella's voice, at least, held firm. "Wear them down over time and try not to get cornered."

"That's a terrible plan," Carl moaned.

"Yeah," Ella said, "but it's the best we've got. Unless you found a book on what to do in a fight between a big group and a small group?"

"I think you're supposed to try and be the big group," Carl said. He wilted under the combined stares from Alan and Ella. "Right, not helping."

"Screw this," Alan said. "They won't attack until the timer runs down but there's nothing saying we have to wait."

Bracing himself to be hit by a rock - or worse - Alan straightened up and stood tall behind the top of the wall. Behind him, he heard Carl curse and Ella sigh. Alan didn't let that stop him; he called lightning to his hand and above him, the clouds rumbled in sympathy. He held it in his hands for a few seconds, channelling in enough power to hit more-or-less true, then let it fly at the biggest, meanest bandit he could see. The bolt struck the bandit square-on in the chest, small fingers branching off to ground themselves in the metal studs of their armour. The man convulsed and fell sideways from his saddle.

**** Bandit Fighter killed (+200 XP) ****
**** Faction Reputation (Riverside Bandits) lost! ****
**** Invasion countdown advanced! ****
**** Invasion has begun! ****
**** Enemy Force remaining: 24 ****

CHAPTER SEVENTEEN

As the dead bandit fell from his saddle, the bandits around him roared - literally - into life. The front row abandoned their vehicles - bikes, Alan suddenly recalled - and dashed towards the village gate on foot, dragging large rusted chains behind them. Alan didn't have time to focus on them, however; the rest of the bandits didn't wait to fill the air between them and the gate with a barrage of rocks. Some of them wielded small slings; others just used their bare hands. The effect, either way, was the same - a driving rain of projectiles that forced Alan back down behind the relative safety of the top of the wall, arms over his head as Ella and Carl hunkered down and swore. Alan was sure they were swearing at the bandits and not him. Mostly sure, anyway.

"Well there goes any chance we had of thinking up a better plan," Ella yelled.

"We had a minute left," Alan yelled back, "what sort of plan were you going to come up with in a minute?"

"It was a work in progress!"

"Well think fast!"

"Guys, the gate!" Carl, who was laid prone on the walkway, pointed down at the archway and Alan turned to see what was happening.

The bandits with the chains had made it to the gate easily under the cover of the barrage and had looped the chains through the grille that blocked their access to the village. Alan swore as he realised what they were trying to do and - ignoring the cries from Carl and Ella - crawled his way to the ladder down. By the time he had made it to the gate - in the shadow of the wall he was at least able to sprint, shielded from the rocks - the bandits had secured four separate chains to the wood and metal and fled back to their bikes, which they were already turning around. Alan didn't wait to give them a chance to rev up their engines; he grasped the nearest chain and cast lightning directly into it. The chains glowed with the heat of the bolt that crackled through them, scorching the wood around them black. The grille made it hard for Alan to make out any detail on the other side but even he couldn't miss the thudding explosion that flared into life at the other end of the chain. His dad had once told him that Old World vehicles had been powered by explosions; the lightning had let them all out at once.

**** Bandit Fighter killed (+200 XP) ****

**** Enemy Force remaining: 23 ****

The sudden shock of the explosion cost Alan precious seconds; by the time he had recovered his wits and cast Lightning Strike on the next chain in line the bandits had already disconnected it. That trick would only work once. Alan doubted he had another 23 tricks left in him.

"Ladders!"

Alan whipped his head around as Carl cried out; over the top of the wall, a dozen metres down from the brother and sister, appeared the grizzled face of one of the bandits. Ella was there in seconds, whirling her mace around in an arc that carried it directly into the bandit's teeth; even from the gate, with a rain of rocks still thudding into the ground around him, Alan heard the horrible crunch of bone. The figure dropped back out of sight but up and down the wall, in both directions, more bandits appeared, pulling themselves over the sharp spikes with no apparent regard for their own bodies. A distant part of Alan wondered if the minds inside them could still feel the pain - or had the system controlling them stolen even that?

**** Bandit Fighter killed (+200 XP) ****

**** Enemy Force remaining: 22 ****

"Where the -" Alan started to yell, then realised there was no way they could keep up a conversation over the distance and rapidly approaching combat.

**** [L. Disciple Alan]: Where the hell did they pull ladders from? ****

**** [Fighter Ella]: No idea - they just appeared! ****

**** [Scholar Carl]: Duck! ****

Alan saw Carl launch a wild stab over Ella's head with his dagger, causing an approaching bandit to jerk back and giving Ella time to introduce her mace to his ribs. The figure fell back but didn't stop moving; he was too far away for Alan to be sure but he'd guess that it was one of the more experienced bandits.

**** [L. Disciple Alan]: Hold on, I'm coming to you guys! ****

**** [Scholar Carl]: No way - we can't let them trap us up here! ****

**** [Scholar Carl]: You need to get out of here - we'll meet you somewhere! ****

Alan heard the dull thud of bodies hitting dirt behind him; he turned to see half a dozen bandits dropping down from the wall, not bothering with the ladders. His first cast of Lightning Strike missed; his second only caught the lead bandit on the arm. While the woman screeched and fell back, clutching at burned flesh, she was on her feet again in seconds. Her companions stalked towards Alan, not paying any attention to the stench of burned skin and leather that now filled the air.

**** [L. Disciple Alan]: Guys I'm getting cut off down here. ****

**** [Fighter Ella]: Why do you think we want you to run? RUN! ****

His MP was too low to cast another bolt of lightning at the approaching bandits, low enough that he could feel the emptiness inside of him gnawing away. Alan didn't dare look back up at the wall, back at Carl and Ella - he knew that if he saw them fall or be threatened there he wouldn't be able to leave. Instead, he ran; darting through the hail of stones that had all but stopped, one arm over his head. Behind him - as though they had been waiting for the hunt to begin - he heard the bandits break into a run after him. As Alan passed out of range of the barrage he heard a rumble overhead and felt the first few drops of rain smack into his head.

If there was one advantage that he had, one slim hope, it was that he knew the village and the bandits didn't. He'd spent his entire life ducking and running through the streets. He knew which alleys ended blind; he knew which walls dropped off sharply on the other side. Memories of a dozen years spent exercising what little youthful energy he'd had in the confines of a village that felt far too small were now his best chance of losing the bandits. He just had to be careful not to lose them all.

He snared the first bandit thanks to a sharp turn and a low garden wall; in the precious seconds that the former broke line of sight with the bandits he hopped over the latter, hugging himself into the shadow of the brickwork. A few seconds later he heard the bandits charge past; only when they had all passed did he pull himself shakily back over the wall and - against all his better judgement - jog after them. He caught up to the rearmost bandit with ease once the group began to slow, confused and without a target. He didn't allow himself time to think of the bandit as anything but a threat, didn't allow himself time to hesitate, sinking his dagger - the new, serrated one that he had gained the night before - into the bandit's back. The man stiffened then fell limp, crying out with a choking, gurgling moan as he fell. Alan barely had time to pull the blade free before the rest of the bandits turned on him and charged once more, with no apparent concern for their fallen friend.

**** Bandit Fighter killed (+200 XP) ****
**** Enemy Force remaining: 19 ****

Alan blinked away the rain as he ran, focusing on the message. He had missed a few in his initial dash away from the bandits; Carl and Ella were doing their part as well. As he watched, the number ticked down again - but this time there was no message about experience gain. He hadn't missed any either; he decided that there must be a maximum range, outside of which the party didn't share in each others' kills. Despite the rain - which was now falling hard, fat droplets ricocheting off of the ground - and being chased by murderous bandits, Alan found himself strangely annoyed by the lost experience. Was this why Carl and Ella had been so annoyed with him for tackling the dungeon solo? The drive to gain experience and get stronger made sense but there was more to it than that. Whatever. Now wasn't the time to puzzle over exactly what influence the rules of the game had over him.

**** [L. Disciple Alan]: Where are you guys? ****

**** [Fighter Ella]: Argh! ****

**** [L. Disciple Alan]: Ella! ****

**** [Fighter Ella]: I'm fine, dumbass - you startled me, that's all. ****

**** [Scholar Carl]: We're by the old well - there are maybe seven or eight bandits chasing us but we managed to get away for the moment. They're not too bright. ****

**** [L. Disciple Alan]: Only seven? ****

**** [Scholar Carl]: Or eight. I'm sorry, I didn't stop to ask them. ****

Alan looked quickly back over his shoulder, not trusting his feet to keep their grip on the rain-slicked ground for too long. There were only four bandits chasing him that he could see but he was sure there had been more than that chasing him to begin with.

**** [L. Disciple Alan]: I've got four, where are the rest? ****

**** [Scholar Carl]: Shit. ****

**** [Fighter Ella]: Shit. ****

**** [Scholar Carl]: That's at least seven missing. Where the hell have they gone? I thought they were here for us? ****

**** [Fighter Ella]: Here for Alan, you mean. ****

**** [L. Disciple Alan]: Thanks. ****

**** [Scholar Carl]: You know what I meant. ****

Alan ducked around another corner and squeezed himself into the doorway of a house. This time he got to see the bandits charge past, running in perfect unison with blank faces and absolute silence. He didn't wait for them to get far; he ran after them at full speed, hoping and praying that the rainfall would mask his footsteps. Already the world was beginning to turn grey and close in, the torrent of water now falling from the sky veiling everything in the distance. He caught up to the trailing bandit quickly and this time he grabbed for them with his free hand, channelling Static Shock into his palm as he did so. The bandit seized and fell, dragging Alan down with him, paralysed and silent. Alan finished them off with the dagger and tried not to vomit as he did so. The bandits had tormented the village for years, had tried to kill him and his friends - and yet, when he got up close and personal, he still couldn't stomach taking another human life.

**** Bandit Fighter killed (+200 XP) ****

**** Enemy Force remaining: 17 ****

He looked up to see that the other bandits had disappeared into the storm. His plan had worked too well; he had lost the last three that had been chasing him. He hoped they would keep charging straight ahead, following the street around the edge of the village back towards the gate - but he didn't fancy rushing after them by himself in this weather. If the rain got much heavier - and even as he thought it, the force of the raindrops battering into him continued to increase - he'd end up running into them before he saw them.

**** [L. Disciple Alan]: Where are you guys now? ****

**** [Fighter Ella]: Back by the old well again; we managed to lose the bandits that were chasing us. ****

**** [Scholar Carl]: Hit and run was only going to work for so long against them; I don't know, it seems like they're getting smarter. ****

**** [L. Disciple Alan]: I've lost all mine. That's seventeen bandits running around somewhere in the village - where the hell are they going? ****

Part of Alan hoped they'd decided to cut their losses and go home but it was a small, cowardly part of him that he knew not to listen to. There was no system message saying that the invasion was over and his luck wasn't that good. There had to be a -

**** Sanctuary under attack! ****

Sanctuary. The church.

Alan didn't even bother sending a message to Carl and Ella. Even if he hadn't been vaguely aware of their position - an awareness that grew sharper as they grew closer - he knew the steel in them well enough to know that they'd be charging towards the church already. Towards their parents. His dad. At the thought of his dad, Alan's stomach clenched. The villagers had to know what was happening on some level. Trapped in bodies they couldn't control, trapped in the church with bandits beating down the doors - well he could only imagine the terror they were feeling. He was up and running in a heartbeat, vaulting over garden walls and dashing down alleys. He didn't have to think of the route - he knew it by instinct, a jagged path that would take him to the church as quickly as possible. He just hoped that was quick enough.

His feet kicked up waves and he charged recklessly through the rain. His visibility was next to nothing; only the world immediately around him held any colour or form and even that was obscured by the water running down his face. The air sizzled and the clouds overhead seemed close enough to touch, thick and boiling and black. A distant flash of light broke through the rain and several seconds later the distinct crack of lightning - a noise Alan now knew all too well, that he could feel in his soul - cut through the rain and the rising wind. After waiting so long he found himself curiously uninterested in seeing it strike.

A dark shape emerged out of the rain ahead of him; Alan didn't slow down. He threw lightning wildly and didn't care when it missed spectacularly; the bolt superheated the rain and threw up a cloud of hissing, spitting steam along its path. The figure flinched and fell back and Alan leapt over them, racing ahead. He was close now, far too close to be distracted.

The church loomed into being, its bell-tower stretching up into the storm and only visible due to the light that streamed from every crack and window. The main doors were closed; great thick wooden things that were always closed, the know-how of opening them lost to time and apathy. Light - soft, golden light - streamed around their edges, casting their outline out into the mid-day dark.

A lone figure was silhouetted against that outline; as Alan charged at them he realised it was the bandit woman from before, the one whose arm he had burned. The one he must have lost early on. That she had wound up at the church once she had stopped chasing him and started trying to break her way in - well, that was a terrible sign.

He skidded to a halt, kicking up water across the flagstones of the road, channelling Lightning Strike for several seconds. When he was sure of his aim he let it fly straight at her - only for the bolt to crash harmlessly against the stone wall of the church a dozen paces away, darting from raindrop to raindrop in a jagged, random path that went nowhere near the bandit woman. Alan got the sinking feeling that his earlier miss hadn't been as solely unlucky as he had first thought.

It did alert the bandit woman to his presence, though, and got her to stop attacking the church door. She wielded a long, broken section of metal pipe that had left more than a few ragged tears down the wood doors and she spun it easily around in her hand as she turned to face Alan.

"Please," Alan said, holding both palms up. "You don't have to do this."

It was an empty plea; he knew she wasn't in control, not really. Whatever the system was that controlled her now, he doubted it understood mercy. It certainly didn't seem too talkative - the woman stalked towards him, jaw set, in utter silence. Alan felt the weight of his dagger in his hand. The woman's weapon had the reach, for sure, and when he concentrated on her he realised she matched him in terms of levels. If he could just get inside of her guard -

He almost didn't get the chance to try. The bandit darted forward suddenly, moving with enough speed that Alan couldn't react fast enough to dodge her pole as it swung around and cracked into his side. He felt the pain flare through him and grasped at the metal - but fell away from it too fast, his hands clutching at air and rain. The bandit approached him again, this time bringing the pole down in a double-handed overhead swing that threatened to smash his face open. Alan managed to jerk his head out of the way at the last second but then the bandit's foot came crashing down, smashing into his chest and knocking the wind from him. His breastplate - and he'd thank Ella for that if only he lived through this - spread the force a little but he still choked and gasped as he was struck, barely keeping down the contents of his stomach. It was hard to believe that he had the bandit where he wanted them.

He grabbed for the bandit's leg, lightning streaming between his fingers, and channelled as much power through her as he could bring himself to, eyes clenched shut against the terrible light that ripped through her body. There was a thick wet splat and the weight above him fell to one side to smack messily against the cobbles. Air flooded his lungs as he took a deep, ragged breath and rolled away from the body. Only then did he open his eyes again, taking care not to look at where the bandit had fallen or where the rain was beginning to spread across the street in a pinkish hue.

**** Bandit Champion killed (+250 XP) ****

**** Enemy Force remaining: 15 ****

He retreated to the church doors with shaking steps, letting himself fall against the wood and stare out into the rain. The bandit's body was a distant lump on the ground. The world was a small stage curtained with rain and roofed with the clouds overhead. Another flash briefly lit up the sky and this time the sound came a little quicker. Again and again, the light flashed, every few seconds for nearly a minute, each time showing just enough of the distant houses and alleyways to renew the threat in Alan's mind and cast darting shadows everywhere he looked.

Only the awareness he had of Ella and Carl's positions stopped him from crying out in fear when the two dark shapes raced out of an alley towards him; their features resolving into the faces of his friends. They saw the body on the ground and Alan slumped against the doors and redoubled their speed; only when Carl reached down and cast healing magic into Alan did their faces return from terror to generalised fear.

"They're coming here," Alan said when his heart stopped trying to drill its way out of his chest.

"The bandits?" Ella looked back at the body on the cobbles. "Are you sure?"

"This is a game, remember?" Alan forced himself to stand. "Or it's at least trying to be a game. This is - this is keep-away."

"But the bandits are here for you," Carl said gently. "I mean, yeah, they're probably going to mess up the village but even so -"

"They came for me - for us - but when they lost us or we lost them … they came here," Alan said. "They tried to break into the one building in the village where everyone is sheltered and the system knew it. This whole thing has twisted up everything into the game and the bandits are twisted up too."

"Makes sense," Ella said slowly. "Explains why the system knew to send out a message that the church was being attacked."

She craned her head to look up at the building.

"… and why it's glowing too, I guess."

"So what do we do?" Carl said, brushing rainwater out of his eyes. "Just wait for them to come to us? There's more than a dozen of them out there - there's no way we can take on a dozen!"

"We don't have a choice," Alan said flatly. "If they get into the church, our parents - hell, the entire village - they all die."

"You don't know that," Carl said, "you don't know!"

"Carl," Ella said softly, laying a hand on her brother's arm, "we can't risk it. You know that."

Carl fell silent and placed his hand over his sister's, shutting his eyes in prayer.

"Maybe they won't all arrive at once?" he pleaded with the thin air.

There was no such luck. Out of the corner of his eyes, Alan saw movement in the rain; dark shapes approaching the church from the cover of the buildings ahead.

"Guys," he whispered, grasping for his dagger. "Look."

They moved forward, slowing as they came: bandits. Three at first, then another, then several more, more and more, until there were fully fifteen of them, fifteen figures standing in the storm, oblivious to the rain and the wind, all staring at Ella and Alan and Carl as they huddled in the doorway of the church. The rain ran down them in rivulets and the bandits stood as unmoving as if they were made of stone, carved and painted and left behind.

Alan stood tall and clutched the serrated knife in his hand. Carl found some steel inside of himself and stood too, a dagger in one hand and a book in the other. Ella moved in front of them both, buckler on her arm and mace in her hand, loosely hanging by her side.

"Love you guys," she whispered.

Alan tensed himself for the charge, sure that at any moment the bandits would rush forward as one. How many times could he cast Lightning Strike? Five? He'd take down five of them, he swore to himself. After that … well, he had a knife and a hand to hold it in. He knew it would hurt but he'd go down swinging. Hopefully, it wouldn't hurt for too long.

And then something happened that he hadn't been expecting: the bandits started clapping.

It was a jerky, puppet-like motion but it was clapping all the same; muffled by rain and distance and the awkward way they held onto their weapons at the same time. There was motion in their ranks; movement as the group split, making way for one at the rear to step forward between the ranks. He was tall and powerfully built, dressed in dark clothing and a strange black chest plate with faded letters stamped across the front in white. His face was - well, it was unremarkable to Alan. Whatever mask of horror and cruelty, whatever twisted monster of a man he had been expecting, it wasn't to be found here. Just another face in the crowd.

"Well done," the man at the front said. "You've put up a hell of a fight for a bunch of farmers. Pity you didn't play along like the rest of your lot cowering back there."

<Bandit King Flynn>
<Level 10>

Peering closer at the man, Alan frowned, confused, as the expected description of the man's class and level appeared over his vision. There was something wrong with it. It took him a second to realise what was missing but when the realisation hit him, it hit him hard. This man wasn't an NPC.

This man was as free-minded as Alan was.

CHAPTER EIGHTEEN

The first thought in Alan's mind was that this was some sort of trick. He tossed it aside quickly; the system so far had been honest - if not clear - about the information it gave out. If the man wasn't listed as an NPC then he must be free and fully under his own control. The second thought was that they were saved; that this man had somehow brought the bandits under control at the lost moment and the battle was now over. He dismissed that too, although not as quickly and not without regret. It was a lie he was all too eager to believe.

The third thought - the one that stuck - was that this man had been in control of the bandits from the start. It was the worst possible reality. They'd been counting on the bandits being about as intelligent as the rabbits or the goblins. At the very least, Alan had hoped they would prove no more organised. Without that edge, if it just came down to numbers, they were well and truly screwed. They had been from the start.

"You're the little lightning boy, eh?" The man - the bandit leader - pointed one finger straight at Alan. "The one who's been raising so much hell for me? The one who's been stealing from me?"

Alan stared at the man's label again:

<Bandit King Flynn>
<Level 10>

"I haven't taken anything that belonged to you," Alan replied. He hoped the rain would mask the note of terror in his voice. "The rest was all-self defence!"

A crack of lightning lit up the sky.

"Oh you've got nerve, kid," Flynn growled. "You broke into my camp! You attacked my men! You took lives that belonged to me! I couldn't even get a decent night's sleep without coming out and finding half my camp knocked out because of you! I'll show you self defence, you cheeky little sod. Gordon!"

One of the bandits staggered forward on unsure legs, carrying something in their hands. At first, Alan thought it was another rod or pipe, built from long lines of black metal. It was only when Gordon hefted it up into the crook of their shoulder, resting its length along his arm to point at Alan, that he recognised it for what it was - a gun. He'd only seen anything similar once before, also in the hands of bandits, but the older members of the village had all made it clear to the children what it was, what it represented. Alan had no idea if the system would keep him alive if he was shot by a gun but he doubted it - and he had absolutely no desire to find out.

Lightning split the sky again and in that instant of light, Alan saw the finger hooked across the trigger pull back. He opened his mouth to cry out but it was too late. A burst of light flared around the end of the gun as Gordon struggled to keep it under control. The noise - if there was any noise, although he seemed to recall that guns were supposed to be loud - was masked by the thunder and lightning. Alan flinched - and then looked down, sure that he would see a bloody mess where his body was supposed to be, his brain too slow to realise he was already dead. Nothing. His HP was full. Nothing had changed except for the look of confusion on the bandit leader's face and -

And a slight haze across the air in front of him, punctuated by a round dot of metal hanging in mid-air. As Alan watched, water began to stream down across the open air as though it was solid, an invisible window-pane hung between him and the bandits. A second later it flickered out of existence, the bullet and collected water hitting the ground with a splash and flowing quickly away.

** [Scholar Carl]: Don't say anything guys - want to keep him guessing. **

** [L. Disciple Alan]: Was that you? Since when could you do … whatever that was? **

** [Fighter Ella]: Since he went digging through the rest of his books last night, found some dull tome about walls or something. Hasn't shut up about it since. **

** [Scholar Carl]: It's called 'The History of Modern Architecture' and it just saved your life, so maybe show it a little respect. **

** [Fighter Ella]: Alan's life. I'm tougher than that. **

While the silent conversation only took a moment, that was long enough for the bandit leader to go through several emotions judging by the state of his face: confusion, doubt and finally rage, a rage that looked entirely at home on him despite his plain features. He jabbed a finger at the group again; enough warning for Carl to throw up his invisible wall and catch half a dozen metal projectiles before the gun stopped firing. Flynn snatched it from Gordon and pulled the trigger himself but nothing happened, whatever mechanism powered the weapon failing or running dry, and he threw it to the ground with an inarticulate snarl.

"Fine," he spat, "we do this the hard way. I'm going to enjoy this you little shit."

As one body, the bandits stepped forward past their leader, closing ranks to hide him from sight. Weapons were unsheathed, feet planted astride and fourteen sets of glassy eyes focused on Alan, looking straight past Ella - who still stood protectively at the front - and ignoring Carl entirely.

"I'll teach you to mess with me," Alan heard Flynn yell from behind the rest of the bandits. "Ready, and -"

"CHARGE!"

The cry came from off to Alan's right and cut through the wind, thunder and rain as though they weren't there. It reverberated down Alan's spine and he felt his heart beat faster in his chest - suddenly the bandits seemed far less significant than a second before. This, something told him, was a battle they could win. Would win. The hammer-blow of forced positivity crashed against his fears and doubts and washed them away. No message flashed across his vision - this, he realised, wasn't something the game had cooked up. This was something real: hope, as fragile as it was.

A horde of small dark blurs shot out of the storm, thundering down the street like a wave and crashing into the side of the massed bandits. The bandits turned too slowly to face the new threat and as it swept into and over them several of the men and women fell beneath it, clawing at dozens of small figures that clambered over them. The bandits fought back and any one swing from the larger bodies sent several smaller ones flying; it was only when one of the smaller assailants was sent skidding across the street to fall still at Ella's feet that Alan, by the light from the church, saw what it was.

A goblin - only, far removed from the goblins that had chased them through the forest what felt like an eternity ago. This goblin looked more complete - rather than a slack sack of flesh and branch-like limbs, this goblin had visible muscles and coarse grey hairs, spots and pores and a wrinkled little face. It was alive - or, at least, had been until a few moments ago - and fully formed, not some rough puppet. It even had clothes (albeit crude ones, little more than rags) and a long, rough knife still clutched tight in its hand.

"What the hell?" Carl leaned down to peer closer at the goblin. "Are they on our side now?"

"No idea," Alan said, "but they're hitting the bandits hard and I'd rather not waste the opportunity."

"Agreed," Ella said. "Try to keep up."

With that she darted forward, propelling herself across the street and kicking up a small bow wave as she sped through puddle after puddle, throwing herself into the melee, her mace illuminated by another bolt of lightning as she dove at the nearest bandit.

"And she gives you grief for being reckless," Carl chuckled, hefting his daggers. "Ready?"

"Hell no," Alan said. "Let's do this before I have a chance to think."

Together, the two friends dove into battle. Alan had just begun to pull together a plan in the seconds it took to reach the fray - then it was immediately rendered obsolete as took a solid blow to the face. He found his feet in seconds and a warm wave of healing magic popped his nose back into place but any desire for a plan was gone. He simply moved; moved out of the way of weapons, moved into the path of enemies and struck. With the rain and the risk of hitting allies, he didn't bother trying to throw lightning; instead, he cupped it in his palms and strove to grab and slap the bandits, pulsing lightning into them and hopping back.

It worked - partly. The bandits he struck were incapacitated with pain, even if the lightning didn't cook them outright, but for every one he struck true, another deflected his blow at the last second, sending lightning arcing out over the brawl. Within a minute of the chaos starting he was running on empty, only a sliver of MP remaining and his HP dropped by a dozen different cuts and blows. There were bodies all around him and he couldn't block them quickly enough; the world became a tangled mess of bandits and goblins and sharp metal, all of it seemingly aimed at him no matter where he stepped. He tripped backwards over a fallen bandit and was saved only when three goblins jumped for the throat of a woman bringing a rock down on him. This was torture; this was hell; he had to get away. He scrabbled along the ground for the light of the church but more bodies fell in his path - goblins, dead by the dozen and still falling.

A hand reached down to him. At first, Alan flinched away but the hand was empty and when it found him it pulled, yanking him to his feet and out of the fight. Alan found himself staring into the ruddy, sweating face of Samuel. Samuel, who had ordered him to give himself up for dead. Samuel, who had dismissed this all as Old World nonsense. Samuel, who was currently covered in blood and slime, wearing a tattered mess of rags and wielding a rusted sword and wooden shield. Behind him, the largest, meanest-looking boar Alan had ever seen brought razor-sharp hooves down onto an unlucky bandit, roaring over the sound of the rain.

"Do I want to know?"

Samuel laughed, an uncharacteristic twinkle in his eye. The effect would have been charming, were it not for the dried blood that matted his moustache. Instead, it was slightly unnerving.

"Adventures, my boy! Adventures!" There was the slightest slur to his words and a bloody wound on his forehead. Samuel patted him on the back and swung his sword - which, Alan realised, was the first sword he had ever actually seen - at a bandit. Alan didn't have time to see the outcome of that particular fight before a black mass of wings and claws burst across his vision, a cloud of birds that swirled and dove and tore through the bandits, brandishing talons like knives. Alan saw Elaine sheltering in the lee of a wall, tracking the birds with her eyes and her hands. When she spotted Alan staring at her she gave him a quick smile and a wave before focusing once more. Her husband Arthur crouched near her wielding a knife in each fist, a bandit slumped over the cobbles at his feet.

Catching his breath - and with his MP beginning to look a little healthier - Alan realised with a start that the tide had turned. The counter in the corner of his vision listed less than 10 enemies remaining while a backlog of messages hinted at plenty of experience gains from the madness. The ground was covered in goblin bodies but they had clawed the bandits down with them too. The melee had broken down into individual fights, rather than an all-encompassing war. They were almost there.

"ENOUGH!"

The bandit leader stood tall in the midst of his remaining men, snarling and kicking at a pair of goblins that danced around his feet. Alan reached out towards him - to hell with the rain - but the man uttered a word too low for Alan to hear and was gripped with a sudden red glow. It seeped out from his pores and streamed from his eyes in an instantaneous flash that mocked the lightning overhead. Veins bulged in his forehead and his next kick sent the goblins flying as though they weighed nothing at all. With an inhuman roar, he charged at the closest non-bandit. That was Samuel, who met the charge with a roar of his own - and was sent flying across the street by a back-handed blow that split his shield, smashing into the church door and falling limply to the ground.

**** [L. Disciple Alan]: Carl! Get to him now! ****
**** [Scholar Carl]: What? Oh shit - on it! ****

Swinging his two daggers fast enough that it looked like he was wielding three, Carl tumbled out of the fight and sprinted for the prone man. The goblins followed, all of them streaming away from whatever bandits they were fighting and wailing as they ran for the body of Samuel. The remaining villagers were suddenly exposed; Ella facing off against two men, her mace gone, blood streaming down her bunched fists. Another bandit fell beneath a shadowy mass of beaks, futilely beating at them in silent terror. Even with the mass of casualties, the standing villagers were still outnumbered two-to-one.

And then there was the leader. The red glow still suffused his body and left his mouth in great steaming clouds of blood-tinged vapour. In a gut-wrenching moment of horror, Alan saw that the label above his head had changed.

<Bandit King Flynn>
<Level 15 (+5)>

Flynn kicked his way across the body-strewn battleground, sending fallen bandits and goblins flying with every stride, a bloody length of metal-studded wood clasped in his hands. He moved inevitably towards Ella, who was barely holding on as it was. Alan nudged at his MP reserves; low, but enough for a distraction. He pulled the star rod from his pack with one hand, waving it above his head, and struck out with the other.

"Hey!" he yelled, throwing as much lightning as he dared at the bandit leader. "Over here!"

The lightning didn't hit anywhere near the leader but that didn't matter; the steam and light-show grabbed the man's attention. He turned and began to accelerate towards Alan, stumbling here and there when his foot came down on a body but recovering fast enough that it almost didn't matter. Alan stood his ground, waiting for Flynn, judging the timing with a cold sense of detachment. Three steps, two steps - He leapt under Flynn's swing, feeling the wood scrape the back of his pack, and flung both arms around the man's waist, capturing him in a bear hug that caught the older man by surprise. Alan didn't waste the moment; he cast Lightning Strike, his palm flat against Flynn's back, and tensed himself against the pain.

The pain never came. The lightning crackled through the bandit's chest and hit Alan too but danced across the surface of his skin. The sensation was … intense but not painful as such. Flynn, meanwhile, roared and twitched - until he grabbed Alan by the back of his cloak and shirt and pulled hard, throwing Alan clear across the street. Alan tumbled across the ground, his ribs smacking into the cobbles, until he came to a halt against a garden wall, one hand still clasped around the star rod.

**** HP: 102 / 180 ****

Groaning, Alan pulled himself to his feet. At least it was over, right?
Wrong.

The bandit king stood in the middle of the street, backlit by the odd flash of lightning and the bloody melee in front of the church. His skin steamed and seemed pinker than before but that could have been a trick of the red light that still swirled around him. The odd flicker of electricity trickled here and there across his skin, his teeth were bared in a pained snarl, but he still stood. When Alan looked at the health bar above his head he felt as though he'd been hit again, his chest seizing as the breath left his lungs. Flynn's health had dropped by only a sliver; Alan could have repeated the trick a dozen times and only reduced the man's health by half, if that. The bandit king apparently realised the same thing as his snarl turned into an equally vicious grin and he began to charge after Alan again, roaring as he did so. Alan ran from him, diving blindly into the storm, not letting himself look back. The sounds of battle disappeared almost instantly, eaten up by the rain and the wind, leaving only the thudding rain to match his heartbeat.

And footsteps. Behind him, barely audible over the rain, running footsteps. Footsteps that were growing louder with every passing second. Alan ran faster. He had to; it wasn't as though he had a plan. Only an instinct, a drive to run, a base level of fear that told him that he was prey - and prey ran if it didn't want to become dinner. He had no idea how Flynn had gained 5 levels in a heartbeat but it didn't matter; his lightning wouldn't even tickle the man with that great of a difference. The storm above him screamed down, his lungs and his ribs screamed at him from within, and behind him, Flynn just screamed; a low scream that shook Alan's soul. So he ran.

The sky flashed with lightning and the instantaneous peal of thunder that followed temporarily masked even the rain. It was so close now that Alan felt as though he could reach out and touch it. He passed Carl and Ella's house at a dead sprint and stumbled for a second over the thought of them back in the square, fighting for their lives. They'd put so much faith in him and he had no idea what he was doing, no idea where he was even going! Flynn was a monster even without his new level boost. With it, Alan realised the man could have taken the village almost single-handedly. He couldn't take Flynn down by himself; he needed something else, some kind of edge.

And then he saw it, silhouetted against the skyline as lightning struck again. A wheel began to turn in his head, unbidden. He had - well, not a plan. A plan involved thinking. This was still gut instinct but that had gotten him this far, at least. He knew the route in his bones and he turned, darting away down a side-street, past house after house. Behind him, he heard the low scream again - not quite as loud as before but closer now and no less murderous. His hands fumbled in his belt and he downed the vial in one go, coughing as a little of the sour liquid fire went down the wrong way.

They passed the edge of the village through another of the fortified gates, this one thankfully wide open. The mystery of where they had come from quickly fell behind as Alan raced. The cobble streets turned to grass and the grass turned to mud and he strained and struggled to keep upright and moving forward. Lightning, again and again, far outclassing anything he had ever conjured. It struck the church bell tower twice as he climbed up and around the side of the hill, each strike freezing an instant of time before his eyes in black and white.

His legs finally betrayed him as he reached the top. He crawled forward, digging deep into the sodden earth and scooping up great handfuls of mud as he pulled himself under the shelter - what little there was - of the dead, split tree. That was where the bandit leader found him, flat on his back with the star rod tucked under his belt, one hand beneath him and one hand clutching his side, trying to massage out the stitch. The man still glowed red but it was paler now and when he breathed his breath no longer steamed. The label over his head now only showed his level to be 12; still a titan compared to Alan. Flynn towered over Alan, a red and black silhouette against the storm, and when he reached down with his club, pressing down on Alan's chest, the strength behind it drove the wind from Alan's lungs.

"Very clever," the bandit leader boomed down. "Taking me away from my men, weakening my power. If only you had a gang of your own waiting out here you might have managed to take me down. But it's just you."

"Just me," Alan gasped. He had no idea what the bandit leader was talking about but he wasn't about to correct the man.

"Pity," the leader said, leaning harder on the end of his club. Pain shot through Alan's chest and he cried out despite himself. "You would have made a good gang member. With a few more like you and a few less of those idiots back there, I'd be unstoppable. Heirloom Online -" He spoke the words with a halting uncertainty and it was clear that they meant even less to him than to Alan. "- is the best thing that ever happened to me. I showed that little shit Gordon who the real boss was, him and all the others you cut down. I'll find more, though, and when I do I'm going to burn your shithole of a village to the ground. Everybody's going to know what happens when they cross me."

"The rod," Alan gasped. "Why ..." He slapped ineffectually at the club with his free hand.

"Because you took it from me." The bandit leader cocked his head, devilish confusion behind the red fog. "What other reason would I need? You came into my house and tried to strut around like you were on my level, like we were equals. A fucking farmer? You're not my equal you little shit. You're nothing."

If Alan had the air in his lungs for it he would have burst into laughter and possibly tears. The man was seconds away from ending his life and Alan couldn't even pretend to be scared of him. After killer vines and goblins and giant, murderous rats it was all just so petty. Flynn leaned down, supporting all of his weight on the club now, crushing Alan beneath the weight of a mountain. One foot came down hard on Alan's wrist, pinning his hand into the dirt.

"You can throw lightning around like it's nobody's business and look at you now," Flynn hissed, as he brought his head level to Alan's, his breath sour and warm on Alan's skin. "Nobodies like you don't deserve power like that. Who have you got under you, eh? Me, I've got an army!"

Anger flashed across his face. "Had an army. Well, I'll get another. Because that's what you farmers don't understand about power, why you don't have any. Hell, power's only power if you use it, keep people in their place. People like you, you don't have the guts."

"No," Alan spluttered, "but I've got something better."

He gathered the last of his strength, his dad's face at the forefront of his mind, and rocked from side to side, yanking his hand out from underneath him. The bandit leader's eyes grew wide at the sight of the sizzling, boiling power contained there, the lightning that Alan had been channelling since he had begun climbing the hill.

"Patience," he spat.

Alan couldn't tell whether it was the sheer power of the lightning or having pinned it for too long but he couldn't feel his hand. That didn't stop him from throwing it up towards the bandit leader and finally - painfully, mercifully - letting the bolt loose. Flynn jerked his head back and the bolt missed. Alan saw it in his eyes that the leader knew he had dodged it - only in the last instant did he see the dawning realisation that Alan didn't care. He had worried that the bandit king would use his last seconds well, to dive out of the way or use some other, previously hidden ability. As it turned out, there was no time. There was only the moment: the moment in which the lightning speared up from Alan's hand, dancing and dodging from raindrop to raindrop, crackling off into a thousand tiny branches that touched here and there in the sky. Only a few of those branches made it to the clouds. Only one needed to.

Alan's world turned white and quiet and very, very still.

CHAPTER NINETEEN

When Alan's mind refocused itself it was into a world of pain. Light and colour and sound bled in slowly but the pain came first; not overwhelming but certainly all-encompassing. It wrapped around him like a cocoon made of knives. It was especially bad when he moved, except for his back - that burned beneath him no matter what he did. He hoped that this meant he was alive. Life had held a lot of pain, especially over the past few days, and it didn't seem fair that death could hurt too.

He wasn't sure if his eyes had opened when he told them too. It was dark, certainly, and not as quiet as he had first thought - outside of his own heartbeat, he could hear a constant, rhythmic sound. After an agonisingly long time, he realised that it was rain. Not rain as he had heard it before. Not the driving, torrential rain that had swept through the town. It was gentle; tapping against the ground and the walls - because if he wasn't wet, which he wasn't, he had to be indoors - with barely any force at all. It was soothing and he lay there for a long, long time with barely any motion or even thought; if it wasn't for the pain he would almost have thought he was dreaming.

Eventually, though, his stomach complained enough for him to try to open his eyes again and at least start to make sense of it all. This time there was light - a soft, creeping light that was unmistakably dawn. It slid in through a set of windows at the far end of the room, drawing everything in outlines and mild shadows. He didn't recognise the sight of the room but something about it spoke to home. Not his home but home nevertheless - a pervasive, practised cosiness to the arrangement of the room.

He pushed back the sheets that covered him and gasped as the fabric brushed across his skin. Every touch was hot and painful and he when he sat up it was worse; the air burned cold against his exposed back. When he stood up, even the soles of his feet seemed burned. He couldn't see any visible injuries when he looked down at himself. The pain on his back was enough that he didn't dare try feeling back there for wounds.

Memories of the flight up the hill came rushing back. Suddenly a few things made more sense - although not, strangely, how he was still alive. It hadn't been a suicidal plan, as such, in a large part due to a lack of actual planning. He had very much wanted to live through it. He just hadn't expected to. At least now Ella would get her chance to kill him.

He found a ratty old dressing gown hanging on the back of the door and pulled it around himself. The fabric was far rougher than he would have liked even if he hadn't felt like his whole body was an open wound but it was all that he could see. The landing outside was no more familiar to him than the room had been and lit with even less light. There was enough, though, to let him find the stairs. Halfway down he began to hear quiet noise and conversation; a little further and the smell of something warm and savoury tickled at his nose. Once that happened, any complaints of pain were drowned out by the pull of his stomach. He found his bearings at the bottom of the stairs; he had stormed out of this house twice now. He stepped lightly across the tiles and through the door, into a cloud of quiet voices and heavenly smells.

Ella and Carl had their backs to him at the table, hunched over in their seats and staring at the wood. Samuel sat dozing in one corner, while Bess held her usual position at the stove, stirring a pot of something and humming to herself. She looked up as Alan entered and gasped, sprinting around the table with surprising speed to wrap him in a tight embrace. She stopped, embarrassed, when Alan hissed in pain. Sadly that warning didn't stop Ella and Carl from leaping up and crushing him too. By the time they stepped back and let Alan loose he was sure he was on the verge of passing out again.

"Good to see you up man," Carl said, slapping Alan on the back and laughing at his pained groan of a reaction.

"Feels like I've got the world's worst sunburn," Alan gasped. "How long -"

"A day-ish," Ella said. "Little less - the fight was yesterday."

"And we ..." Alan trailed off, unable to comprehend that they might have actually pulled it off.

"Won?" Ella grinned. "Yeah, we won. Do I look like a bandit to you?"

Alan decided not to answer that question; it didn't look like Ella had washed or slept since the fight. She was covered in dried blood and he was pretty sure none of it was hers. He only got a glimpse of her mace resting on the floor by the door but there were definitely hairs and matted ... something stuck to it. Instead, he slipped into an empty chair and groaned as he took the weight off of his feet. His back screamed at him but all that escaped his mouth was a strained whistle.

"And the bandits?"

"Dead." Ella crossed her arms and Alan was sure she was trying not to smile. He appreciated the effort but that didn't make it any less unnerving. "Every last one. We finished off the ones by the church and when we found you ... Well, we found bits of the other guy. Very small, very well done bits. You knew you'd survive getting hit by lightning - real lightning - before you went up there, right?"

"... sure," Alan said after a second. "Part of my class - lightning doesn't hurt me. As much, I mean."

"Uh-huh." If she didn't believe him - and Alan was confident that she didn't - Ella at least let him have the lie for a change. "Well, we dragged you back here, healed you up as best we could and stuck you in bed. You looked terrible even after Carl exhausted himself healing you. Then we -"

A harsh crackling sound from the sideboard cut through her words and made everyone jump. While Bess tutted and wiped up a spill that had escaped her pot, Alan turned to see the star rod leaning up against the wall. Only he had never seen it like this - alive, for lack of a better word. It still fizzed in his mind but now it fizzed in the real world too, emitting a harsh buzzing drone that jumped and dropped at random, while bright lights shot up and down the pattern in it in jerky, halting movements.

"Started doing that when we found you," Ella said. "We think - Carl thinks - it happened after it got hit with lightning. Like it brought it to life or something."

"Old World technology ran on electricity most of the time," Carl said. "Lightning's just electricity but ... bigger. Maybe that's what it needed?"

"Maybe." Alan shrugged. "Not like any of us know anything about that stuff."

"You would do well, Alan, not to forget your elders like that."

Bess appeared from nowhere with a steaming bowl of porridge, placing it carefully on the table in front of Alan along with a spoon and a pot of what turned out to be honey. Similar bowls appeared in front of Ella and Carl and at a fourth space, which Bess took. Alan blinked. The pot still stood on the stove, steaming away. The fact that the wooden spoon was still stirring it, moving around and around as though guided by invisible hands, was only mildly surprising after the events of the past few days.

"That horrible sound, my dears, is static." Bess blew carefully on a spoonful of porridge as she spoke, savouring it with an obvious look of satisfaction before she continued. "It was a common problem for radios back in the day and I daresay a bigger problem now, given all the muck in the atmosphere."

Three sets of eyes stared at her as she innocently took another spoonful of porridge. Alan only recognised a few of the words she had used and none of them with any real familiarity. Static? Like his ability? Maybe Carl was right, maybe the rod was full of lightning now.

"How do you know that?" Ella frowned at the older woman. "How old are you?"

Bess laughed. "Oh, old enough not to mind when people ask me my age. It really is very rude though Ella dear - do keep that in mind."

Ella turned back to her porridge, her face flush.

"And old enough to remember when things like radios were a lot more common than they are now," Bess said. "Oh my parents were the real experts, bless them, but I know enough to - well, I suppose I know far more than I need to get by, but you understand my point. That thing is a radio - or at least it sounds like one - and I think somebody is trying to talk to you."

"Talk to us?" Alan's heart beat a little faster. "Who?"

"Well I'm sure I don't know now, do I?" Bess pointed her spoon at Alan's bowl and he remembered how hungry he was. The first spoonful was heaven; the second and third were nearly as good. "But if you still think that it fell from the sky and caused all this ... well, all this change, then I suppose whoever's trying to call you must know something about it. It certainly can't hurt to talk to them."

"Then do you know how to make it stop doing ... that static noise thing? Make it work properly, let us talk back?" Carl's eyes lit up.

"Oh, I don't have the foggiest idea I'm afraid." Bess smiled pleasantly and laid her spoon to rest in the empty bowl. Alan hadn't seen her finish it but the woman had put away enough porridge for two people faster than he ever could, regardless of how hungry he was.

"I never was much good with Old World machines," Bess said sadly. "Not many people are, you know. There's just not enough of them left for anyone to need to know. Not round here. And that thing is very advanced, even for the Old World. The last radio I saw was a child's toy by comparison and I can't have been much more than a child myself at the time."

"That's it, then." Carl slumped back in his seat and his eyes lost a little of their sparkle. "It's hopeless."

"No," Ella said slowly, "it's not." Alan could tell she was thinking it through in her head - and he was pretty sure she was coming to the same conclusion he was.

"We need to find somebody who understands this sort of thing," he said. "Someone who knows enough about Old World technology to fix it and let us talk to whoever's on the other end."

"But there's nobody like that left," Carl said, "not round here".

"So we'd need to go somewhere with Old World tech," Ella said.

Alan nodded. "Somewhere where there are still people who use it."

"There's nowhere like that, though," Carl said. "Nowhere outside of …"

His voice trailed off. After a second of thought, his eyes widened and he jerked as if struck, hissing a curse under his breath - if Bess heard, she pretended she hadn't. His skin paled and he looked to his sister, who just nodded grimly.

"London," Alan said to the silent room. "We have to go to London."

The word hung heavy between them. Old Samuel grunted and shifted in his sleep. London. The Dead City. It might as well have been the moon - nearly two hundred miles away and about as hospitable. A monument to the worst of the Old World, to hear it told. The travelling merchants never went that far south and never spoke of those who did. There were rumours aplenty but only one that Alan's dad had ever trusted: in London, the Old World didn't rest in peace.

"But it's so far," Carl said after an uneasy moment. "It'd take months. And the roads -"

"They'll still be trapped months from now, for all we know," Alan said. "I'm not giving up on my dad. And forget the roads - we can handle ourselves."

"You sure?" Ella asked.

"No," Alan said. How could he be? "Got a better idea?"

"No," Ella said with a laugh and a shake of her head, a dusting of dried blood drifting free from her hair and coating the tabletop. "You going to try and run off by yourself?"

"Hell no," Alan said with a forced grin. "I can't do this without you guys."

Dozens of messages hung at the bottom of his vision. A new message appeared as he spoke - Alan only paid attention to the first line.

**** Quest Gained: London Calling ****

The uncomfortable sensation that something was listening in on them crept over him, clamouring for attention with a thousand other worries and hopes and stabbing pains. Alan ignored the inner churn and the notifications and looked to his friends instead. The twins were filthy and bloody and bags hung heavy under their eyes. By contrast to the neatness of the kitchen, they looked lost and adrift and Alan was sure, in that moment, that there was nobody he would rather be adrift with. He thought back to the bandit leader's final words on the hilltop. He wasn't sure what his place was any more but, with his friends' help, nobody was going to put him in it. They made each other too powerful for that.

More powerful than lightning.

EPILOGUE

The escape pod crashed into the surface of the ocean with a noise like an angry hammer blow, rattling Linette's bones around despite the padded seat she was strapped into. She could feel the water slowing the pod as it sank and the fateful moment before buoyancy commanded it to rise again, popping above the waves and then sinking back down, slowly finding a comfortable equilibrium. Inside, Linette waited for the bobbing to subside to a tolerable minimum before unstrapping herself.

Life since she had been ejected from the *Eden* had been one unpleasantness after another. Orbiting the Earth while the pod skimmed the upper atmosphere, slowly burning off excess velocity, had been dull. Rocketing through the sky in a cone of fire, certain that at any moment she would be disintegrated by some previously unknown flaw, hadn't been dull enough. The thought of sinking to the bottom of the ocean due to some long-ago miscalculation had been even worse and therefore at the front of her mind the entire time. She'd done it, though, with a little help from gravity. She'd made it to the planet where it all began. She'd made it to Earth. Sure, she needed to find food and water and preferably land or she'd do little more than die here but it was a start.

As it turned out, the escape pod had a range of equipment designed for exactly her situation. A clever little device the size of her palm desalinated the water straight out of the ocean while a compartment under the floor held enough emergency ration bars to keep her fed for a year. There was even a motor built into the outer hull for aquatic propulsion - although even turned on, she couldn't be sure it was doing anything. The open ocean looked much the same regardless of how fast or slow you were moving.

She passed the first day sleeping off the events of the past week - and when land remained stubbornly out of sight she spent several more days sleeping off the events of the past month. Ever since the transfer from the

Genesis. Ever since her war began. Not *the* war, of course - that had been quietly smouldering away behind the scenes for years. She had just had the good fortune to turn up as it all turned loud and messy.

She wondered which of the stars in the sky was the *Genesis*. There was no way of telling, of course. Even if she'd known enough about astrology to chart the stars and spot those that wandered when they shouldn't have, she didn't have the tools. All she had was an emergency tablet with a limited media library and too much time on her hands. The pod had a built-in computer but all it did was give out environmental readings and send out a distress beacon. She'd disabled the beacon while she was still in orbit.

The environmental readings, though - they were the vindication she wanted. Needed. She obsessed over the data between sleeping and eating. On the first day, the pollution readings were off the chart - radiation and microplastics everywhere, a testament to why humanity had fled to the stars. The seas were near enough to dead that Linette began to question whether they had waited too long.

On the second day, they were much the same. On the third day, though, the radiation count was down by a significant amount. By the fourth, the readings were looking promising across the board; no plastics, no oils, rising levels of the various microfauna that had historically inhabited the planet's oceans. Linette cried herself to sleep with tears of joy the first time the Geiger counter registered nothing more than historical levels of background radiation. The terraforming probes tried to make landfall on, well, land - it made for a more stable surface from which to work. Now, though, the effects were being seen even in the middle of the ocean. It was working.

When she woke the next morning from the cramped, foetal curl that she had assumed on the bottom of the pod floor, it was to the by-now usual rocking of the waves and the far less usual sight of an elaborate image projected across her vision, several lines of familiar text displayed immediately under it.

**** Welcome to Heirloom Online****
**** <u>Please choose an option:</u> ****
**** Load Existing Character ****
**** Create New Character ****
**** Log Off ****

With a shaking voice, she said "Load" out loud and gasped as the text disappeared, replaced by a new message.

**** Welcome back [Arch Druid Linette] ****
**** It has been 1 year, 1 month and 3 days since last login ****

What on Earth was the interface to *Heirloom* doing on - well, on Earth? How was she logged in to the game when she wasn't wearing a VR set? And how did she have access to her old character data, which should have been stored safe and secure on her old ship? Now, more than at any time since she had landed, she wondered which star in the sky was the *Genesis*. If she could access her character data from its media servers down here on Earth, what did the crew and passengers of the *Genesis* now have access to? How long would it be before they realised it? Had they already noticed? Were they too busy combing over the wreckage of the *Eden* to care?

And what would they do when they found out that they had lost the war while they slept?

THE END

THANKS FOR READING

I hope you've enjoyed reading *Lightning Disciple*. Book 2 is already underway and should release Summery 2020!

If you want to keep up to date on how that's going you can visit www.elliothendry.co.uk and sign up for my mailing list. No spam – just updates on what I'm writing, what I'm reading that I think you might like, and promotional offers.

You'll also receive a **free digital copy** of an **exclusive companion novella** for signing up! Want to know just what Samuel got up to that led to him bringing a small army of goblins - not to mention a giant boar - to the rescue? You can find out in *Side Quest: The Goblin Village*, a fast-paced novella of about 24,000 words. Yours to keep, forever.

You can also follow me at @EHendryWrites on Twitter or email me at Elliot@ElliotHendry.co.uk. Say hello!

Read on for a sneak peek at *Moonrot*, Book 2 in the *Heirloom Earth* series.

MOONROT - PROLOGUE

Waves slapped against the side of the escape pod, the saltwater spray carried upon the sea breeze. Some of the spray fell in through the open hatch at the top of the pod but most fell back into the clear blue sea once more. The pod sat high in the water, the waves rising no further than half-way up its side even when the weather got rough and right now the weather was anything but rough. The sky was empty and cloud-free, the wind gentle and pleasant. Even the waves, as low as they were, were artificial, a bow-wave resulting from the relentless drive of the motor in the pod's base that drove it forwards towards the horizon. Towards land.

At least, that was the theory. From where Dr Linette Cooper was sat, legs dangling out of the pod hatch while she braced herself against the interior frame with one arm, there was nothing on the horizon except more horizon. She wasn't sure whether the motor was damaged during planetfall or just slow - after all, it wasn't designed for long trips. It was supposed to be just enough to manoeuvre while the pod waited for rescue by the ship in orbit, the ship Linette was sure was looking for her even now. The distress beacon, which would alert the ship to her position, had been the first thing she had destroyed.

Linette wondered if the second thing hadn't been her sanity. Some head trauma sustained during the descent, toxic smoke inhalation while on the *SF Eden* or a bad reaction to the emergency rations - something had clearly pushed her over the edge. Several days after the pod had splashed down in the ocean she had woken up to find the login screen for *Heirloom Online*, the great cultural vault slash cryosleep entertainment phenomenon, hovering in front of her eyes. She had even been able to log in to her old character, a level 50 Arch Druid, despite being at least 35,000 kilometres from the *SF Genesis* and its VR equipment.

Now the HUD - which she had, in a moment of dark humour, rechristened the *hallucinating user* display - lurked in the corner of her vision and behind her eyelids, stats and quest notes flashing in and out of focus whenever she concentrated on them. Not that she concentrated on them, not for the past week and a half. After the first curious day she had tried to ignore the whole crazy mess, figuring that indulging in the fantasy probably wasn't helping. Not really, not in practical terms.

That was how she knew she was imagining it, after all - the whole thing was obviously a ploy by her subconscious, cooked up in response to the ordeal that had led her to Earth. Playing *Heirloom Online* had been one of the happiest periods of her life. That had been the whole point of it. That had been why everyone played it. Now her mind was craving the safety of that time, the sense of power and control and certainty it had given. There had always been a nice, ordered list of quest steps to follow, always a fair fight. Not like reality, which right now was pretty damn unordered. Linette didn't feel even slightly in control.

So she sat in the pod hatch and watched the waves and strained her eyes searching the horizon for land, for anything that wasn't just open water. She sat and she watched and she indulged the one guilty scrap of curiosity that she couldn't ignore.

**** Distance to San Francisco: 3,212 km ****

As she watched, the final digit in the display across her vision ticked down to 1.

It hadn't been intentional, at first. She had been trying to figure out where she came down and where she could reasonably expect to make landfall. She'd been able to figure out from the pod's emergency computer that she had splashed down somewhere in the North Pacific Ocean; after that, it had been a case of wracking her memory for countries and cities. Her time spent in *Heirloom Online* had paid off; the terrain had been based on Earth, with cities based around the major population centres before everything went to shit. The in-game San Francisco had been a major base for some of the more nautical-themed activities and quests; not her favourite then and even less so now, having experienced the ocean for real.

As soon as she had thought about that memory the new message - *the new delusion*, she corrected herself - had appeared, rotating with the world and ticking down the distance at a depressingly slow rate. More proof of her hallucination; the in-game San Francisco had been a favoured hangout of some of her closest friends, chief among them Garrett Walsh. She spared a smile at the thought of that impressively-muscled man and the time they had spent together. That was what her subconscious was pulling on, that sense of belonging and safety.

Which didn't explain why she had chosen to follow it. The rational part of her could see no good reason, as it was no better a direction than any other vaguely-easterly course. It was no worse, though, and she had a stubborn desire to see what her mind did when she finally arrived at whatever random point it had set her towards.

Not that she'd find out any time soon. There was no way of telling her exact speed - she didn't count her hallucinations as a trustworthy measure of distance, after all - but she could tell it was slow. Real slow. She had food and water to last her for a year but she definitely didn't have the patience.

The distance message caught her eye again and she snorted back a laugh. If she really had been logged in to *Heirloom Online* the idea of slowly drifting her way to shore wouldn't even have occurred to her. Even without the fast travel system - and for all that she lacked patience, that had been a little too immersion-breaking - she'd had much better ways of getting around. What would she have done? Probably cast *Natural Allies* and -

As soon as she thought of the spell, a swift sense of fatigue hit Linette right between the eyes, like coming down from a sugar rush in an instant. It wasn't much but the sensation was unsettling and, not for the first time, she cursed the lack of a proper medical scanner in the pod's first-aid kit. She just hoped that if she did have a head injury, it took her quickly.

Linette was pulled out of her morbid thoughts by a sudden splashing, the sound of which broke over the sound of the waves on the hull. She looked down to see an amazing sight: two sleek, rubbery creatures poking their heads through the surface of the ocean, staring up at her with comical grins. *Dolphins*, she realised with a gasp. Incredible - they'd been classified as extinct even before the *Genesis* launched. They were even stranger-looking than in the records and the way they stared up at her, as though they were waiting for something … Linette felt a dull pressure against her mind. It was simple but focused. It was one word.

Help?

Her thoughts froze. The dolphins kept pace with the pod, heads above the water, staring up at her.

Help you?

Slowly, she recalled how it had felt to order animals around in *Heirloom Online*. She concentrated, hardly able to believe what she was doing, as she pushed back with her mind, directing the dolphins to swim around the pod. With a clicking cry, they did so, ducking under the waves and darting around the pod in a matter of seconds as black blurs visible through the clear water. When they popped their heads back up again their smiles seemed somehow satisfied.

Help you?

"Push?" She said it in a trembling voice, operating in a daze, and was rewarded by the two animals ducking behind the pod and setting their rubbery heads against its hull, tails thrashing. At once Linette felt the pod lurch forward and almost tumbled back through the hatch. The sound of the waves was joined by the rapid, rhythmic slap of the twin tails working together. Linette stared at the creatures that she now apparently controlled, lost for words, and let her hallucinations speed her towards land.

162